T0288842

BENEATH the LIGHTHOUSE

Other Books By Julieanne Lynch

BENEATH the LIGHTHOUSE

LIGHTHOUSE

JULIEANNE LYNCH

Beneath the Lighthouse

This is a work of fiction. Names, characters, places, and incidents either are the product of the authors' imagination or are used fictitiously.

Any resemblance to actual persons, living or dead, events or locales is entirely coincidental.

Copyright © 2018 Julieanne Lynch
All rights reserved.

Cover Credit: Original Illustration by Sam Shearon
www.mister-sam.com

No part of this book may be reproduced or transmitted in any form or by any means, electronic or mechanical, including photocopying, recording, or by any information storage and retrieval system now known or to be invented, without written permission from the publisher, except where permitted by law.
ISBN: 978-1-944109-18-9

VESUVIAN BOOKS

Published by Vesuvian Books
www.vesuvianbooks.com

Printed in the United States of America

10 9 8 7 6 5 4 3 2 1

For Jenn

"Even if the hopes you started out with are Dashed,
hope has to be maintained."

~Seamus Heaney

PROLOGUE

I cy tendrils of air cut into her throat like shards of glass. The more she struggled to breathe, the more her lungs burned.

The binding cords kept her still—a statue, standing frozen in eternity, shrouded in darkness. Her restraints were so tight her hands had gone numb. She shivered, unable to shake the feeling that she was being watched.

"*Where am I?*" She moved her lips, but her voice failed.

Footsteps echoed all around.

She turned her head toward every sound, hair whipping across her face with each snap of her neck. *Who was there?* She stared hard, searching for a glimmer of light. A scream formed in the base of her throat as the footsteps came closer.

She closed her eyes, shielding them from the coming horror. In a moment of madness, she opened them a slit, but the darkness was gone. She stood on the cobbles of the causeway, her hands still bound.

Confused, she looked at the overcast sky. Gulls swooped down, their calls echoing in her head. The salty stench of the coastal breeze nipped at her nostrils. When she saw the lighthouse, its beacon of light now resting in the day, she wanted to run.

A teen boy leaned against the stone tower.

As she focused on him, a strange sensation swept through her.

His heartbeat thumped in her ears. The trepidation seeping through his veins resounded in her head. The fear. The anger. The desire not to live a moment longer. A jumbled mesh of thoughts— he was lost, just like her.

How was it possible?

She had never seen him before.

He glanced in her direction and their eyes met.

Her jaw slackened. He *saw* her.

CHAPTER ONE

Present Day

The first slap stung the most.

"Would you get the hell up?" Ma shouted.

Jamie opened his eyes and scowled at her. His heart heavy, there was no avoiding what waited for him in the kitchen.

His father's nightly heavy drinking had become routine along with the next morning's confrontation. Jamie sighed. It didn't matter how many times he pretended to be elsewhere, the reality hit him hard in his waking moments.

"Your father is going mad down there. Why in God's name did you do it?"

Jamie pulled the covers over his head.

"Jamie McGuiness, get your arse out of bed before I wallop you." She tugged at the duvet.

"Aye, right, Ma." He sat up, rubbing the sleep from his eyes.

Sonya rested her hands on her hips.

"Jesus, Ma," Jamie said. He stood and inspected her new war wounds—a blackened right eye and swollen lips. His insides churned as he reached for her.

"Don't you dare." She pushed his hand away. "Not today, I

can't be doing with this. Not this day." Her voice broke.

"But Ma, he can't keep getting away with this."

Sonya turned her head, hiding her face from his view. She picked up Jamie's school uniform and threw it at him.

"Get dressed and get down the stairs."

Jamie stared. Her humiliation had turned to anger. He hated Da for turning her into a shadow of the woman she had once been.

Sonya closed the door behind her.

Left alone with his thoughts, Jamie pulled on his trousers and stood in front of the mirror. "Why can't my parents just be normal?"

Normal. Something he'd never be because of Asperger syndrome. But he longed for a family life without all the drama … the way it used to be. He zipped his trousers and kicked his brother's soft stuffed bunny out of the way.

Noise, coming from downstairs, filtered through the closed door as he buttoned his shirt. Doors banging, the baby screaming, his father bellowing—the floor vibrated beneath his feet.

If he ignored it long enough, the noise would fade, masked by his thoughts. He went through this ritual every morning. For nearly three years, life had become something Jamie hated. It never made a difference how many times he tried to help *fix* things. Da undid all the good and wallowed in a drunken stupor, drinking himself to death.

Jack McGuiness had become a shell of a man, trapped in a self-destructive rage. He'd changed right before the eyes of his family, becoming a monster none of them recognized.

Jamie never understood how Da had allowed his family to fall below the poverty line. Jack drank the dole money away, backed horses who never won, and continually blamed Sonya in the process, often knocking her about.

Jamie hated it. He despised waking each morning. He often danced around the thought of just ending it all. He was convinced his death would have been easier than ending up a drunken brute like his father. Once the thought came into his head, another followed.

Where would his parents find the money to pay for his funeral?

Nothing was ever simple, not even planning his own death.

Jamie walked into the small kitchen. He glanced at Ma. She stood by the cooker, holding baby Sarah in her arms, trying to console the child.

Jack banged his fork on the table and glared at Sonya. "Shut the wee fucker up."

"She can't help it. She's cutting a tooth." A tear rolled down Sonya's cheek.

Jamie held out his hands. "Give her to me."

He held her against his chest and rocked her in his arms. The movement helped soothe her, though he earned a look of contempt from his father.

"You're a smart wee bastard, aren't you?" Jack asked. He clenched his fists into tight balls, his knuckles growing white.

"Just leave it, Da," Jamie said.

Jack smashed his fist on the table, causing the beer can to

jump. "Leave it? Who are you to tell me what to do in my own home?"

"Jamie, stop it, please," Sonya said, her fingers curling around his shoulder.

The chair scraped along the floor as Jack stood.

The six-year-old twins, Paul and Thomas, stood in the hallway, their little eyes wild with fear.

Thomas wrapped his arm around Paul's shoulder and held him close. "Come on, let's watch some tele," he said.

Her face laced with worry, Sonya turned her head toward the twins.

"You're some wise lad, aren't you?" Jack asked, and walked over to where Jamie stood. "Thinking you can do whatever the feck you want."

"I took the money because Sarah needed nappies and there was nothing for the boys for tea," Jamie replied.

Jack's nostrils flared. "Give your mother the baby."

Jamie's heart thumped hard.

Unable to look at Jamie, Sonya took Sarah into her arms. The fight had long left her. In its place stood a woman broken, about to crumble.

Jamie swallowed hard. "It was only twenty quid, Da." Knots tightened in the pit of his stomach.

"That money was mine, lad. You had no right going through my things."

"But … the boys would have gone hungry." Tears burned the back of his eyes.

Jack grabbed Jamie by the throat and pushed him against the wall.

Jamie gasped for breath. The crazed look in his father's eyes terrified Jamie as Jack's fingers tightened.

Jamie dug his nails into his father's skin. He had to make Jack loosen his hold, but it was pointless.

"Jack, stop it," Sonya begged. Her pleas echoed Sarah's screams.

Jamie pushed off the wall and twisted his body in a last attempt to break Jack's hold.

Thomas and Paul stood in the doorway, their mouths agape.

Jack drove him back against the wall. Jamie's head hit with enough force, his legs turned to jelly.

"I'll kill you," Jack said. "No one steals from me. I fecking tell you, no one."

Jamie's head grew light. He let out one last desperate breath.

Jack loosened his grip and released Jamie from his clutches. Jack's breath was labored as he breathed into Jamie's face like a menacing beast.

"Next time, I'll put you six feet under." He walked away, taking his can of beer with him.

Sonya cried, holding Sarah close to her chest.

The two little boys in the hallway wailed.

Jamie touched his neck, rubbing the spot where it hurt the most. He choked back the tears, but his pride was crushed and he wanted nothing more than to run.

"Jamie," Sonya said through several sobs.

He ignored his mother, grabbed his school bag, and left the house through the back door. Red-faced, Jamie sucked in a deep breath. He struggled to control the swirling emotions threatening to consume him. Sometimes, there wasn't much else to do other than to walk away.

The wind blew in his face as he walked along the path leading to the old lighthouse. He kicked at stones, staring at the horizon. The salty scent of the water always filled him with a sense of hope that something better lay across the Irish Sea.

Jamie jumped from the path and made his way across the beach. He headed straight for the causeway, seeking refuge in his favorite place.

Jamie didn't care about it being the last day of the school year. He needed time to clear his head—to think. He would go in when he felt like it. He had to decide where he was going once the summer ended. To make choices which not only affected him, but his mother and siblings.

Jamie threw his backpack onto the rocks. He slid down and rested his back against the old stone of the tower. He closed his eyes and tried to clear his mind. No matter how much he willed the bad feelings away, they remained embedded deep within his soul.

Gulls flew overhead, their cries pulling him from his thoughts. Jamie squinted at them, wondering what it would feel like to be free, to come and go as he pleased.

"Not in this bloody life."

His throat ached as he mumbled the words. He drew his knees up and rested his arms on them whilst watching a ferry sail past.

Jamie visited the lighthouse daily—it was his release. A place where he gathered his thoughts and laid emphasis on the good, the bad, and the downright ugly.

School and all its stupid playground politics wasn't something he believed in or wanted to be a part of. He had no intention of becoming a carbon copy of the other boys in the fifth year. The majority were intent on going out, getting wasted, and shagging the first girl who paid them any attention.

Jamie wasn't interested. His duty was to make sure the children were fed, especially on dole day. Wasting his time at school wasn't going to fix the shit going on at home.

He pulled his phone out of his pocket and scrolled down to find he had four missed calls and three text messages from Lenny. "Bloody hell."

Jamie rolled his eyes and switched the phone off. He slipped it back into his blazer pocket. He didn't want nor need Lenny's crap—not this early in the day.

Surrounded by silence, Jamie watched the ships glide over the water—smooth and effortless. It served as therapy. Staring out at the horizon, he found it easy to become lost in his thoughts. Anything was better than having to deal with the present.

He thought about his mother's swollen eyes, Sarah's cries, the looks on the twins' faces. Guilt ate away at him deep within. He shook his head, his eyes filled with tears. He wanted to cry so badly, but refused to give in to the swarming emotions playing havoc with his soul. He hated the dull ache, which never seemed to leave his stomach. There had to be a way of escaping it, but no matter how hard he tried, brick walls met him at every turn.

The feeling of being completely lost was killing him slowly.

Somehow, some day, it would win and he'd never recover. Jamie accepted his miserable, lonely existence. No one seemed to care enough to step in to help rectify things. Resting back against the cold stone, he turned his head and caught sight of a girl standing on the beach.

Her eyes didn't shift from him.

"Weirdo," he muttered.

Jamie rolled his eyes before looking away from her. Then, he glanced at her from the corner of his eye.

She stood much closer to the lighthouse, not moving.

He sat up straight and his brow furrowed. How had she moved so quickly?

The wind gently blew her black hair across her face.

Jamie grabbed his bag and stood. He had only taken his eyes off her for a split second, but as he gazed back at the beach, she had disappeared.

"What the …?"

Walking across the causeway, he looked up and down the beach, across the road, and back at the lighthouse.

Nothing.

Jamie ran a hand through his hair, trying to make sense of what he'd seen. He reached into his blazer pocket and pulled out his phone. He switched it on and found another message from Lenny. Sighing, he dialed his number.

"'Bout you, lad?" he said.

"Jesus, you're a hard man to find. Are you coming in today?" Lenny asked.

"Aye, on me way now." Jamie looked back across the

causeway, stretching his neck to catch sight of the girl.

"Any craic?"

He stepped back up onto the small ledge of rocks. "Naw, nothing, just the usual shite."

"Are you sure?"

"Aye," Jamie lied.

"Then get your arse here. I'm dying a double death without someone decent to talk to."

"Dead on," Jamie replied. "See you shortly."

Jamie took one last look back at the causeway. He shook his head and smirked.

"It's all in your head, lad," he whispered, and headed for school.

The wind whistled behind him. The noise sounded like a sad melody lost in the breeze.

CHAPTER TWO

Lenny slouched against the brick wall, smoking the last of his cigarette as Jamie arrived. He smirked when he saw Jamie's disheveled appearance before he noticed the marks on his friend's neck. His face grew serious.

"Ah, for feck sake, lad," he said, shaking his head. "Your oul man needs a good lamping."

"Tell me about it," Jamie replied. "I'm sick of this shite."

"Is your ma all right?"

Jamie shook his head, his cheeks growing warm. "He beat the shite out of her last night."

"Jesus Christ." Lenny stared at Jamie. "You need to get the feck away from there."

Jamie stood with his back against the wall and sighed. "I know. I just worry about the wee 'uns."

Lenny nodded. "Aye. It doesn't stop me from wanting to beat the crap out of your oul man."

Jamie knew Lenny hated what was happening behind closed doors. He trusted him with every fiber of his being. Despite what took place at home, Jamie wasn't the kind of person to walk away, not when his mother needed him.

"So, what's the craic here?" Jamie asked, changing the subject.

The two of them stared at the bustling crowd out in the schoolyard.

Everyone was hyper, excited it was the last day of term. All of them were eager for their summer holidays. Some were ready to begin their next phase in life, while others pondered over turning another year older.

Jamie dreaded all of it.

"A few of us are heading to a house party tonight," Lenny said. "You should come."

Jamie shrugged, resting his arms on the wall. "I'll see. Not sure if I've any money."

"Feck the money, lad. I'll shout you a can or two."

Jamie glanced at Lenny and smiled. "You're a dose."

"Aye, I am, but feck it, I can't be going to an end of year shindig without me old mucker."

The two of them walked through the gates and headed for the main door, waiting for the bell to ring. Like clockwork, the bell rang, ending morning break.

"Was I marked absent?"

"Aye."

"Feck."

"Who gives a shite? Not you, surely?" Lenny teased.

"Feck off, you dose."

Jamie shoved Lenny playfully on the arm. Walking into the main corridor, Jamie nodded at a few lads, ignored the charms of two girls, and headed straight for his form classroom.

"See that?" Lenny asked, nudging his arm.

"What?"

"Claire gave you the eyes." Lenny smirked, nodding at a group of girls who stood next to their lockers.

"Feck off," Jamie said, and snuck a glance behind him.

Claire smiled and waved at him.

Jamie nodded and looked away. He shrugged, pretending he wasn't interested.

"You've got to get with her." Lenny winked.

"Women are the last thing on me mind."

"That's the problem with you, McGuiness. Too much junk up there and not enough going on down here," Lenny said, grabbing his crotch.

Jamie laughed, shaking his head at Lenny.

"I'm serious, lad. You need to … I don't know, buck the bones of Claire back there and just live a little."

"I'll leave the shagging to you, Lenny."

"Ach, you're no fun when you're all emotional."

"Walk a day in my shoes and then you will know a thing or two."

"Listen, lad," Lenny said. "Jamie Junior down there needs to see some action before you're ninety."

"Jamie Junior is doing just fine." Jamie pushed Lenny into the wall and laughed.

The two of them walked into their form room. The day's schedule was different. It was more relaxed.

"What about you, lad?" another boy asked.

Jamie sat down beside him. "Not too bad, Damian."

"You on for tonight?"

"Doubt it," Jamie said, and shrugged.

"Of course he is," Lenny piped in. "He's just being a twat."

"Feck off," Jamie said.

Lenny rubbed his hands together and winked at Damian. "He's in serious need of a good buckin'."

Damian grinned.

Lenny guffawed.

Jamie slid down in his chair, mortified by his friend's determination to cure his sex life. "You're both shits," he said.

Lenny and Damian laughed, watching their friend squirm.

The day's lessons were far from educational. The whole day had been a mass of overwhelming activity making it easy for Jamie to disappear to the solitude of the library, instead of standing around making chitchat with his peers.

Jamie walked down the last aisle and slumped to the ground. He sighed in relief and let the quiet surround him. At least he could finally think.

Cold crept up his spine and he shivered. He glanced at his phone. He hadn't been there for more than fifteen minutes. Goose pimples prickled to the surface. He rubbed his arms. A warm day outside, it had felt cool walking into the library, but nothing like this.

The cold hurt. It gripped his chest and tightened his lungs. Someone must have played with the thermostat. But ... he couldn't hear the hum of the air conditioner. Another shiver ran through him and he released a pent-up breath. Small crystalline snowflakes hovered in the air in front of him.

On the shelves in front of him, dark eyes stared back at him.

"What … the …?"

He scrambled to his feet and raced around to the other side of the bookcase, ready to knock the lights out of the person trying to spook him. No one stood nearby. Rows and rows of books surrounded him. He scratched his head. Running his hand down over his face, he sighed. The chill had gone.

He didn't believe in the paranormal. No matter how much he searched for a reasonable explanation, however, he came up with nothing. He'd had enough of school, he grabbed his bag and left.

"Where you off to?" Lenny shouted, running to catch up with him.

"I'm done here. Time to head back to the war zone."

"Ah, Christ," Lenny said. "Need an envoy? I know a few hard 'uns who'd be more than happy to deliver a punch or two."

"Are you wise?" Jamie asked. "He'd knock you out and whoever you bring along with you."

"Well, you know where I am if you need me," Lenny replied. "Listen, Finn is driving tonight. We'll pick you up about eight, all right?"

"Lenny—" Jamie said.

"Stop making excuses, lad. It's the summer. It's time for fun."

"Aye, so you keep telling me," Jamie said, raising his eyebrows.

"See ya at eight, and McGuiness?"

"What?"

"Don't let your oul man touch you again."

"Aye, like that will happen."

Jamie continued walking, knowing Lenny wouldn't take no for an answer. One thing occupied his mind, and it wouldn't leave him be.

The television blared as he walked in through the back door. Sarah screamed in the distance, and the breakfast dishes sat on the side. He slipped unnoticed up the stairs.

"Fecking bollocks." His father's incoherent mutters echoed behind.

Jamie walked across the landing. The door to his parent's bedroom stood open. He leaned against the door and looked at his mother, who sat on the edge of the bed, rocking Sarah in her arms.

"You finished early today," Sonya said, looking up at him.

He shrugged and said, "Aye, not much going on there. Glad this year is over."

"Are you all right?"

"Aye."

Her bottom lip trembled. She examined his face.

"Did he hurt you?"

Jamie shook his head. "Naw, I'm all right." He didn't want to give his mother another reason to cry.

"Are you sure?"

"Ma, I'm good," he said, stepping into the room. "How's Sarah?"

"She's just not settling today," Sonya said. The dark rings around her eyes crinkled as she held back a yawn. "I took her to the health center. They said it's just her teeth, nothing to be worrying over, but he's going mad down there—"she nodded at the door, "—and won't let me downstairs with her."

The thought of his mother being a prisoner in her own home made his stomach churn.

"Can't you go to Granny's?"

Shaking her head, she turned her face away from him, the tears seeping from her swollen eyes. "No, I can't let me ma see me like this. It's bad enough that nosey witch, Bernie, kept looking at me at the doctors."

"Ma, you can't keep doing this. He's going to end up killing you."

"What can I do, Jamie?" she asked, looking at him. "He's my husband, the father of my children. I just can't up and leave, not after everything."

Everything meaning Emer. In his heart of hearts, he knew his mother couldn't go. It was still so new and raw. Jamie grabbed her hand and held on for a few minutes.

Jamie sat in silence, afraid to mention Emer's name, terrified of what would consume them if they had to face the truth. She was gone and would never be coming back.

Even after three years, the devastating knock-on effect of Emer's death haunted them. They were unable to move on, unwilling to accept things had changed. Despite how hard they prayed or pretended she hadn't died, an emptiness existed in every room of the house.

Emer's room had been left untouched for the past three years. Jamie refused to step inside. If he went in there, the finality of his twelve-year-old sister's death would hit him hard. It would have crushed him more than his father's fists.

He had been numb ever since Emer's body was found. The vision of her lying in her coffin would never leave him, not for as long as he lived. Thirteen years old at the time, he'd tried hard to digest the fact that someone had taken his sister's life. It didn't stop the terrible dreams that came weeks after her funeral. He never believed it had been accident, something he insisted upon, but his words had fallen on deaf ears.

Shaking his head, he willed the memory away, focusing his gaze on the little miracle in his mother's arms.

"I'll look after you, Ma. I won't let anything happen to you," he said. He rested his arm around her shoulder and kissed her head.

"You're a good lad, pet," she said.

"I've a good mother."

"Go on, now. Let me settle your sister," Sonya said, wiping the tears from her cheek.

"I love you, Ma."

"I love you, too."

Jamie disappeared into his room and sat down on his bed, staring at the palms of his hands. Unable to escape it, the memory came at him like a flood.

CHAPTER THREE

March 16, 2012

J amie finished his breakfast.

His father sat across the table, tying his boots. Jack smiled at the three-year-old twins, Thomas and Paul, who stood watching him getting ready for work, mimicking every expression he made.

"Are you two going to be good boys for your mother today?" he asked, winking at them.

"Yup, going to nursery, Daddy," Paul said. His squidgy little face creased when he spoke.

"Me, too," Thomas said. "Going on the slide, and then the sand pit."

"And me." Paul turned to Thomas and smiled. "Me go first."

"Then make sure you look after each other," Jack said, giving them both a kiss.

"Okay, Daddy," they said in unison, and ran from the kitchen, racing down the hall with their arms stretched out like planes taking off.

"How's about you, son?" Jack asked.

"Got an assessment," Jamie replied. He couldn't muster any enthusiasm for it.

"You'll do grand."

"So Ma keeps tellin' me."

"Your mother is a wise woman." Jack smiled and glanced at Sonya, who stood in front of the kitchen sink.

Emer walked into the kitchen, scrolling through her phone.

Jamie dropped a spoon in his empty cereal bowl. *What had she done to her face?*

She ignored both her brother and father, too busy smiling at the text she'd just received.

"You're not going to school wearing all that make-up," Jack said, his warm expression changing fast.

Emer groaned. "It's only a bit of foundation and eyeliner."

"I don't care. You're not going out looking like a trollop."

"God, I hate you," she said, storming out of the kitchen, making sure she slammed the door behind her.

"She'll be the death of me," Jack replied, rubbing his temples.

"You're not the one who has to deal with all the drama," Sonya said, and loaded the dishwasher.

Sonya turned around and rested her hands on her hips. She smiled at Jack, who moved in for a quick kiss before grabbing his lunch box and flask.

"I'll not be late tonight." He kissed her one last time on the cheek.

"See you later, love," Sonya said. "Have a good day."

"Bye, Da," Jamie called after him.

"Be good, son." Jack closed the kitchen door behind him, leaving for the day.

Sonya turned toward Jamie.

He chewed on an apple, looking over his last-minute notes.

"Don't be worrying about the test. You'll do grand."

"Easy for you to say."

"Well, you have a good head on those shoulders, so stop stressing."

Emer walked back into the kitchen with red lipstick on, her school skirt shorter than before. "Has he gone?"

Sonya scrunched her face. "Jesus Christ, would you wipe that stuff off?" She handed Emer a dishcloth. "You look ridiculous and much too old for your age."

"Do I look like I care?" Emer said, scowling at her mother and tossing the dishcloth aside.

"Emer McGuiness, don't you dare test me."

"Oh, am I meant to be scared?" Emer threw her hands up and burst into laughter.

"Emer, stop acting like a bitch. You're not impressing anyone," Jamie said.

Emer rolled her eyes at Jamie. "Feck off. You're just jealous." She turned her back on them.

"Jealous of what, exactly?" Jamie asked.

She whipped back around. "That everyone likes me and no one gives a crap about you." Emer looked him up and down, like he was nothing but a piece of shit on the ground.

"All right, stop it the pair of you. You!" Sonya pulled Emer by the arm. "Get your face cleaned up, and you." She pointed to Jamie. "Go and wash your teeth."

Emer pushed past her mother and laughed. "Make me." she said. "You're just an old sow who knows she's well past her sell-by date."

Before Sonya could get to her, Emer strode out the front door.

Jamie shook his head, sensing his mother's frustration. "She's just acting like this to fit in with the older girls at school."

"Aye, while killing your father and me in the process," Sonya said, and sighed. "Go on, you better get on, otherwise you'll be late."

"All right, but I'll kick her arse if she keeps this up," Jamie replied with a serious look.

"Ach, would you get away with it?" Sonya laughed and playfully clipped him over the head.

"See ya, Ma."

"Have a good day, pet."

Jamie hurried on to school, eager to take his seat next to the radiator at the back of the classroom. No matter how many times Mr. Harron ushered him to the front of the classroom—a tactic his teacher used to stop him and Lenny from chattering—it failed. He kept repeating the same mistakes. In some cases, it would have been seen as a habit of getting the wrong attention. Both he and Lenny had the best craic winding their history teacher up.

"Did you get any revision done?" Jamie asked.

Lenny eyed Michelle's legs. "Naw, I watched the footie instead," he said, not once taking his eyes off the pretty redhead. "Do you suppose she wears one of those yokes?"

"Yokes?"

"Those push-up bras," he whispered.

"Jesus, is that all you think about?"

Winking at Jamie, he nodded and replied with a hearty, "Aye."

Jamie laughed. Lenny was a character. A sex-crazed—or so he hoped to be—ejit, but a harmless one.

Lenny Bannon had been a solid part of Jamie's life. Their mothers were friends. They'd grown up together and experienced almost everything around the same time. Lenny had confidence—something Jamie failed to possess—or so he had convinced himself.

Jamie often wondered what it would have been like to be as assertive and outspoken as his best friend. Every time he opened his mouth, however, he became a shadow of who he wanted to be.

"You do know your sister is meant to be texting some older lad," Lenny said, raising an eyebrow.

"Eh?" Jamie said, leaning on the table. "What do you mean?"

"Well, your sister does look a lot older, so you can't blame a lad for wanting to, ya know …" Lenny said, raising his eyebrows and biting his bottom lip.

"Feck off. Me da would break a few necks."

"Just saying." Lenny held his hands up in mock defense.

Jamie's cheeks flushed. Heat bubbled across the back of his neck. "I'll be having words with her."

The door to the classroom closed. Mr. Harron made his presence known.

"Now, who here has prepared for today's assessment, and who will be clocking in extra hours after school?" His voice bellowed to the back of the classroom. "McGuiness, Bannon, get your tails up here to the front."

The classroom went quiet.

Jamie and Lenny grinned. They walked to the front of the classroom and took their seats at two tables a few feet apart.

Jamie sat down and kept his focus. He forgot about Lenny and his banter, concentrating on the set of questions on the paper in front of him. He bit into the side of his cheek, trying his best to ignore Lenny's gossip about Emer and the older boys. Regardless of how much he pushed it to the back of his mind, it continued to irk him.

His brain went blank.

Come on. Don't lose it now. He tapped the top of the pen against the paper.

The ticking clock on the wall behind the desk became a constant observation point. Each move of the hand signaled another minute lost.

Sweat seeped across his brow. He struggled to make sense of the questions on the test paper. Looking from left to right, up at the clock, and back at the paper, he closed his eyes and willed the sensation of unease to go away.

The bell rang loud, resounding in his head. Jerking upright, he dropped the pen. Light-headed, he looked around at the class and found it hard to make sense of the dread overcoming him.

"Jesus, lad, it's only a stupid test," Lenny remarked, grabbing his bag and throwing it over his shoulder.

"I don't feel so good."

"You don't look so hot." Lenny looked at Jamie with enquiring eyes, and then shrugged. "You'd be a jammy shite if you get off from doing PE this afternoon."

Jamie faked a smile. He stood and exited the classroom with the rest of his peers.

Laughter coming from the corridor caught his attention. He looked up. Emer stood next to the emergency exit, flirting with one of the boys from the upper sixth form. His blood boiled. He marched over to where they stood and grabbed Emer's arm.

"What the feck are you at?" he asked.

Emer scowled at him before she smirked. Her eyes narrowed. She tilted her head and met Jamie's glare.

"You're a dose, Jamie. Go on to class. No one wants you here."

"If you don't stop this crap, Emer, I'm telling Ma," Jamie warned, much to the older lad's amusement.

"You need me to teach your brother some manners, Princess?" he asked.

"Aye," she replied, folding her arms across her chest. "It might be the most fun he'll ever have in his sorry life."

Jamie looked at the lad, and then at Emer. Shaking his head, he wanted nothing more than to smack Emer hard, regardless of the consequences.

"You'll get what's coming to you," he said, and turned his back on them.

"That's right. Run along to class, you loser," Emer shouted.

Sometimes, he hated his sister, a spoiled little bitch who had been ruined by Jack. She'd grown up too fast once she'd begun secondary school. Though he ignored the way she looked more like a woman, he still saw her as the snotty-nosed brat who used to steal his sweets.

The rest of the day dragged by. Jamie hated when he couldn't stand to be around his friends. Every so often, he felt trapped by them and their banter. He didn't want to be a spare part or a boring shite, but there came a time when he didn't connect with it all.

His mother blamed his low attention span on his Asperger syndrome and his reluctance to listen to everything. Instead, he'd focus on one thing at a time. All his devotion went into it, and the outside world rarely got a look in.

It had always been this way. Different from many of his peers, most of them knew not to say anything. Jamie flew off the handle when things got a little too much for him. As the years went by, Jamie found he could control himself.

His attentive mother didn't understand how different Jamie was. She saw the bright, wonderful boy shining underneath. She wanted him to reach his full potential, regardless of the obstacles standing in his way.

Later, as they walked home, Lenny chatted about the one thing occupying his mind twenty-four-seven.

"I'm tellin' you," he said, his eyes wide with surprise. "Sinead has huge ones. They're way out here." He held his hands out in front of his chest.

Jamie laughed.

Damian shook his head.

"You're not wise," Jamie remarked.

They turned down his street.

"Did you talk to Emer?" Lenny asked.

"I did."

"And?" Damian asked.

"What do you think?" Jamie rolled his eyes. "She's a stupid bitch."

"Aye," Lenny replied. "But to be fair, she's kinda hot."

Jamie hit the back of Lenny's head.

Damian grinned, but said nothing.

"Okay, point taken," Lenny conceded, curling a hand around the back of his head and pouting in mock pain.

They neared the front gate leading to Jamie's house.

Damian bid them his farewell and crossed the street. "See youse over the weekend," he shouted.

The two boys waved at him, immersed in conversation.

"Are you on for footie tomorrow?" Lenny asked.

"My name's down on the list," Jamie replied.

"Then why the long face?"

Jamie sighed, dropping the bag he carried near his feet and resting his back against the stone wall that surrounded his house. "The dose Emer talked to will be there. Not sure I want to be on the receiving end of him."

"This might sound out of turn, but your sister is going to end up the duff if she's not careful," Lenny said.

Lenny's assumptions were spot on.

"That's what me da is freaking over," Jamie said. He stared at the house standing behind him. "She's so stupid, she doesn't see the slut she's making herself out to be."

"Aye."

"Anyway, I best be getting in." Jamie picked up his bag. "I

told them I'd help out with the twins tonight."

"See you tomorrow, lad," Lenny replied before he went on his way.

Jamie stepped inside the house.

His mother ran about, tidying up after the boys. It was his parents' monthly night out, and Jamie always did the honors of babysitting. He didn't mind. He liked being in charge, which the twins loved. Being a big brother had its perks.

They were a happy family, but beneath all the contentment, something darker stirred. Jamie sensed it every time his father had a drink. Something always snapped with Jack, and ripped the joy momentarily out of their lives.

CHAPTER FOUR

March 18, 2012

Sunday was a day filled with Mass, dinner at Granny Reilly's, and then fun in the park. It had always been this way, ever since Jamie could remember. For the most part, he couldn't get enough of the extra helpings of gravy and Yorkshire Puddings. His grandmother's was ten times better than his mother's.

Jamie chased the boys around the swings before he noticed Emer slipping off behind the trees, lighting a cigarette. He shook his head, unable to believe the boundaries she crossed. She had no sense, whatsoever, convincing herself she could do whatever the hell she wanted.

Jamie ran over to her. He coughed and blew the smoke from his face.

"What's wrong with you?" he whispered. "Da is only down there. He'll kill you if he sees this."

Emer stuck her tongue out at him before taking another drag. "Feck off. Who asked you for your input? I'm not a baby anymore."

"Oh, and standing here smoking makes you a grown up?"

"Jamie, leave me alone. I don't care what you think," Emer

said, blowing the smoke into his face.

"You're going to end up grounded, you stupid bitch."

"*If* they catch me." She smirked. "Why, are you going to squeal on me?" She sniggered and looked away from him.

Jamie refused to listen to her a moment longer. Emer and her incessant need to grow up too fast pissed Jamie off more than anything else.

Jamie swallowed his retort and walked away. His jaw tightened, as though it had been wired shut. He kicked at the stones on the path and made his way to the twins.

He pushed the boys on the swings and stared up at Emer.

Emer sat under the trees and lavished all her attention on her phone.

Jack and Sonya sat on the bench lost in conversation.

Emer smiled at her phone.

Jamie bit down on his bottom lip, curious about what she was up to.

Emer stuck her tongue out at Jamie. She made her way over to her parents.

"Ma, can I've the key to the house?"

"Why?" Sonya asked, looking at the boys, and then straight at her.

"I've just got me watsit," Emer replied, holding her tummy.

"Oh. Aye, go on, then, pet." Sonya handed her the key. "We won't be much longer, will we, Jack?" Sonya turned her head, looking at Jack.

"No, another half hour, maybe." Jack glared at Emer. "Straight home, you hear?"

"Yes, Da," she said, taking the key from her mother's hand.

Emer pushed her luck. Her lies, using people against one another, and never taking responsibility for her actions would ultimately destroy any chances of her being trusted. She didn't care and wanted to have fun, regardless of the consequences.

Present Day

Jamie sat on the edge of his bed crying. Unable to stem the flow, he pounded his fist against the bed. The guilt-laden emotions swelled until they crushed him from the inside out, battered by the past.

If he had told his parents sooner about the things Emer had been doing, she'd still be alive. Every time he thought of her, all the things he should have done to save her flooded through his mind. But he still ended up facing the harsh reality—he had failed her. It was his fault. A void like no other existed, leaving him in a limbo worse than death.

Jamie took off his school shirt and pulled on a t–shirt. He looked hard at his reflection in the mirror. How would it feel to not exist? The mirror showed the Jamie everyone knew and loved, yet his blue eyes were empty. The young lad with dreams of playing for his favorite football team no longer existed. In his place stood a shadow, a living, breathing shell of the person he used to be. The ugliness of his home had become a constant reminder of the person he no longer was. There was no escape or happy ever after.

Desolation and depression hurt almost as bad as Emer's death.

Jamie closed his eyes for a moment.

A chill, the same kind he'd felt in the library, pricked at his skin. The air grew thick and icy. *What was happening?* Each labored breath became sharp. Every nerve in his body stood on edge, his senses on overdrive. He opened his eyes.

A shadow loomed behind him in the mirror's reflection. He blinked hoping the shadow, some sort of trick of the light, would go away, but it remained. Its presence dominated him. He attempted to turn his head, but couldn't. His heart pounded hard.

The shadow flowed, a discordant and uncoordinated swirling mesh of movement.

Jamie's gaze remained locked on the mirror, unable to break free. The apparition descended upon him, shrouding him in its dark, wet residue. It entered his body.

Thump.

Thump.

Thump.

His heart was in a vise, compressed by whatever moved through his core. His eyes bulged, and he gasped for breath. Cool air washed over him.

Water lapped around his ankles. A strange odor assailed his nostrils. Unsure of where he was, or why he was there, Jamie scrambled to make sense of it. One minute, he stood in his room. The next, he was confined in a pit.

Scream after scream ripped through his throat. Jamie struggled to find a way out. He caught sight of his hands ... only they weren't his. The shock silenced his screams. He wasn't in his body. He saw things through someone else's eyes. Darkness crowded the edges of his vision.

Back in his room, he stood in front of the mirror, trembling and soaking wet. Jamie searched the room, trying to figure out what had just happened. Nothing was out of place. He shivered. Nothing would ever explain what had just occurred.

Jamie took a few deep breaths and dried off. The adrenaline coursing through him caused sweat to trickle down his brow as the chill left the room. He put on a fresh change of clothes, doing his best not to think. Taking a step towards the door, he glanced around the room. Unease swelled within him. He grabbed the door handle and swallowed the tight ball which had formed in the back of his throat.

He closed the door tight behind him. *"It's all in your head."*

Jamie walked down to the causeway. Standing on the rocks, he gazed at the tide coming in. His mind raced. The vision of the dark, wet pit flooded his mind. The smell had been familiar, but everything else confused him.

His phone chimed. He dug it out of his pocket and glanced at the screen.

Lenny.

"'Bout you, lad?" he answered.

"You're a hard man to find. I just called to yours, and your ma said you left," Lenny said.

"Aye, I had to get out of there."

"Where are you?"

"Where do you think?" Jamie said, knowing Lenny would understand.

"Hang around. I'll be there soon." Lenny ended the call.

It had been this way for a while now. Jamie found himself coming to the spot where Emer had been found. A daily habit, he sometimes visited the causeway twice a day. He felt close to her here, as if her soul was out there, listening to him. He begged for forgiveness, for not being a better brother.

Jamie held on to so much anger and regret. He wished it had been him who died. Then again, who would have stepped up to protect his mother from the drunken, violent wreck his father had become?

He looked out at the rising tide. His mind had been blank since the unexpected weirdness in his room. He would never tell anyone about what had happened. It would be a means to have him locked up in the nuthouse.

Fifteen minutes later, Lenny appeared with a plastic bag in his hand. "A little something for your troubles," he said, handing Jamie a bottle of Frosty Jacks. "It helps chase the ghosts away."

"You're a stupid clart." Jamie chuckled.

Jamie wasn't much of a drinker. The best way to rid his mind of his troubles was at the end of a bottle of cider, however. After taking a swig, he handed it to Lenny.

The two of them sat down on the rocks. A beautiful summer evening, the sun's amber glow hovered over the horizon.

"I don't know why you keep coming here," Lenny said, shaking his head and rolling a cigarette. "It gives me the creeps every time I sit here."

"Not me," Jamie responded. He looked up at the old tower and squinted. "I wish I knew what went through her head during those last moments."

"That is some fecked up shite you're talkin'. Seriously, lad, you're gonna end up mad like your da if you keep on doing this. Emer's dead, long gone, and buried. Doing this isn't going to bring her back. You can't keep lingering in the past, lad."

Lenny had a point. Who in their right mind held on to the ghosts of the past? But Jamie couldn't let go.

"I can't *not* think about it," Jamie said, looking down at his feet. "It's there every time I close my eyes. Her face and the marks on it, as well as the blue of her lips. Those things can't be unseen. And the smell …"

"Jamie, I'm not sure if I've answers to all this stuff you're going through, but the way I see it, you're alive. You have the whole future in front of you. Do you really want to lose it all to something you never had any control over?"

"I know," he replied, and took another swig of the cider. "I just can't look at me ma. Every time she looks at wee Sarah's face, all she sees is Emer. Do you have any idea how much it hurts watching her slowly die, pulling herself apart to keep a man who's long given up being happy?" Jamie's voice broke. "It's not fair, Lenny. They deserve so much more. I deserve something better than this."

Lenny shook his head, took a drag of his cigarette, and looked out at the ferry sailing by. "Honestly, if it was me, I'd be long gone. But you're not like me—you have sense. Too much of the stuff, if truth be told. Still, you're a good person, and it's what makes you stand out from the crowd. It's why you think the way you do."

Jamie sighed. His temples throbbed and he couldn't focus. Lenny and the causeway faded as he lost his balance and fell to the side. Ripples of movement pulsed through him. Bile rose to the back of his throat.

Clouds rolled in and the dark ominous sky rumbled above him. Thunder echoed in his head. An eerie silence surrounded him. A deathly stillness—and the putrid stench of decaying flesh assaulted his nostrils. On his feet—with no memory of having stood—his mouth grew dry as he tried to speak, but no words came out. *What had happened?*

Through the murky shadows, the breeze carried a female voice.

"Jamie," the voice whispered. *"Look at me, Jamie."*

The voice whispered a command, but it didn't feel real. Everything around him spun, but he stood still. The coolness of the causeway seeped into his feet, the sickening scent of the salty air wafting into his nostrils. Gulls screeched in the distance.

He looked around, searching for the source of her voice, but there was no one there. Darkness descended upon him, the cold air making him shiver. His breath froze with each exhale.

She tore through him, her voice vibrating, screaming his name. *"Jamie. Jamie. Jamie. Jamie. Jamie."*

Her cold, dark eyes bored into his; a piercing painful glare full of rage. A wicked inferno of black embers burned him from the inside. His mouth opened, his jaw line stretched, the pain unbearable. Then, nothing.

He gasped and coughed, lying on the stones. He looked up to find Lenny's worried face gawping at him.

"What the feck? Two sips and you're down." Lenny laughed

and helped Jamie to his feet.

"I felt weird as hell there," Jamie replied, rubbing his temples. The headache eased off.

The sharp, dark eyes remained at the back of his mind. Like they were watching and waiting, biding their time.

"I told you, this place isn't good for you," Lenny remarked, looking up at the lighthouse. "Come on, we can take this back to mine. Me da is out for the evening, and Ma is at bingo. I'm sure we can have a drop or two of the hard stuff before we hit the party."

Jamie didn't want to say no. He hated lacking the confidence to say how he was feeling or mention what he wanted to do. Lenny did have a point, though. The causeway and the lighthouse brought back bad memories, which would eventually consume him alive if he allowed them to.

CHAPTER FIVE

March 23, 2012

E mer had set her alarm clock for 1:00 a.m. The house would be quiet. She didn't want to stir her parents from their sleep. Emer snuck down the stairs. She unlocked the back door and slipped out.

Steven had parked his car close enough to the house so Emer wouldn't have to walk too far.

Emer approached the car, staring at the back of his head. She'd piqued his interest with the picture she'd sent him. He'd texted her saying he couldn't wait to see them in the flesh.

Emer slid into the front passenger seat and smiled at him. She had him exactly where she wanted him.

"Aren't you the right wee madam sneaking out at this hour?" Steven winked at her.

"Aye, maybe, but who gives a feck about it?" Emer replied, trying to sound a little older.

"So, you going to show those pretty titties or what?" he asked, looking down at her ample cleavage.

"It depends."

Steven smiled and looked at her. "Okay, I'll show this, if you get those out." He winked at her once more and grabbed his crotch.

Emer lifted the top of her pajamas, giving Steven an eyeful he'd never forget.

"No touching, okay?" she warned.

He stared at her chest for the longest while. His fingers twitched.

Smiling like it was Christmas morning, Emer pushed her top back down and folded her arms across her chest. "Okay, now you show me what you have down there," she said, eagerly waiting to catch sight of his privates.

Steven unbuckled the belt of his jeans and slid down the zipper. He pushed his hand inside, intent on releasing his erection. Before he could do so, the door to the car opened.

"What the feck is going on here?" Jack asked, his eyes blazing. He looked at Steven with his hands shoved into his trousers. "You dirty wee bastard. Do you have any idea how old she is?"

Jack pulled Emer's arm and twisted it. His nostrils flared.

"Daddy, stop this. You're hurting me. Let me go," Emer cried.

"You! What have I raised?" Jack roared into Emer's face. "You trollop. Get into the house before I break your legs."

"I'm sorry, Mr. McGuiness. It won't happen again," Steven cried.

"You're fecking right, it won't. If I see you sniffing around Emer again, I'll kill you, and that's a promise, lad," Jack shouted before slamming the car's door shut.

Steven sped off down the road.

Jack's jaw clenched, his muscles tight. His eyes were narrowed, rigid, cold, and hard.

Emer had never seen him this enraged before. She panicked

and ran back up the path.

Lights were turning on inside most of the houses on the street. People peered out of closed windows. Some opened their front doors to get a better view.

Stomping up the path, he ignored the concerned faces of his neighbors. Jack couldn't see past the red blazing in front of him. He wanted nothing more than to rip Steven apart. His little girl behaving like a grown woman made his stomach churn. He burst through the front door, slamming it shut behind him.

Emer sat on the couch, crying in her mother's arms.

"Bad wee bitch," Jack roared, pointing at Emer. "What in God's name have we raised?"

Sonya looked at him, shaking her head. "Not now, Jack."

"By feck, this will be dealt with now."

The twins crept down the stairs, fear spread across their tiny faces. Jack pointed at them and they scarpered, half running, half crawling, back up the stairs.

"The wee bastard had his hands on his dick." Jack's voice broke. "God only knows what would've happened if I hadn't seen them."

"We weren't doing anything, I swear," Emer cried.

"Then why were his jeans undone?"

She shrugged, looking at the ground.

"I'm sick of it, Emer. Sick to the back teeth with your

behavior. You can't go on like this."

"Like what? Growing up?" Emer shouted.

"Don't you dare, young lassie." Jack reached out to grab her.

"Jack, please, just let me handle this," Sonya begged.

Jack sat down and shook his head, shocked and let down by his only daughter's behavior.

Jamie stared at Emer.

Jack noticed the burning hardness in his glare.

"You're nothing but a slut," Jamie said. "I wish you were dead."

Emer ran from the room and darted up the stairs. She slammed her bedroom door behind her.

Present Day

Parties weren't Jamie's cup of tea, but Lenny lived for them.

The two sat in the back of the car. Jamie listened to the tunes, whilst Lenny drank a few cans of Tennents.

They had driven the short distance into Larne, joining a few of their friends from school. They celebrated the start of eight weeks of leisure, drinking and not caring too much about rules and schedules.

The night wore on. Jamie's mood changed the more he drank. For someone who never had any real intention of becoming a miniature version of his old man, he failed miserably.

"You looking for a bit of something to perk you up?" one of Lenny's cousins asked.

"Nah, I'm grand with these," Jamie replied, shaking the almost empty can of beer in the lad's direction.

"No bother, just hit me up if you fancy having the trip of your life." The boy chuckled and walked away.

"Did you see Claire?" Lenny bounced over to where Jamie stood, nodding at a group of girls.

"Nope," Jamie replied, refusing to look in their direction.

"Are you blind?" Lenny smacked him across the back of his head.

"No, but I'm guessing you're not." Jamie laughed.

The smile spread across Lenny's face.

"You know Claire is mad for you, right?"

Jamie glanced in Claire's direction. His cheeks reddened. He'd kissed a few girls in the past. Two of the experiences had led to his lip bleeding on an untightened brace.

"Aye, so you keep telling me," Jamie replied, trying not to make eye contact with him.

"Jesus, you're mad if you pass up the chance of getting in between her legs."

"Ah, for Christ sake, lad, not everyone is continuously horny like you," Jamie said, and pushed past Lenny.

Lenny stared down at his feet, raised his eyebrows, and nodded. "Aye, you're right."

As much as Jamie wanted to be one of the lads, there were some things he wasn't comfortable with. Using a girl for the sake of it was one of them.

Walking towards the wall of the car park, Jamie pretended not to hear his name mentioned, happy to play deaf and dumb.

"I take it Lenny is busy with the matchmaking," Claire said, startling him.

Jamie didn't want to look at her, finding it hard to ignore the pretty girl he'd had a crush on since they were both in primary school.

"Aye, he's a stupid dose when he wants to be," Jamie replied, looking at her for the first time without feeling the heat rise to the back of his neck.

"But he's harmless," Claire replied.

"So why are you out with this lot?" The blunt honesty caught him by surprise.

Claire looked back at the crowd and shrugged. "Sure, what else is there to do?" she asked. "Go to bingo with me mother? Are you wise?" She laughed.

Jamie glanced at Claire. He liked the fact she was much more down-to-earth compared to her friends. "I suppose you're right."

"I never had you down for these things anyway," Claire commented.

"How come?"

Claire jumped onto the wall and looked at Jamie. Her smile disappeared.

"I suppose with what happened to your sister an' all."

Jamie grew silent. Unsure of what to say, he was glad Claire wasn't afraid of speaking her mind.

"Lenny doesn't give me much choice these days," Jamie replied, trying not to be a complete tosser. "Drinking and going out spinning in cars just isn't my idea of fun."

"Want to know a secret?" she asked.

Jamie nodded and smiled.

"I hate all this," Claire whispered. "I hate being made out to be this slapper who's up for a laugh and shag. The truth is, I'm not like that at all. Never have been. Never will. I don't fancy catching the clap anytime soon."

"Then why do you surround yourself with people who make you feel like that?" Jamie asked, looking at her directly.

Claire shrugged and stared at her fingers. "Sometimes, it beats sitting at home listening to my mother going mad at me for not doing something right, or Granny insisting I go to Mass with her."

"And I thought I had it tough," Jamie said, flashing his teeth with a broad smile.

"Aye, I guess none of us has it easy."

Jamie and Claire looked at each other, their awkward silence laced with something new and exciting. For the first time, Jamie relaxed whilst being in her presence.

"So, what are your plans for the summer?" Claire asked.

Jamie shook his head and noticed how pretty Claire was. A line of small freckles dotted the bridge of her nose, making her natural beauty stand out. She wasn't made up like the other girls. Not a false eyelash in sight or the tangoed complexion. Just a pretty girl who seemed to be lost in the crowd.

"I've nothing planned yet. Maybe try to get a bit of work. Depends on home, I suppose, and what's available," Jamie said, setting the can of beer down on the wall. "What about you?"

"As little as possible." She giggled. "I've applied for a job at Spar, but I've not even been given a call back yet so I wouldn't hold my breath."

"Maybe if neither of us is busy, we can hang out?" Jamie asked.

"I'd like that." Claire beamed.

Jamie grinned, excitement coursing through every inch of his body. He never imagined wanting to spend time with a girl, especially Claire, regardless of his childhood crush. The newfound idea of being friends with more than just one person flustered him.

"I'll be seeing you, then," Jamie said. He looked at her, his insides all over the place.

"Yes, Jamie McGuiness, you will."

Claire jumped down from the wall and kissed his cheek before running back to her friends.

A glimmer of hope, something he never truly understood, filled Jamie's head. Something good would finally come from all the darkness that had taken over his life in recent years.

CHAPTER SIX

J amie awoke with the bitter taste of the sea in his mouth. He retched, barely making it out of his room before vomiting on the carpet. The nausea pulsed through him, like a wave descending upon him. Relentless, it pushed down his throat. He gasped and rested on his hands and knees, waiting for the moment to pass over him.

Sonya came out of her room. "What's happened?" she asked, dropping to her knees and resting her hand on his back.

Water poured out of Jamie's mouth.

Sonya's words became a distant echo in his ears as the house around him faded. Impending doom overpowered his senses.

The temperature plummeted to freezing point. Screams reverberated in his ears. Sweat drenched his skin. Agony rippled through him at the hands of a perilous monster. Punches came hard and fast. His eyes bulged. Bones broke. Blood pooled in his mouth. All thoughts were knocked to the side. He struggled to breathe.

The power behind the hands pounding down on him left him weak and disorientated. He threw a punch at his attacker ... and missed. He looked to the side and focused on the dark door, the stairs leading upwards, and the boots that looked familiar.

Smack.

The fists slammed into his face, resulting in a pain he had never experienced before. Warm metallic-tasting blood slipped down his throat.

Jamie spat the warm crimson from his mouth. He punched, kicked, and clawed at his attacker, but never connected. Overwhelmed by the onslaught, he used his arms to block as many blows as possible, but it was still too much.

Crying, Jamie shivered, rolled onto his side, and wrapped his arms around his torso.

He closed his eyes and played dead, trying to ignore the pain.

Warm hands slid across his arm. "Jamie." His mother's soft voice called out to him. "Jamie, pet?"

Jamie opened his eyes and glanced up at Sonya. His head throbbed. The wooziness subsided. He panicked and scrambled to his feet, curling a hand around his face.

"Jamie, are you okay?" she asked.

Confused, he shook his head. "I don't know. It must have been a bad dream," he whispered.

He walked into the bathroom and locked the door behind him. Jamie walked to the sink. He turned on the tap and splashed his face with water. He grabbed the towel and dried his face, looking in the mirror.

Someone else's eyes stared back at him.

The darkness bored into Jamie. An unnatural chill enveloped him. He was no longer alone.

BENEATH THE LIGHTHOUSE

March 31, 2012

Jack and Sonya spent the best part of a week without talking.

Sonya tried to convince Jack that Emer wasn't a bad person.

Jack refused to believe a word she said. Whenever he looked at the twelve-year-old, he turned away in shame.

The drinking began. Nothing serious, at first, just a few jars at the pub every evening. Sonya suspected her husband wanted to avoid having to come home and facing their demons. It wasn't easy for him to come to terms with the fact that their little girl was far from innocent.

Emer sat in her room for most of the evening. She refused her dinner and wouldn't talk to Sonya.

Jamie sat in the living room, watching Transformers with the twins.

Sonya went upstairs.

"Jamie!" she shouted. "Jamie."

Jamie thundered up the stairs. "What's wrong?" he asked, standing at the door.

"She's gone," she said, staring at Jamie, her eyes filling with tears. "The bad wee bitch has done it this time."

Emer's window stood wide open, and the room was empty. Sonya opened the door a little wider.

Jamie followed her into the room.

Sonya's heart thumped hard in her chest. Her body absorbed the unease running through her veins. Her mind refused to fathom as to why Emer would do this.

An hour later, Emer still hadn't come home. Sonya paced the floor of the living room. She dialed the number for Mac's Bar to let Jack know, but the calls went unanswered.

"She's with Steven, I know it," she said, holding her fingers to her temples.

"Maybe she's just with her friends." Jamie shrugged. "You know what she's like. She gets a thick head on her and doesn't think."

Sonya stopped dead in her tracks and turned to face Jamie. "She's breaking my heart."

Jamie walked over to his mother and wrapped his arms around her.

As five a.m. came, Sonya sat on the sofa, waiting for Jack to come home.

Padraig, Sonya's brother, had spent most of the night driving around town, looking in the usual places where the teens liked to hang out, but no one had seen Emer.

Sonya dozed off. The sound of the doorbell ringing startled her, seconds later. She stiffened and sat upright. Her head pounded from the need of sleep.

Jack cursed and repeatedly rang the doorbell. He was plastered.

Sonya made her way to the door, her stomach churning with dread. Her palms grew wet, and her mouth went dry. Emer was missing. The sheer thought of telling Jack frightened her.

"Jack, where have you been all night?" she asked, and opened the door.

"Don't be at it, woman." He pushed past her.

"Emer's not here," she said, her eyes burning from all the crying. "Do you hear me, Jack? Our daughter's missing."

Jack ignored her and held onto the railing. He stomped up the stairs and slammed the door behind him.

Padraig appeared and walked over to her. He rested his hands on Sonya's shoulders.

"He's too drunk to care. Let him sleep it off."

Sonya turned to face her brother and fell into his arms, crying. The anger left every inch of her, leaving a terrified woman in its wake. The possibilities of something bad happening to her daughter frightened her. Images of Emer lying drunk somewhere, or in a car wreck flickered in her mind. She pushed the horrors to the back of her mind. The more time passed, the deeper the emptiness embedded itself inside.

Sonya broke their embrace and walked to the door. She stared out of the pane of glass, praying for her daughter to come home.

Present Day

Eight days had passed since the weirdness in the bathroom. No matter how many times he showered or used the toilet, he wouldn't look at his reflection.

Jack had been drinking all weekend, and Jamie avoided him

like the plague. Sonya had taken to sipping cups of cold tea, whilst the twins had gone to stay at their granny's.

Jamie pushed Baby Sarah in the pram, trying to give his mother a break. She looked tired and thin. Despite how much Jamie coaxed her into eating a slice of toast, she refused.

"Ma, ya have to eat something," he said, pushing the plate in front of her.

"I'm not hungry, pet. Would you mind taking Sarah out for half an hour so I can rest my head?" she asked, looking at him with such sad eyes.

Jamie found it hard to swallow past the lump in his throat.

"No bother," Jamie replied, popping a fresh bottle of milk in the changing bag. "She loves spending time with her big brother, don't you?" He cooed at the baby and pulled a face, earning a big grin from Sarah.

Sonya wearily got up from the table and walked to the living room.

Jamie left the house, pushing the pram in front of him, whilst making faces at his baby sister. The warm July air felt good on his skin. He couldn't wait to stretch his legs.

Sarah's cute little blue eyes stared up at him.

For a moment, he wondered what she made of all the madness. He turned onto the main road.

Claire walked towards him with a smile of surprise on her face. "Aww, look at you," she cooed.

"Ach, would you quit it?" he replied, shaking his head.

"Is that your baby sister?"

"Aye, this is Sarah," he said with pride.

"Ah, she's a wee dote." Claire reached for the infant.

"And a screamer when she wants to be." Jamie smiled at Claire.

"So, where are you off to?"

"Giving the oul doll some rest," he replied. "I'm taking Sarah to the park. She won't give a shite. It's a nice day, so sure, why not?"

Claire glanced at him and smiled. "Fancy some company?"

Jamie nodded, glad she'd offered. "I'd like that."

The two walked side by side, happy and content.

Jamie sat on the swing, holding Sarah in his arms. She babbled away as Claire looked on. Jamie's face lit up every time Sarah smiled up at him.

"God, she really loves you," Claire remarked. "You're so good with her."

Jamie's cheeks flushed. "She's a great wee thing, really, and I love helping out when I can."

"I can't stand my sister. She's a bloody nuisance. Sometimes, I wish her dead."

Jamie glared at her. "Why would you say something like that?"

"Oh, Jamie, I'm sorry. I didn't mean it. I ... I wasn't thinking straight." Claire awkwardly played with the small necklace around her neck, running her thumb over the vial-shaped pendant. "Sometimes I forget my mouth, and whatever I'm thinking just comes out—the good and ugly."

Jamie sighed and relaxed. "I guess I'm guilty of thinking like that, too. We're only human, right?"

"Exactly." She smiled and swung back and forth.

As the evening progressed, Sarah needed a change. Jamie decided on going home.

"I better head on home," he said. "This one needs a change and another feed."

"I enjoyed spending time with you," Claire replied.

"Maybe we can do this again, minus my sister?"

Claire chuckled. "Aye, as much as I like babies, it would be nice for just the two of us to hang out."

"How about Monday?" he asked.

Claire nodded and smiled. "Absolutely."

"Good stuff," Jamie replied. "I'll meet you by the Diamond at lunchtime."

"I'll see you then," she said, and kissed his cheek.

Jamie's cheeks grew hot. He wanted to act mature, but his nerves were dancing all over the place. Each time he saw Claire, a warm sensation he never experienced before consumed him.

By the time he got home, Sarah fussed, ready for her spoon-feed.

Sonya sat in the kitchen, her face unchanged, looking more tired than ever.

The twins were happily watching an episode of *Doctor Who*.

Jack sat nearby, snoring in his chair.

"Ma, Sarah needs feeding and changed," Jamie whispered.

Sonya looked up at him, her blackened eye had begun to change color. "Ah ... there's some spud and gravy in a bowl in the microwave. Would you mind doing it, love? I don't feel so good."

Jamie wanted to go his room, but his mother looked too spent and needed the rest more than he needed the solitude. "Okay."

He sat Sarah in the highchair. Jamie heated up the small bowl of food and fed the hungry tot. He made airplane noises and pulled funny faces.

Sarah laughed as each spoonful made its way down to her.

"You're such a good boy," Sonya remarked.

"Sure, I'm the golden child," he replied, smiling at his mother.

"That you are, pet."

Once he fed Sarah, Jamie pulled her into his arms and walked towards the back of the house. The extension remained incomplete. Work on it had stopped the moment Emer died. The back room served as a constant reminder of the past. Holding his sister in his arms, Jamie found himself drawn to the room.

Jamie was such a different boy when compared to others his age. He wasn't your stereotypical teenager, not when it came down to the heart and soul of things. Sensitive, and sometimes too perceptive, it made him the perfect candidate as she observed him feeding the baby. She'd never known anyone to care as much as him.

She kept an eye on him, sensing everything that reminded him of death—the coolness of the room, the breeze pricking at the skin behind his ears, and the stale scent of mold and decay.

So many painful memories flitted through his mind. For a

moment, she felt sorry for him. It was odd reading him. Seeing Emer lying in her coffin, his mother's bloodied face, the empty beer cans——the bad thoughts left a hollow mark on his soul.

He stood there, looking around the uncompleted room. Jamie held the baby close to his chest. The desire to protect the small child became an overwhelming force. She reached out to touch him, reminding herself of how beautiful that kind of bond was.

Before she made contact with him, he turned his back on the boarded window and walked back towards the kitchen. She followed close behind, immersed in his pain.

"Jamie," she whispered his name.

CHAPTER SEVEN

Jamie's sleep was anything but restful. He twisted and turned.
He ran across the causeway, unsure of what he ran from. Jamie had to get away, to find shelter—anywhere as long as he wasn't seen.

Chased by something dark, he panicked and stared behind him before he was pushed hard into a wall. He looked down at his feet; he wore a pale blue skirt and black shoes, his knees bloodied and scraped.

What the hell?

Someone grabbed his hair, tossing him through a huge door.

He fell hard onto the wet ground.

"Please," his voice echoed, but it didn't sound like him. No, this wasn't his voice.

His head ached. The jarring maze of visions continued to beat through his skull.

A hand grabbed him by the throat, squeezing the life from him. Another blow sent a ringing noise hammering inside his head, the pain deafening.

Bang.

He came to, lying on the floor, lip split and bleeding.

April 1, 2012

"May we come in, Mrs. McGuiness?" the police officer asked, holding his cap to his chest.

Sonya opened the door wider to let them in.

The two officers entered the house, walking into the living room.

"This is just typical," Sonya complained. "Youse weren't interested last night, but today, you're here bright and early."

"Mrs. McGuiness, can you take a seat, please?" the tallest of the officers asked.

"We tried to report her missing last night, but we were told she was probably out getting drunk," she said, slightly higher in pitch. "You didn't take us seriously last night, and now you're here? This is just scandalous."

"Sonya," Padraig interrupted. "Let them talk."

"Mrs. McGuiness, is your husband home?"

"Yes, he's in bed."

"Can you wake him, please?"

Sonya looked at the two of them and held a hand to her chest. Her jaw clenched, and her posture grew rigid. She looked at Jamie, who stood near the doorway, and nodded at him.

Jamie returned the gesture. He turned to fetch his father, tiptoeing into the bedroom, moments later. The stench of stale alcohol nipped the back of his nose. He walked over to the bed and shook his father.

"Da … Da, wake up. The peelers are here," he said.

Jack groaned and burped before rolling over onto his side. "Tell them to feck off."

"Da, they're here about Emer," Jamie said.

Jack's eyes flickered open. He stared at Jamie for a brief moment before scowling. Sitting up, he ran a hand over his face and looked at the clock on the bedside table.

"Tell them I'll be down now," he said.

Jamie nodded and left the room, taking one last glance at his father before pulling the door closed behind him.

After a few minutes, Jack came down the stairs, buckling up his belt. His eyes narrowed when he saw the cops.

"What's the problem?" he asked. "What brings you lot into my home?"

"Mr. McGuiness, could you take a seat, please?"

Jack shook his head and raised his voice. "Don't tell a man what to do in his own home."

He shooed Jamie away and closed the door behind him.

As if I'm not going to listen. Jamie pressed his ear against the door.

"Mr. and Mrs. McGuiness, I'm afraid we have some very upsetting news," the older officer said. "A young girl, who goes by the description of your daughter, Emer, was found washed ashore on the causeway this morning and pronounced dead at the scene."

A long pause followed. Nothing, not even a pin drop, would have gone unnoticed.

Jamie's heart seemed to stop beating. The officer's words reverberated through his head.

"No ... no ... no! It isn't our Emer," Sonya shouted. "You've come to the wrong house."

"Mrs. McGuiness, she was found by a member of the public shortly after 8:00 a.m. We will need you to come with us to formally identify the deceased."

A loud, piercing scream filled Jamie's head. A noise he'd never forget, not for as long as he lived.

His mother's cries penetrated through every inch of the house. The twins appeared.

Jamie looked at them, his eyes filling with tears. He didn't have time for crying, however. Instead, he switched on his autopilot and ushered the boys into the kitchen. He grabbed two bowls and filled them with ice cream. It seemed like the right thing to do.

"Why's Mammy crying?" Paul asked, spooning some of the chocolate ice cream into his mouth.

"Is Mammy sad?" Thomas asked. His bright blue eyes focused on Jamie.

Jamie shook his head, unsure of what to say. "I'm not sure. Daddy will let us know. Eat up before it melts."

They sat in the kitchen for another twenty minutes before Padraig came in. He glanced at Jamie and shook his head. Looking at the twins, he reached his hands out to them.

"How about a little trip to Granny's?" he asked.

Paul and Thomas jumped down from the chairs and ran to their uncle.

"Is it true?" Jamie asked. His voice broke.

Padraig nodded and led the boys out the back door. He left Jamie alone in the kitchen, whilst the sounds of his mother's sobs echoed through the house.

Present Day

Jamie didn't stop running, not until he reached the causeway. The light summer breeze blew in his face. He looked up at the lighthouse. His mind raced. He tried to remember the dream.

It had felt so real.

Standing on the stones, he bent down and touched the coarse surface. Dread vibrated through his fingertips. Jamie raised his head and focused on the waves swirling in the distance.

"Why?" he whispered. "Why did you have to keep pushing?"

With a heavy heart, Jamie lost himself in the past, trying to imagine the last moments of his sister's life. Every time he pictured how it happened, his mind went blank. No matter how often he read the report, he never understood why she had been down near the water, not when he knew she hated the sea.

A hand touched his shoulder, startling him. He looked over his shoulder and relaxed when he saw the friendly face.

"Jesus, I near shat myself," he said before bursting into laughter.

Lenny laughed, throwing his head back. "Aye, I can get a whiff of it already," he joked. "Thought I'd find you here."

"I always knew I was transparent."

"Fecking right, you are. And a dark horse, too, might I add."

Jamie glared at Lenny, watching him roll up a cigarette. "What do you mean?"

"Claire." Lenny raised an eyebrow.

"Ah," Jamie said, scratching the back of his head. "We just agreed to meet up and hang out."

"Aye. It makes me wonder if Jamie Junior down there is finally on his way to becoming a man." Lenny pointed at Jamie's crotch.

Jamie rolled his eyes, trying to avoid having to talk about sex and Claire. He refused to demean a girl just for sexual gratification.

"I'll leave the sexy times to you, my friend," Jamie replied.

"Well, there's no better lad, my friend," Lenny joked.

The two of them chuckled.

"Do you ever wonder what Emer was doing out here?" Jamie asked, changing the subject, focusing his gaze on the melting horizon.

"Why do you have to keep asking these kinds of questions?"

"Because I'm a glutton for punishment." He shrugged. "I think way too much."

"Sometimes," Lenny said, and nodded, "more than you should. But this is just how you work, Jamie. There's been way too much crap in your life. Your old man doesn't make things easy, and your poor mother has had her plate full."

"I just worry about the twins, about Sarah. I often wonder what would happen if I just left, but I'm not sure I can. Not until I am certain they'd be all right."

Jamie's words were carried on the wind, right to the top of the lighthouse. He glanced in its direction and nudged Lenny's arm.

"How many ships has that old thing guided back to safety?"

"Me da said it was a great lighthouse at one point, but then, they got the new modern ones, and there wasn't a need for the old light keepers," Lenny said.

"I bet this old place could tell a tale or two."

"But lighthouses don't talk, Jamie. Even if they did, would you really want to know what happened to Emer?" he asked. "Seriously? Is that the kind of shite you want to remember for the rest of your life?"

"Maybe. Maybe not," Jamie replied, staring at the top of the beacon.

"Lad, you need to get a grip. Otherwise, you're going to wake up one day an old man who did nothing but live in the past."

Lenny had a point. For some reason, he couldn't break the cycle. The obsession refused to let him be. So many questions remained unanswered. The closure his family needed never came.

For the most part, Jamie went with the flow, incapable of taking his own life. The more the pain swarmed inside, the closer he came to ending it all.

Deep within his heart, he knew things were changing. All the pent-up anger, sadness, and frustration slowly worked its way to the surface, making him a ticking time bomb. The cluster of wrought emotions would either kill him, or leave those he loved broken or dead.

She stood at the top of the lighthouse, her eyes focused on Jamie and Lenny as they walked back to town. Was Jamie ready to accept the truth? Guilt consumed her. Nevertheless, she wanted to show him the past. Unfortunately, he needed a harsh lesson on the value of life. He couldn't throw his life away because of his grief. His responsibilities went further than blood. The pain was no longer about him. He was the missing link, the key to everything.

The truth alone would set her free, but Jamie needed to do the bulk of the work. Closing her eyes, she channeled all the festering anguish and the memories of her last moments. The energy bustled through her as she made her voyage to his soul.

CHAPTER EIGHT

April 3, 2012

The pallbearers carried Emer's coffin into the living room of the small house.

Jack stood by the stairs. The oak casket was set a few feet from the fireplace.

Sonya looked on, her face full of pain. Her cheeks wet with tears, she held a hand to her mouth. It trembled with each small breath she took.

The twins were in the kitchen, watched over by two nuns. A wake house wasn't a place for small children, but they had nowhere else to go.

The house was full to the brim with every member of their family and well-wishers calling, who gawped at the pale face of the once lively twelve-year-old. From the looks on some of their faces, they were relieved it wasn't their child lying cold and still.

Human nature did this to people. They came and gave their sincere condolences. When they left, their body languages changed. Jamie noticed their relaxed posture, faces not so ashen, and their changed demeanors.

Jamie hadn't even attempted to look at Emer. Not once. Even

when they were at the Chapel of Rest, he refused to look at his sister. He couldn't face it.

Lenny walked into the house with his parents, dressed in trousers and a shirt. The sorrow etched across his face mirrored every other mourner in the house. Lenny opened his arms and embraced Jamie.

The two hugged hard.

"I'm so sorry, lad," Lenny whispered.

"I can't believe it," Jamie muttered.

Jamie blinked and pressed his lips together. A bright sheen of moisture shone in his eyes. The pain was too much for him to contain. He shook his head and sat on the bottom step of the stairs, holding his trembling hands together.

Lenny sat down beside him. "Do they know what happened?" he whispered.

"They said she had been drinking, banged her head, and drowned."

Jamie looked at his best friend, searching for a sign that this was a bad dream, unable to escape the truth. This was very real. Nothing would bring his sister back from the dead.

"Jesus Christ!" Lenny ran a hand through his blond hair.

"Do you know what the worst part of it is?" Jamie asked. "I told her I wished she was dead a few weeks back. I should never have said those words. I'm such a fecking idiot."

Jamie closed his eyes, refusing to give in. Being the strong lad his parents had raised seemed paramount now, more than ever before. Underneath all his bravado and willpower, he was a just a boy. One who needed the freedom to cry like the rest of them.

Once Father Darcy began the Rosary, Jamie joined his parents in the living room, doing everything in his power to avoid glancing at the open coffin.

Sonya sobbed, unable to control the flow of tears dripping down her cheeks.

His jaw rigid, Jack clenched his fists into white balls. His face was devoid of emotion. Underneath it all, Jamie suspected his father was a broken man.

When the time came, the mourners retreated to the front street, giving the family their last moments with Emer.

Father Darcy stood by Jack and Sonya as they stared down at their precious little girl.

Sonya made a sign of the cross on her forehead, brushing her hair from behind her ears. "Always so pretty, pet," Sonya muttered, and sobbed.

Jamie wanted to run, to leave, to do anything other than having to look at his dead sister. There was no avoiding it, however.

Sonya reached her hand out to him and tugged him close to her side. She kissed the top of his head and looked at his face.

"Say goodbye to her, pet," she said.

Jamie opened his eyes. His heart skipped a beat. Darkness enveloped the entire room. The only light visible focused on Emer in her coffin.

Disbelief filled every inch of his body. The girl looked like Emer, yet at the same time, she seemed so different. The blue of her lips had been painted over in the hopes of trying to make her look like her usual self, which was impossible. Everyone had remarked at how peaceful she looked, but to Jamie, she looked anything other than at peace. She looked haunted. The marks on her face, blue and deep, were hidden under a pile of ridiculous make-up. Her skin had a waxy look about it.

It had to be a bad dream, but the reality of the coffin cracked through his denial. Anger swirled in his stomach. He wanted to shout at her, tell her to wake up, to stop being a drama queen. He reached for her, unable to bear the coolness of her skin.

Tears leaked out of the corners of his eyes. Shaking his head, he bit down on his lower lip to keep from crying. He wanted Emer to open her eyes and tell him it was all just a bad joke. That she had many more years ahead of her, but no, not Emer. She remained solid in her coffin, unmoving, and the grief became unyielding.

He hated everything he had ever said and done to her. He had been a selfish brother, a self-centered brat who should have known better.

Nothing would ever be the same again.

Present Day

Jamie sat at the dinner table. His stomach churned. He looked at his mother.

"Can I go to my room? I don't feel so good."

Sonya reached over to check his forehead and looked into his eyes, aware of how sad and lost he was. The corners of her mouth tilted downward.

Jamie sighed. They'd all become accustomed to the loss and sadness. In their world, life was an endless struggle. Nothing brought them a sense of hope.

She nodded at Jamie.

Jack drunkenly walked in through the back door. "Your mother cooked that grub, so you better eat it." He pointed his finger at Jamie.

"Leave him be, Jack," Sonya said, standing up. "He's not well."

"Aye, not well, me arse." Jack cursed. "Sure, isn't that the thing with all you young ones? Too fecking lazy to do a day's work. Pissing my food and drink up against the wall."

Jamie left the kitchen before Jack made contact with him. His father's bulging eyes told him a beating would come his way.

His mother's voice echoed down the hallway. "Please, pet, just sit down and have something to eat."

Jamie stood still, wanting to go back in and lamp his father in the face. He would have been walloped, however, something he wanted to avoid. It was bad enough he felt less of a man for not being able to protect his mother. To add insult to injury would have been another blow to his confidence.

Jamie escaped into the sanctuary of his room and lay on his bed. He rubbed his eyes. A subtle, but noticeable chill nipped at the skin on his forearms. Sitting upright, he pulled his quilt up around his neck, gazing around his room, pretending he wasn't spooked.

The sun was setting early, and the light from the large window to his right was now a soft grey. A burnt orange strip of radiance glowed on the horizon, silhouetting the coast. If things had been different, it would have made a wonderful evening to watch the sunset.

His heartbeat pounded in his ears, and the clock ticked beside his bed. Jamie wasn't alone. He could sense *it*, though he couldn't see *it*. He slowly reached out to switch the light on.

It grabbed his wrist the moment his fingers touched the lamp, materializing before his eyes.

"Follow me," she whispered, her dark eyes staring hard into his.

Jamie plummeted down a vortex that had no beginning, middle, or end. His heart raced.

She held on to him, her grip burning his flesh. The pain alone proved it was quite real.

With a loud boom, he suddenly stood looking at the lighthouse, the girl holding onto him tightly. Cold and damp, the scent of death reeked from every pore of her flesh.

"Who are you?" he asked. "What do you want from me?"

Before she answered, she evaporated. Her presence moved within him.

He gasped and groaned, the sound unrecognizable. His eyes widened. He caught sight of Emer standing on the causeway, shouting and crying. Frozen in place, he reached for his sister.

Emer's face purpled with rage. Her arms thrashed. She fought someone he couldn't see.

Stepping closer, Jamie focused on the dark figure in front of Emer. Her disheveled hair blew all around her, shielding the identity of her attacker.

Water dripped around his feet. Jamie looked down. His black shoes were torn at the toes. His toes poked out of them, the chipped nail polish visible. Confused, he raised his head. He no longer stood near the causeway.

Jamie stood inside the lighthouse. The thick, potent stench of death permeated through the air.

Awareness gripped him tight. Something lurked in the shadows.

No longer inside his own body, Jamie saw things through someone else's eyes and it wasn't Emer's. He turned his hands over and examined the long feminine fingers. Blue, chipped polish covered the round nails. Heavy breaths coming from behind him caught his attention. He glanced over his shoulder. His heart raced, and his mouth grew dry.

It's not real. It's not real.

The blow to the back of his head propelled him forward. He smacked his face against the cold stone of the tower. Blood oozed from his nose, trickling over his lips. The taste of his own blood turned his stomach. His hair was pulled back, his head held down by a familiar hand.

Jamie stared into the cold drunken eyes of his father. A sickening realization hit him at a shocking rate. His head pounded from the immediate onslaught of a headache. Thick, rancid breath puffed in his face.

"Please, I won't tell anyone."

The female voice bursting from his lips caught him by surprise.

No form of a reply came from his father. Blow after blow crashed down on his face. The crunch of bones cracking echoed all around him. Pain rippled through every inch of his body.

Jamie accepted that his life would never be the same again. The monster living under the same roof hid a very dark secret. There was only one thing for it—vengeance.

CHAPTER NINE

Like a bullet, Jamie raced from his room, down the stairs, and out into the night. He didn't stop running, not until he stood outside Lenny's house, banging on the door.

Mrs. Bannon opened the door, surprised. She welcomed him in, nonetheless.

"This is late for you, pet," she remarked. "He's in his room."

"Thanks," Jamie replied. He ran up the stairs and burst into Lenny's room seconds later.

Lenny peered at Jamie. "What's happened?"

"Nothing," he said, sitting down on the edge of the bed. "I just had to get out of the house before I did something I'd regret."

Lenny gawped at Jamie and nodded.

Sometimes, Jamie needed to get away. Tonight happened to be one of those moments.

"Is your da being a shite?" Lenny asked.

"You could say that." Jamie sighed, his head still aching. "I can't stand being around the bastard."

Lenny shook his head.

Jamie had been pushed around by his father one too many times.

"Wanna head into town for a bit of craic?" he asked.

"Feck, do I know?" Jamie said, touching the top of his head.

"Come on, you might even get to cop a feel with the pretty Claire," Lenny joked.

For the first time in a long while, Jamie nodded. He needed to do something to rid his mind of what he'd seen.

Several minutes after eleven p.m., they met up with a few of the lads from school. Cans of Tennents and Carlsberg were shared amongst them as they sat on the ramps in the park.

Jamie drank two cans, the buzz from the beer going straight to his head.

"You all right there, lad?" Lenny asked.

"Aye, I'm grand, just you be worrying about yourself," Jamie replied, snorting as the words left his mouth.

Maria pulled up in her newly purchased Golf and smiled at Lenny.

Claire got out of the passenger side and walked across the car park to where the lads had congregated.

"Fancy seeing you here," Maria remarked when she caught Lenny looking at her.

"Where else would I be, huh?" Lenny said in a flirty tone.

Jamie shook his head and opened another can of beer. He accepted another beer from Lenny and offered it to Claire.

Claire smiled and took it.

"I didn't expect to see you here," he remarked.

"Aye," Claire replied. "Maria came by and we went for a drive. There's not much else to be doing on a Sunday night."

"Are we still on for tomorrow?" he asked, trying not to sound desperate.

"Absolutely."

Claire sat on the ramp, her leg brushing against Jamie's.

Smiling, he sipped his beer and looked at Claire. Her beauty drew his attention. He noticed everything. When she smiled, a small crease appeared on the side of her nose. Mid-conversation, she brushed her hair behind her ears and rubbed her thumb across the vial of her necklace.

Claire gently rested her arm under his.

"Wanna go for a walk?" he asked.

"Yes."

"I'll dander on home," Jamie shouted over to Lenny, who smiled at them and waved them on.

"Aye, no bother," Lenny replied. A knowing look spread across his face.

"See you on Wednesday," Claire said.

Maria giggled.

Jamie held his hand out.

The two walked away, surrounded by silence for five minutes, holding hands. Her hand fit perfectly in his.

Jamie soon broke the silence. "So, this is nice," he remarked.

"I think so, too." She smiled, making eye contact with him.

Jamie's nerves were wearing thin. Claire must like him to hold his hand and smile at him in that way, but he didn't want to make a fool of himself.

Minutes later, they arrived at the halfway point between both their homes. As they walked along the old road that led to the causeway, Jamie stopped. A new sensation consumed him, and a kaleidoscope of colors burst in front of his eyes. He'd never kissed a girl before. The surge of adrenaline strengthened his resolve. He wanted to kiss Claire, and silently prayed she wanted it, too.

Wrapping a hand around Claire's waist, he cupped her face with the other, and their lips met. The kiss was gentle, but captivating, a mixture of all the hope and desires of a newfound romance.

Awestruck as their lips moved together, time after time, the moment transported them to another world.

Jamie found it impossible to imagine the kiss ending. He wanted to stand there, holding Claire close, her warmth pressed against him. The kiss of life injected new hope and dreams he thought he'd never have again.

They were lost in a sea of lust. Fiery, powerful, and beautiful— the combination of emotions within the kiss sent waves of passion crashing over them. Their lips pulled apart. A gentle breeze fluttered past, the calm and cool air blowing in from the sea.

Jamie had never felt anything like it before. It was exciting, frightening, and encouraging.

"Wow," Claire whispered, her arms wrapped around his waist.

"I know," he muttered, dizzy from the kiss. He didn't want the moment to end.

"I could get used to you kissing me like that, Jamie McGuiness." She giggled.

"And I could get used to having you in my arms, Claire Brannigan," he replied, brushing his nose against hers.

She watched them from the sidelines. A pang of jealousy pulsed through her. She didn't want to share him with anyone else.

April 7, 2012

The days that followed the funeral were some of the hardest Jamie had ever lived through.

His mother went to bed on the afternoon of the burial and didn't stir from her room, not until Father Darcy stopped by four days later.

"Is your mother not up for visitors?" he asked.

"Mammy isn't herself at the moment," Jamie replied.

The floorboards at the top of the stairs creaked. Jamie looked up.

Sonya appeared at the top of the landing. "It's okay, Father. I'll be right down," she said, her face haggard.

Jamie went into the kitchen, filled the kettle, and waited for it to boil.

Out in the back of the house, Jack made no effort to talk to anyone. He moved around the extension, refusing to engage with his family.

BENEATH THE LIGHTHOUSE

Once the kettle was ready, Jamie filled the teapot with hot water and put it on a tray beside the teacups and biscuits. Jamie carried it into the living room and set it down on the coffee table. He weakly smiled at the priest.

"You're a good lad, Jamie," Father Darcy remarked, watching Jamie fill a cup with tea and milk.

"Here you go, Father," he said, offering him the tea.

Sonya strode into the room and sat down on the armchair near the fireplace. Her hair unkempt, lines of strain were etched around the corners of her mouth. Dark circles surrounded her eyes, her complexion pale.

"I stopped by, Sonya, to check in on you all," Father Darcy said.

"Thank you, Father," she replied.

"I was saying, Jamie is a good lad. You and Jack are lucky." The priest looked at Jamie and smiled.

"Aye, he is." Sonya reached over and touched the back of Jamie's hand. "He's been a godsend."

"Sometimes, even in our darkest hour, it's amazing where the strength and hope can come from. More often than not, it's from the love of a child."

Sonya nodded and agreed with the priest. She looked at Jamie once more, her eyes filled with tears ready to burst from their dam.

"Do you mind if I go?" Jamie asked.

He didn't want to listen to the priest waffling on about how God had a plan for everyone, putting the blame of Emer's death on fate and destiny. Everything was still too fresh.

"No, pet, off you go," Sonya replied.

Jamie couldn't wait to leave the room. The more he had to

listen to Father Darcy, the more he wanted to run away. He strode into the kitchen and observed his father, who stood behind the thick plastic sheeting that led to the extension.

Jack mumbled, scratching the back of his head.

Jamie stepped outside and walked up to the sheeting. His father looked like a disheveled wreck of a man.

In the space of a few days, Jack had fallen apart, completely disengaged with his family. They needed him more now than ever before, but Jack was lost in his own misery—a selfish place to be when his wife and children needed him to be strong.

Jamie stared at him.

Jack ran to the sheeting and glared at him. "What do you want?" he growled.

"Nothing, Da, just checking to see if you need a hand," Jamie replied, wanting to be a man, but still needing the comfort of his father.

"Go away. I don't want to be bothered." Jack turned his back on Jamie.

He would never forgive his father for shunning him, but he finally understood. Full of pain, Jack grieved like the rest of them, blind to the needs of his family.

Jamie walked out the back door, his heart heavy with burdens others his age would never understand. Not unless they were going through the same pain.

He walked to the causeway, visiting the very place his sister had lost her life. Lost in a past he tried to piece together, nothing made sense.

CHAPTER TEN

*S*he cried and opened her eyes, peering down from the tower. Her tears fell like a torrential downpour that refused to stop—not until she was set free.

From deep within her, the light had been diminished. The void left behind became a constant loop of dread and sorrow. She had been the subject of so much needless pain. The vortex of doom refused to stop moving, the endless surge of torment pushing her existence into limbo, a fate worse than hell.

Jamie awoke with tears fresh on his cheeks. His pillow was soaked, the ache in his chest an ever-present reminder of the day he buried his sister.

Regardless of how many times he washed his face, the tears and sadness wouldn't stop. He cried for so long, he was sure there couldn't possibly be any tears left. They were relentless.

Sobbing, he wiped his face and got out of the bed. He stepped to his dresser and looked in the mirror, searching for the girl he'd seen not too long ago. He needed her to stop what she was doing to him. Whoever she was, she needed his help, but having him become an emotional mess wasn't going to help things.

"Please," he whispered, glancing at the wall in his reflection. "Just tell me how I can help you."

The wall behind him rippled like the sea. Black hazy waves moved towards him like a living, breathing entity.

Jamie held his breath before he relaxed and turned around to face the entity head on.

A hand reached for him. Her cool flesh pressed against his.

"Jamie," she whispered.

Her breath brushed against his skin. He found himself being absorbed within the embryo of the past.

Iliana Crumlish finished cleaning up the last few boxes from the stall.

Her grandmother looked at her, taking note of the restlessness inside her. Shaking her head, she pointed her finger at Iliana.

"Child, you need to stop pouting. How will you ever get a husband if you keep scowling?" she asked.

"Granny, I'm just … bored," Iliana replied, sitting down on the stool outside the small caravan.

Her grandmother lifted the hem of her skirt and stepped down from the mobile home. She took a seat beside Iliana.

"You're just restless. It's normal. Most of the girls your age are marrying, starting their lives. You are just feeling a little left out."

"Thanks, Granny, like I need reminding." Iliana scowled.

"Stop the huffing. Go take a walk, get a bag of chips and a can of Coke, and spend time with that wee friend of yours. Just come back smiling." The old woman smiled, revealing a gold tooth at the front of her mouth.

Iliana sighed. There was nothing else for her. Not unless she caught the eye of one of the older boys and he proposed. She despised turning sixteen and being seen as over the hill because she wasn't married.

In their culture, they married young and had children young. Their lives were lived doing the same things their ancestors had done before them. It was the Irish Travellers way and nothing would ever change it.

Iliana stood. She picked up her last box and set it down in the trailer.

Her father walked down from the carousel and smiled. "Just one more day in this town, and then we move south," he said.

"I know, Daddy," she replied.

"Make sure you help your grandmother out."

He looked at her, his face stern. His features warmed as he pulled her in for a hug.

"Aye, I have, and I've permission to go for a walk," Iliana replied, hugging her father back.

He looked at Iliana and cupped her face in his hands. "As long as you're back before it gets too dark, okay?"

Iliana nodded and smiled. Content, she strolled back to the caravan, picking up her purse. She checked her skirt and shoes, brushed her hair, and pulled a face when her grandmother licked her thumb, pretending to clean a spot of dirt on her chin.

"Ah, Granny, would you stop?" She laughed.

Her grandmother chuckled and rolled her eyes. "I sometimes forget you're a woman."

"I'm sure you do." Iliana pushed her grandmother's hand away in a playful gesture.

Opening up her small jewelry box, Iliana grabbed her locket. Smiling, she secured it around her neck. She only wore the pendant once the fair had closed for the day. It had been a gift from her mother before the cancer had taken her from them. To Iliana, the precious heirloom would always connect her to her mother.

Her grandmother took her hand before she had a chance of stepping outside. Closing her eyes, she mumbled something to herself. Her eyes opened and she gripped Iliana's wrist tight.

"Don't go. I've changed my mind." Her grandmother panicked.

"Granny, don't be silly. I'll be back soon." Iliana laughed.

"Please, Iliana, don't go. There's something dark out there tonight. I felt it when I touched you." The old woman cried.

Iliana stepped in close and kissed her cheek. "I'll be back, I promise. The only darkness out there is the sea, and I won't be taking a dip anytime soon."

Iliana left the campground and happily walked the short distance into town, anxious to be alone with her friend and excited for a small measure of freedom.

Jamie gasped when Iliana let go of his hand.

She stood before him in her ghostly form. Her eyes were dark and full of pain.

Jamie wanted to understand what had happened. "Why me?" he whispered.

Iliana opened her mouth, but nothing came out. She shook her head. Her anxious movements caused her silhouette to shift around the small bathroom like a mist blown around in a storm. With wide eyes, she took control and moved within him, a sensation he had become accustomed to.

With a sharp thud, he was back on the causeway. He didn't understand why the girl kept showing him the place where Emer died. Nothing made sense.

The darkness of the night resembled a painting. It didn't look real. None of it did. Even the lighthouse had an animated look about it with its thick black outline and bulging walls. The chilly air blowing from the sea reminded him that it was real.

He glanced down at his feet. Jamie saw things through Iliana's eyes. Frightening and liberating, he would never have imagined such a thing possible.

He stood on the rocks, the breeze blowing around his bare legs. Iliana's voice echoed inside his head.

"I didn't mean to stumble here," she said. *"But when I heard the screams, I had to see for myself."*

The water stopped rippling and the breeze stopped brushing his skin. Minutes later, the booming sound of heavy footsteps approached.

He ran. His desperate breath burned in his chest. Falling over the rocks, he cut his knees. Wincing in pain, he got to his feet. A small cry escaped him before he continued running.

Jack cut him off at the lighthouse, stopping Jamie from making a getaway to the road. Anger burned across his face.

For a moment, he wanted to close his own eyes. He refused to believe it to be real, unable to accept who his attacker was. His father stood before him, as real as the day, in the flesh and stinking of beer and whiskey.

"Please," he begged. "I won't say a thing. I promise."

Jack growled and made a beeline for him. He hit him hard across the jaw. The pain alone from the slap stung, the blood dripping into his mouth.

Scrambling to his feet, Jamie searched for something to hit him with. He reached for a rock and cried out. His nail ripped and tore from his finger.

Shallow, sharp breaths gripped Jamie tight. He had no time to assess the damage to his finger.

With one clean move, Jack grabbed his hair and thumped him hard in the face. Jack gripped his neck tight.

The pressure burned at the back of Jamie's throat. As he struggled to fight back, the locket was torn from his neck.

Jamie cried out, desperately reaching for it, but his efforts were futile.

The door to the lighthouse opened and Jack threw Jamie down onto the cold, damp ground of the old building. The stench of stale water sickened him.

Each slap, each punch landed across his flesh—the pain and fright a very real experience. Then came the boot to the face.

The ringing in his ears deafened and disorientated him. He scrambled to his feet, blood dripping from his broken nose. Jamie staggered and pleaded with Jack.

"I promise I won't tell ... anyone," he said. "I just ... want to go back to my ... daddy."

Jack charged towards him, hitting him hard with the back of his hand, full of a rage unlike anything Jamie had witnessed before.

This wasn't the man he knew. This wasn't the man who had taught him to swim, ride his bike, or play football. This was a monster. A maniac killing an innocent girl.

"You just had to stand and watch." Jack growled, ramming Jamie's head against the stone floor of the lighthouse. "You just couldn't walk away."

He continued smashing his head until his rage subsided.

Jamie sensed the moment death came. When the darkness surrounded Iliana and became stilted and motionless. Pain no longer burned through him. The sensation of her heart beating its desperate thumps while trying to stay alive disappeared. Emptiness now stood in its place.

No light or tunnel existed. Nothing but the stench of death and blood, and Jack, who looked down at the bloodied, crushed body of the innocent bystander. Spitting on her, Jack turned away. He left the lighthouse, not once looking back at the fresh body on the ground.

Fright rippled through him. His eyes opened, and there he stood, looking down at Iliana's lifeless body.

Her spirit stood beside him, her face emotionless. The energy emanating from her told him exactly how she felt. Jamie realized he had been wrong, and his father was a murderer.

"I'm so sorry," Jamie cried. "I had no idea he was capable of this."

Jamie sobbed and closed his eyes, unable to look at what his father had done. He turned, intent on looking at the ghostly girl beside him, back in his bathroom, alone.

Bile rose to the back of his throat with such force, he vomited hard. His pulse pounded in his ears. He retched, finding it hard to digest the fact that his father was a cold-blooded killer.

Jamie sat on the floor and cried. Rubbing his eyes, he shook his head. All these years, all the lies, the pain, and the anger, all vented towards his mother and him. His father hid behind the mask of grief. All the while, he was nothing but a menace. A wicked person who had no remorse, no regret, and everything to pay for.

He would destroy his father. Even if it meant revealing the ugly truth to his mother.

CHAPTER ELEVEN

Jamie stared at the ceiling for the longest time. He found it hard to switch off his anger. The visions of his father and the brutal killing flashed before him every time he turned over. Iliana's cold stare embedded itself beneath his skin. The way her mouth jerked and the ghastly noise that erupted from the back of her throat as her life slipped away would never leave Jamie's mind again.

His thoughts wandered to Emer. Had her death been an accident? What were the odds of two girls being killed on the causeway? Why hadn't Emer come back to visit him? Why Iliana? So many questions raced through his mind. For the first time, he wanted to know if a connection existed between Iliana and Emer.

The stench of the tower refused to leave him. His stomach churned. He recalled the repulsive odor the stagnant water lapping around Iliana's body left behind.

There was so much to fear. His father slept next door. He had raised him and cried at Emer's graveside, yet he was nothing more than a monster.

No matter how many times he washed the vision from his mind, it remained, like a dirty stubborn stain. He had to find the strength to overcome his fear, even if it meant looking his father in the eye.

Jamie sat up and switched on the lamp. He rubbed the back of his neck. A photograph of the family together in happier times sat on the dresser across from his bed. Jamie got out of the bed and strolled over to the dresser. He took the small silver frame in his hand.

"Why didn't you just stay in?" he whispered, running his thumb over Emer's smiling face.

He shook his head and sighed. The pressure in his chest left him depressed. The dread and despair became one with his grief and agitation.

The smiles on their faces were real. They weren't putting on a show or hiding something from the rest of the world. This was his family at their best. A time before the darkness had taken over.

Jamie set the frame down and walked to his window. He stared at the dark street. The trees in the garden were ghostly silhouettes in the dim light of the moon. When he thought about how bad life had been before, nothing compared to the fear creeping through his soul. It made him remember the things he wanted to forget the most.

April 10, 2012

Jamie sat alone on the swing. The light, cool wind blew around him.

A few boys played football in the nearby field. Their laughter and shouts were nothing more than distant echoes in his head.

Lost in his own little bubble, he thought about Emer and how her body would have begun to decompose. For the first time in his life, he became acutely aware of his own mortality. Death and its destruction were now a part of life. Despair filled his every waking moment. At night, it refused to leave. Emer's waxy face, the cuts, the bruising, and the scent of incense tumbled through his mind.

"Your ma said I'd find you here," Lenny said from behind.

Jamie turned his head and shrugged. "Aye, sure. What else is there to be at?"

"You didn't turn up for registration." Lenny sat down on the swing next to Jamie and swung back and forth, waiting for an answer.

"I couldn't face school today." Jamie sighed.

"Aye, I can tell." Lenny glanced at Jamie. "Do you want to talk about it?"

Jamie shook his head. "No … I don't know. I'm just so confused."

"Me da told me how it felt when he buried his brother, Finbar," Lenny remarked. "He said it was terrible and you will be going through a lot upstairs." Lenny tapped the side of his head.

"I'm not mad. I'm just … I don't know, feeling a bit shite."

"I know." Lenny smirked.

"Me da is acting like a nut job, and me mum won't eat and spends all day in bed. It's fecked up, lad." Jamie shrugged and looked at his friend. "What am I meant to do when they're both falling apart? They're meant to be the adults, looking after me and the twins. Instead, it's down to me to make sure things are done. It's not right."

Lenny jumped from the swing and nodded at Jamie. "Come on. Let's get something to eat. I've a few pounds here from me granny."

Jamie sighed, glanced up at the cloudy sky, and then back down at his feet. "I suppose I could eat a bag of chips."

"Good," Lenny said, and pressed his fingers against Jamie's arm. "Because I can't have you failing away now, can I?"

"Thanks, lad."

"What else are friends for?"

Lenny had hit the nail on the head. When it came to depending on someone other than his family, Jamie could always count on Lenny.

They walked to the chippy and bought two bags of chips and two cans of Coke. After sitting down on the causeway, they ate and watched a few ferries sail by.

"Am I a weirdo if I say I feel like I'm close to Emer when I come down here?" Jamie asked.

"Yup, you are. Maybe I'd feel the same if it were me own sister who had, you know, died."

"I'll never get used to it, not really."

Lenny chewed on a chip and sighed. "We're never meant to get used to death, but none of us gets out of this world alive."

"I know."

"Listen, lad, Emer's death was just a tragic accident," Lenny said. "You can't go around thinking about it all the time. It's not right."

Jamie set the can on the stones and rested his arms on his knees. He closed his eyes and inhaled the salty air deep into his lungs. Everything Lenny said made perfect sense to him, but a part of him refused to listen. A hidden place in his heart had been broken. He would never recover.

"I best be getting home," Jamie said. "I bloody hate going back there."

"Aye, but you can't hide away forever, lad." Lenny grabbed Jamie's shoulder, gently squeezing it. "Will you be at school tomorrow?"

"Probably, there are only so many days I can get away with not going in," Jamie said. "Besides, if the truancy officer goes near the house, I'm done for." He shrugged and sighed.

"See you then." Lenny nodded at him.

"Dead on," Jamie replied, and headed in the opposite direction.

He walked home, the sun setting fast the closer he got to his house. Jamie approached the corner of his street. Dread raced through him. He didn't want to have to listen to his father cursing or his mother crying.

Swallowing hard, he kept moving until he made it home. He pressed his hand against the back door and heard the first thunderous roar coming from inside.

"I told you to stay the feck out of my way," his father roared.

"I'm sorry," Sonya cried.

Jamie entered the kitchen. His heart thumped hard. He reached his hand towards his father.

"Da, don't do it."

Jack cocked his head up and glared at Jamie. "Get the feck out of my sight before I clock you one, too."

Sonya stared at Jamie. Her bloodied lips trembled. She shook her head.

"Ma, please."

"Jamie, just go up to the boys," Sonya muttered.

Jamie stepped back and rested his hands against the counter. His stomach turned over and spun with unease. Rage boiled inside him. He wanted to be a man and stand up to his father, but fear stopped him. Instead, he swallowed his anger and looked away from his mother in shame.

Jack stomped over to Jamie. His nostrils flared.

"You think you're some big hero coming in here, do you?"

"No, Da," Jamie replied.

His voice shook. He lifted his arm, intent on shielding his face. Without taking his eyes off Jamie, Jack backhanded him hard.

Blackness curled around his vision. Jamie's ears rang, and he lost his balance.

"Don't you dare answer me back, you wee shite." A feral look flashed across Jack's face.

"Jack!" Sonya screamed.

The soft, warm touch of his mother's hands on Jamie's arms eased some of the fear and hurt. The darkness receded. He shook his head to clear the confusion. Jamie took a deep breath and glared at his father.

"Please, pet, just go to your room. Take the boys with you," Sonya begged.

She pushed him from the kitchen counter and out the door, closing it behind him.

His father's muffled voice followed Jamie as he crept up the stairs. The sound of the chairs scraping on the kitchen floor screeched.

The twins sat on the edge of their parents' bed. Their faces were wet with tears. He held his arms out to them, and they ran in unison to him.

"What's Daddy doing?" Thomas asked.

Jamie took hold of their hands and led them to his room. He closed the door behind them and switched on the television.

"Nothing to be worrying about. Let's watch some cartoons, yeah?" he suggested, masking the sounds of carnage from downstairs.

"I'm scared," Paul said.

"There's no need to be. I'm here. I won't let anything happen to you," Jamie said, hugging Paul tight.

"Daddy's angry," Thomas remarked.

"Aye."

Jamie swallowed hard, almost choking on his anguish. His brothers' fears were enough to make Jamie wish he was strong enough to change their lives.

"I wish Emer was here," Paul muttered, and hugged his teddy tight to his chest.

"Me, too," Jamie whispered. "Me, too."

He held on to his brothers, afraid to let them out of his sight. The three of them huddled together in the small room. Jamie lay awake, watching the bedroom door.

His mother had gone quiet. Jack's shouts had ceased. A horrible sense of something not being right descended upon the household.

His father had finally snapped. His mother was just a tool for his father to take his anger out on.

Present Day

Jamie stepped away from the window and shook his head. He hated how he remembered failing his mother. He felt like a stupid, sniveling wreck of a child. He despised himself for not being a man. For not having the balls to stand up to his father.

His regret was a living demon torturing him in his waking hours. Iliana's presence opened his mind to the atrocities his father had committed. The premonition of something terrible looming on the horizon followed him with every step he took.

CHAPTER TWELVE

Jamie darted down the stairs and straight out the front door. He didn't bother saying hello or goodbye. He needed air. The desire to be away from his family crushed him from within. Guilt crippled him. Running away would be the right thing to do, even if it hurt those around him.

He didn't stop running, not until he made it to the causeway. Jamie stood on the stones and composed his breathing. The sun shone down in bold, luminous light. Jamie squinted and looked at the glass of the tower. The memory of Iliana's death toyed with his emotions. Confused and angry, he resented Emer for destroying their family more than ever before.

Jamie slipped his hands into the pockets of his jeans. He ignored the burning need to go to the very place where Iliana died. An internal battle roiled within him. Afraid of having to face the truth, he wanted to feel something other than what raced through his veins.

What if she's still in there? He strode towards the lighthouse.

The vision of her remains flitted through his mind. He shook his head, trying to erase the vision.

Jamie bit down on his bottom lip, pinching hard. His hands grew clammy, his breathing heavy. His stomach felt like it had been laced with lead. His mouth grew dry. Once he stepped across the threshold of the tower, there would be no coming back from the reality of his father's wickedness.

He grabbed the doorknob. Twisting the handle, he pushed the door open. The world fell away, and the blood drained from his face. The stench from the stagnant water brought him back to the night Iliana perished.

The desperation of the memory crept through him. Jamie couldn't stand it. The horrific truth surrounded him—his father was a monster.

Iliana stood behind him. Her hands trembled.

"Jamie," she whispered. *"Can you hear me?"* Her voice floated through the air. She hadn't expected him to return so soon. Not after she'd revealed what his father had done to her.

Jamie's anguish seeped into her. She hadn't meant to cause him this much pain, but she needed him to become aware of her desolation. To feel her anguish and acknowledge her existence.

She reached out her hand. Her fingers lightly brushed the back of his arm.

"Jamie," she said. *"Look closer."*

The hairs on his skin stood on end.

"Iliana," he whispered, and turned his head to the side.

The light outside peeked in through the crack of the doorway. Jamie walked across the threshold. Dizziness consumed him. The memory wrapped its arms around him and pulled him back to the night Iliana died.

All sense of time ceased.

Blood filled his mouth. He lay on the wet ground, staring up at his father's face.

Jack glared down at him, his fists clenched and his breathing rapid. "You stupid brat."

Jamie watched his father's posture change. The rage on his face settled. Deep creases lined his eyes, and his lips were pursed.

"Feck!" Jack spat.

He kicked Iliana's legs. They were heavy and didn't move. He cursed again and again.

Blood trickled down the back of his throat. Metallic and thick, it turned his stomach. The cold seeped into his bones. No matter how awful he felt, nothing compared to the sharp grey eyes of his father staring down at him.

Jamie wanted to close his eyes, to hide from his father. Iliana wanted him to see it all, regardless of how ugly it was.

Jack grabbed Jamie by the feet, dragging him across the wet floor. Jamie felt every bump. His head hit the cobbles on the ground. Each time, the ache rippled through him.

This isn't right. Iliana, make it stop. Please.

Dragged along, Jamie understood the point of bearing witness to his father's brutality. To be conscious of the horrific violence, he had to endure Iliana's demise.

His head cocked to the right. His fixed gaze focused on the moonlight. It beamed in through a small window at the side of the building. The soft silver light was a reminder that time became distorted in the memory.

"Look closer." Iliana's voice echoed through his head.

Jamie couldn't move. He didn't understand what she meant.

Jack heaved the body towards the exit. Grunting, he opened the door and peered outside.

Jamie shifted his head. He propelled the sheer force from within. Nothing in his body responded to what he wanted.

Jack pulled hard on his legs.

The force alone caused the gravel of the lighthouse to rip through the flesh beneath his shirt. Liquid oozed from his body. Hauled through the door and into the chill of the night, blood streaked the stones beneath him. The moon glimmered faintly above him. The salty scent of the sea surrounded him. The undulating waves crashed on the causeway.

"Get the feck out of here," Jack said, his voice raised.

He bent down and grabbed Jamie's face, squeezing his cheeks together.

"You shouldn't have been here, you stupid bitch," he cried. "You stupid tinker, always sticking your nose into other people's business."

Jack turned Jamie over onto his stomach. He pushed his face down against the rocks. His foot pushed against Jamie's back. He pulled his hands behind him, his clammy fingers pressing against Jamie's skin.

"Make it stop. Make it stop," Jamie whispered. "Please, make it stop."

His chest constricted, and his eyes grew heavy. A black fog surrounded him.

His eyes adjusted to the darkness. His heart raced. The light of the moon glinted across a small object buried in its obscure grave between rock and sand.

Jamie's mind buzzed with curiosity. He *had* to know.

A sudden pop erupted inside Jamie's ears, causing them to ache. The ringing inside his head pulled him out of the past and into the present.

Jamie stood by the doorway and retraced his steps. He looked down into the rocks beneath his feet and searched for the small gold object. Iliana had led him there for this very reason.

Slow and steady, he moved back towards the place he'd seen himself lying face down. He dropped to his knees and ran his fingers over the stones. A breeze blew around him, ruffling his hair. He looked up at the tower, wishing it would reveal more to him. From the corner of his eye, he saw the glimmering metal twinkling in the sun's reflection.

He sucked in a deep breath and slipped his fingers between the stones. His stomach twisted into a tight knot. He grabbed the small locket and ran his thumb over the face of the inscription.

Iliana, forever in my heart.

Dread squeezed his chest. A sensation pulsed through him, like the vibrating wings of a caged bird. His body trembled.
Is this what Iliana wanted me to find?
Jamie swallowed the dread swarming through him. Still on his knees, he peered up at the tower, tears filling his eyes.

"I'm so sorry," he whispered.

Tears coursed down his cheeks. He tried to get hold of himself, but he bent forward and sobbed.

Everything became too much for him. His father had to be brought to justice. There was no other way around it, even if it meant climbing into the lion's den and meeting the monster head on.

CHAPTER THIRTEEN

By the time Jamie made it home, he had composed himself. He didn't want his mother catching sight of him crying, or finding the locket he had tucked away inside his jeans. He slipped in through the back door and took off his shoes.

"Is that you, Jamie?" his mother called from the living room.

"Aye."

"There's some dinner in the microwave."

Lost in a haze of thoughts, mixed feelings, and apprehension, Sonya's words barely registered.

Jamie ran a hand over his face and sat down at the table. Slouching forward, he rested his chin on his hands and closed his eyes.

"Are you okay, pet?" his mother asked.

Opening his eyes, he looked at his mother. Her soft smile hid her silent torment.

"I'm okay," he replied, trying not to sound too depressed. "I'm just tired."

"You left before I got a chance to tell you."

Jamie froze. His posture became rigid.

"Tell me what?"

"The wee cutty, Claire, rang here this morning," Sonya said.

"She really shouldn't be calling here. You know how your father gets about the Brannigans."

"Oh," Jamie replied, his cheeks flushed.

Sonya switched on the microwave and folded her arms. "She's a lovely girl. Why didn't you tell me you had a girlfriend?"

"She's not me girlfriend, Ma. She's just a friend."

"Are you sure?" Sonya asked, raising an eyebrow.

"Ma, will you stop it?" Jamie said. The burn of embarrassment seeped through every pore of his body. "Where's the oul man?"

"Down at the pub."

"Great," Jamie mumbled.

The prospect of a night listening to his father rant and rave wasn't on his agenda. His mother would either be the love of Jack's life or a living, breathing punching bag.

"It might not be so bad." Sonya shrugged.

The microwave pinged. Sonya turned her back on Jamie, trying to hide her shame.

Full of guilt, he said, "I didn't mean to upset you."

Sonya kept her back to him. Her shoulders slumped with defeat.

He pushed the chair back, stood, and walked over to where his mother stood. "I'm sorry," he said, reaching his hand out to her.

Sonya shook her head and sniffed. "It's okay. You didn't mean anything." She turned around and handed Jamie his plate of food. "I made your favorite."

Jamie looked at the plate of sausages, mash, and gravy. "Thanks," he said. "Sometimes, I wish I was little again."

Sonya touched the side of his face and ran her thumb across

his cheek. "I know the feeling, pet. Now, go sit down and eat. I've the twins to bathe yet, and Sarah will be ready for her bottle." She bit down on her bottom lip.

Jamie took the plate from her and smiled. "You know something, Ma?"

"Yes, Jamie?"

"One day, I'm going to take you away from all of this. You won't ever have to worry about me da coming in drunk and hitting you again."

Sonya put a hand to her mouth. Her eyes were full of sadness.

Jamie couldn't wrap his head around why she stayed with Jack when she clearly feared him. Wouldn't she be happier somewhere else?

"You're such a good lad, Jamie," she muttered. "More's the pity your father doesn't see it. But it's his loss and my gain."

Sonya walked out of the kitchen and didn't look back at Jamie.

He sat down at the table and ate a mouthful of mash and gravy. The whole time he chewed, the more vexed he became. What normally would have been a good meal was now tainted with his newfound knowledge. His stomach turned.

Jamie didn't want his mother subjected to another night of abuse. Unfortunately, he didn't know how to avert the drama. His father was capable of anything. Jamie thought of a way to get his mother out of the house, but something pulled him in an entirely different direction.

Jamie lifted the pendant out of his pocket and set it on the table. He pushed his plate away and stared at the gold necklace, reading the inscription over and over.

After a few minutes, Jamie lifted the chain and closed his fist tight around it. His chest felt like a brick sat inside him, weighing him down, crushing him from the inside out. The pent-up frustration was an all-consuming feeling, a mixture of rage and fear—neither a desirable prospect.

His temples throbbed, making his every effort to think straight a battle.

The phone rang. The sound pulsed through his head. He grabbed the phone lying on the counter nearby.

"Hello," he answered, rubbing the front of his head, trying to push the pain away.

"Jamie, it's Claire."

"Oh, hello."

"I called this morning, but your mum said you were already out," she said.

"Yeah, she's just told me I'd missed your call." Jamie relaxed a little. "How are you?"

"I'm good. Do you fancy coming 'round to my auntie's with me? I've to babysit, and I know I'll get bored."

A smile spread across Jamie's face. "Are you sure?"

"Jesus, Jamie, I've called. Doesn't it tell you I'm very sure?" Claire laughed.

Jamie rested his back against the wall next to the back porch. The sound of Claire's voice eased some of the anxiety tumbling through his mind the past few days.

"Will I come by yours?" he asked.

"Yes. I need to be at Kate's for half eight."

"Then I'll be at yours for eight." Jamie's stomach fluttered.

"Great, see you then. Bye."

"Bye."

Once the line went dead, Jamie stood in the partition between the back porch and the unfinished extension. His heart raced with excitement. Claire was the distraction he needed.

Jamie set the phone down on the kitchen counter and faced the plastic film covering the entrance to the expansion. At first, the exterior extension had been an exciting venture for him. Jack had wanted him to be a part of the building team, and Jamie had loved spending time with his father. Now, the unfinished work was a constant reminder of how much their lives had changed.

Sweat chilled his skin. He stood frozen and stared through the plastic layer. Shadows danced behind the makeshift wall, their silhouettes casting shapes along the ground. A dark shape moved past the boarded window at the back of the room.

Jamie's breath caught in his throat. His heart thumped in his ears. He pushed past the plastic covering and entered the room.

Stillness enveloped him. Jamie strolled over to the workbench. He ran his fingers along the work surface. Dust covered his fingertips. The chill of the air pierced through the light layers of his summer clothes and pricked his skin.

Jamie glanced over his shoulder towards the plastic sheeting. The distant noise came from the television in the living room.

The smaller children giggled, a stark contrast to where he stood.

Dread clamped hard in his chest. With wide eyes, he slowly turned his head and listened.

Drip.

Drip.

Drip.

Water—he heard water.

Where's it coming from?

No rain seeped inside. The room was dry, yet the dripping sound continued.

He pressed his ear against the wall. An irregular trickling and a whimper echoed behind it.

Jamie jumped back, his eyes wide with terror. Frightened, he didn't want to make a sound.

The hairs on the backs of his arms stood on end. A formidable pressure weighed heavy on his shoulders.

A cold, black, malevolent mist swirled around him.

Jamie held his breath. His jaw tightened. His stomach turned. Rooted in place, his feet refused to move. Like a piece of bait on the end of a rod, he waited for the big bad monster to come and gobble him up.

"Who's there?" he whispered.

He exhaled. His breath wafted around his face, the freezing temperature turning it to ice. His eyes followed the shadow descending from the wall in front of him. It floated in his direction.

"No, no, no," he muttered.

He had nowhere to run. The entity was in the house with him and his family. His heart slowed down, the sound of his blood pumping in his ears replaced with the sharp breaths he took.

"Calm down. Just … calm down," he breathed. "Hail Mary, full of grace, the Lord is with thee."

Thump.

A hammer from the workbench fell to the ground.

Closing his eyes, he pushed his hand inside the pocket of his jeans and pulled out the pendant. He gripped it tight in his hand and said her name.

"Iliana."

The darkness made it easy for her to dance in the shadows. To creep around the floors and watch his trepidation with grand amusement. She hadn't meant to scare him. It had never been her plan.

His presence had awakened the energy of the afterlife. Trapped for far too long, he was the key to setting her free, even if it meant unearthing the truth.

Iliana stood beside him, watching him inspect the wall in front of him.

Would he be brave enough to break down the walls?

She reached out and curled her hand around the side of his face, the very spot his mother had touched mere minutes before.

Poor Jamie. He really hasn't got a clue.

Rage bubbled inside of her. Her anger was like a tsunami, pent-up frustration from a life cut short, and all for bearing witness to something no father should ever do.

Closing her eyes, Iliana found herself behind the wall. Her tears dripped down her face. Until Jamie found the strength to believe in the impossible, he would never be able to reach her. She had unlocked his mind, but the hard part was convincing to him to open the gateway to hell.

"Set me free, Jamie."

Jamie fell to his knees. He gasped for breath. His head ached. Staring at the wall, his eyes burned with tears.

Nothing made sense to him. He thought he was going mad.

Maybe madness feels like this. Maybe I'm not right in the head, after all.

"Jamie," his mother called from the kitchen.

He cocked his head up and wiped his face. He didn't want her seeing him like this.

"What are you doing in here?" she asked, pushing the plastic sheet aside.

"I thought I heard something," he replied, stuffing the chain into his pocket and pretending to tie the lace of his shoe.

"I hate this room."

Sonya looked around the room. Her eyes were red and filled with tears.

"Me, too," he agreed, and stood.

"What did you think you heard?"

Jamie shrugged, forcing a smile. "Water or something dripping."

"But it's not been raining."

Jamie sucked in a deep breath and walked towards his mother. "Maybe it was some pipes. I don't know." He shook his head. "Anyway, it's stopped."

Jamie stood beside his mother, watching her gaze around the empty room. Seeing her like this filled him with pain. Before Emer died, he'd never witnessed his mother being anything but a strong and happy woman.

She stood there, not uttering a word, staring at a space that was meant to bring them happiness.

Even the strongest of souls could be broken, he realized.

"Who was on the phone?" she asked, turning her back on the room and walking towards the kitchen.

"Claire."

Sonya smiled and glanced back at him as he followed her. "Ah."

"Don't start. She's just a friend. I'm going to see her later." Jamie's cheeks burned.

"Hmm, that's what I said about your da back in the day."

Jamie smirked and shook his head. "Yeah, the olden days."

Sonya playfully smacked him on the side of the face.

"Will you be all right if he comes back drunk?" he asked.

"Sure, what can I do?"

"You can go to Granny's," Jamie suggested, his face serious. "She won't let him near you if you take the wee ones with you."

"I'm not going to be bothering me mother with silly things, now am I?" Sonya said, her voice rising several octaves.

"I can't stand the thought of him coming back here and beating the shite out of you."

Sonya stood with her hands on her hips. "Jamie McGuiness, less of the tongue."

"I'm sorry," Jamie mumbled, irked by his mother's refusal to help herself. "I'm going. I can't stay here. Not like this."

"Jamie, please. You've got to understand. A woman can't just walk away from a marriage."

Jamie looked at his mother. He narrowed his eyes.

"Really? Women leave abusive men all the time. You're just making excuses to stay with him. I can't always be here to protect you or the wee ones. It's not fair on them."

"You're just a boy. You haven't a clue about what you're talking about." Sonya grabbed a bottle of milk from the fridge and walked to the microwave. "You don't understand how marriages work. You just can't up and leave."

"I know plenty. The longer you stay, the harder it will be to leave. Can't you see he's fecked up?"

Sonya struck the side of his face.

The burning sensation spread across his face. His eyes filled with tears. He'd pushed her buttons and regretted it.

"Don't you ever talk about your father like that again. Do you hear me?"

Jamie swallowed his pride and nodded. He pushed past her, grabbed his jacket, and left the house.

Once free from the peering eyes of his mother and siblings, he let his defenses down. His tears peaked and he choked back the urge to cry. Through all the pain and hurt, his mother had broken down his walls in one go.

He marched away, refusing to look back. He had one thing on his mind—Claire. She eased the emptiness swirling around inside of him. Claire was his distraction, albeit a temporary escape.

CHAPTER FOURTEEN

C laire sat on the wall outside her house.

Jamie's heart skipped a beat.

She fiddled with her phone and didn't notice his approach from the corner of the street.

"Busy, I see," he said.

Claire gasped and smiled. "Aye, nothing like using all my free data." She giggled. "Why are you so early?"

"I needed to get out of the house." Jamie rested against the wall and kicked a loose stone on the ground.

"Are things bad?"

Jamie shrugged and sighed. "When are they never?"

Claire jumped down from the wall. Stepping in close to Jamie, she nudged his arm.

"If you ever want to talk, I'm a good listener."

Jamie smiled and relaxed a little. He glanced to his left and caught Claire staring at him. Unable to throw caution to the wind, he yearned to pull her close. She was so pretty, much prettier than any other girl in his year at school. Kissing her in broad daylight in front of her house wasn't the way to her heart, and certainly not a way to impress her parents. Especially when so much bad blood existed between their families.

He drew in a sharp breath and swallowed his need to seek comfort in her arms, turning the conversation around. "Babysitting, huh?"

"Yup," Claire replied. "Sometimes I help out. It's not a job I like doing, but it's easy money, and I get to hog the TV to myself. There's nothing worse than fighting with the oul man over the remote control."

"Aye," Jamie replied, folding his arms. "Your aunt won't mind me tagging along?"

Claire giggled, much to Jamie's amusement.

Jamie loved the sound of her voice when she laughed. Mischievous and contagious—he never realized how much he liked her until now. She reminded him of a beacon of light on a stormy night.

"You're a dose," she said, smiling at him. "Of course, she won't mind."

Heat flooded his cheeks. "I just might start getting a complex about myself."

"Ah, don't be getting all serious on me, not when I've a bag of foosies in the house." Claire pouted and crossed her arms. "It'd be a shame to waste them all on the little ones."

Jamie smirked and shook his head. "I've a feeling you're going to be putting me through my paces."

"And right you are," she replied, taking his hand. "Come on, we can go around to Kate's early, get cozy, and see what the night brings us."

Jamie felt comfortable in Claire's company. As much as he liked being with the lads, Claire brought out the best in him.

Claire led Jamie down the path and into her house. She ran to the kitchen and left Jamie staring at a little girl with freckles strewn across the bridge of her nose.

"Are you Claire's boyfriend?" she asked, picking her nose.

"I'm her friend, Jamie."

"Do you kiss her? I bet she has dog breath, right?"

Jamie tamped down the urge to laugh. He had half expected to get the third degree from Claire's father, not her seven-year-old sister.

"Well, do you?"

"That's a question for Claire," he replied, winking.

"Well, Mammy says Claire better not be up to any badness, or she'll get a hiding." The little girl kept her finger up her nose as she spoke.

"Okay," Jamie replied, and glared at the little girl.

"Jesus, Tammy, get a fecking baby wipe," Claire said, walking up the hallway.

"He reckons you two be kissing, tongue and all," Tammy mocked.

"Mammy," Claire roared, "Tammy is at it again."

"She's okay," Jamie said. "She's just being a kid."

"Yeah, a fecking dose of a kid." Claire gritted her teeth and opened the front door. "See you later, you little runt," she shouted, and banged the door closed.

"Well, that was interesting." Jamie laughed.

"Jesus, she's not right in the head," Claire said. "She's a lamper."

"Ah, pay no heed to her. She's only little." Jamie held out his hand to her.

Claire smiled and took it. "She's still a bollocks."

Jamie nodded and pursed his lips, thinking carefully about what he'd say next. "Quite possibly, but I can bet you anything we were no different back then."

Claire cocked her head and looked at him. "Speak for yourself, McGuiness. I'll have you know I was pretty bloody perfect."

"Aye, right." Jamie bit down on his lower lip to keep from laughing. "And I thought it wasn't only me."

"You and Lenny? Ha! A right pair of lampers," Claire replied, sticking her tongue out.

Jamie found the banter amusing. It served as an outlet to forget all the ugliness of his home life. Claire was everything he needed, then and there.

"So how about a kiss then, Little Miss Perfect?" Jamie said. The unexpected words escaped his lips.

Claire stopped in her tracks. Her face grew serious.

Had he made the wrong move?

"I thought you'd never ask," Claire replied and stepped closer to him.

Their lips crushed together.

Walking on air, he could have died and he would have been fine with it, as long as he was kissing Claire. Nothing else mattered.

Jamie settled down on the settee and flicked through a few pages of a magazine. He patiently waited for Claire to come back in from checking on her sleeping cousins. He rested his head back against the soft fabric of the seat and closed his eyes for a few seconds.

The day had left him weary. It would have been too easy to fall asleep. Of course, had it not been for the pendant sitting inside the pocket of his jeans, he would have easily forgotten the noise he heard inside the room.

Drip.

Drip.

Drip.

He opened his eyes slowly. The prickles on his skin had the hairs on his arms standing on end. He held his breath and looked around the living room.

The low hum of the TV show played in the background. The window sat ajar and a light breeze blew in. The curtains moved in small ripples.

Jamie's stomach spun with unease.

I'm losing my mind. He rubbed the back of his neck.

Iliana stepped into view in front of Jamie. Her long damp hair hid her face. Her arms hung down on either side of her body— grey and wet. She twitched before raising a hand and pointing to Jamie with a skeletal finger. Her form dripped to the floor, creating a small puddle of black liquid.

Jamie found it hard to avert his gaze. Her powerful presence enveloped him. Jamie's mind flitted back and forth to the room in his house. His stomach churned. Bile rose, causing him to gasp for breath. A chill descended, and the smell of the stagnant water filled the room.

He closed his eyes and rubbed his fingers into his temple. "Please, not here, not now," he whispered. "Go away, please."

Lost within his thoughts, the sound of the door swinging open startled him. His eyes shot open, wide with dread. Jamie jumped to his feet.

Claire looked at him and frowned. "Jesus, you look like you've seen a ghost," she muttered. "Here, give us a hand with this."

Jamie swallowed hard, the bitter taste of terror hard to stomach. He walked over to Claire and took the bottle of pop and two glasses from her.

"Are you okay?"

Her eyebrows furrowed. She stared at him.

Jamie nodded and shrugged. "Of course. I just get stupid sometimes."

"Hmm, I'm not convinced," Claire replied, and glared at him.

Jamie sat down, his posture tense. The cold still burned through his bones. Unable to shift the chill, he shivered. The sensation of something crawling over his body enveloped him, implanting itself beneath his flesh.

"Want me to close the window?"

"If you don't mind?" Jamie said, his teeth chattering.

Claire shut the window and closed the blinds. She switched on the lamp and took a seat on the settee beside Jamie. Taking his hand in hers, she asked the one thing he didn't want to address.

"Are you going to tell me what's going on?"

Jamie sat forward and pulled his hand away. Warming up, he glanced to his left and looked at Claire.

He sucked in a deep breath before asking, "Do you believe in ghosts?"

Fear lurked within him, though he had calmed a little.

Having Claire nearby helped. However, saying the words made him feel like he was losing his mind.

Claire gawped at him. She raised an eyebrow and shook her head.

"Are you serious?"

"Deadly." He swallowed a hard lump.

"Well, talk about a mood killer," she remarked, and sat back.

"You asked me if something was going on, and I'm telling you."

"Yeah, but ... ghosts, seriously?"

Jamie leaned back against the cushions and closed his eyes. Turning his head to the side, he took Claire's hand in his. He rubbed his thumb over the back of her knuckles and looked at her.

"Sometimes, I feel like I'm going mad," he said. "And then, other times, I wonder if I'm not so mad after all. Everything is so messed up, but I know what I saw, and it's freaking me out."

Claire's face grew serious. She moved closer to him.

"Okay, you've got my attention."

"I remember hating the smell of the room when they brought the coffin home. My grandmother had lit scented candles to mask the decay," Jamie said, his voice soft and steady. "I hated having to look at her. I didn't want to have my last memory of her alive replaced by the stillness of her death, but they made me."

"I'm so sorry, Jamie. I can't imagine what it was like." Claire hooked her arm under his.

"So, when I first smelled death, I thought it was my imagination, but there is no denying what is happening." He fell silent for a few moments. "I've been feeling a bit down lately because of how things are going on at home," he said, and glanced at her. "I doubt anyone in town is that blind. I tend to escape to the causeway. Morbid, in a way. Lenny says it creeps him out, but I always feel closer to Emer when I'm there. It's where I first saw her."

"Saw who ... Oh, my god, like ... Emer?" Claire asked, her eyes large.

Jamie shook his head and shivered. "No."

"Then who? Someone you know?"

"A girl. A girl who died in the old lighthouse on the causeway."

The words leaving his mouth made him question his own sanity. Claire's expression was unreadable. Jamie hadn't meant to freak her out, but she left the door wide open by probing him for answers.

"Have you told anyone else about this?"

"Are you mad?" he asked. "They'd lock me up and throw away the key."

"Good," Claire replied. "First thing we'll do tomorrow is go and meet a certain someone."

"Who?"

"Well, if you're being haunted, you'll need a man in cloth at your side."

Jamie smirked at her response. "Are you trying to be a wise arse?"

"No, I just want to make sure nothing weird and evil has latched onto you. That, I can't be dealing with." Claire shook her head and rested it on his shoulder. "Have you not seen all those horror movies? Seriously, I know the very man we can go to about this. Trust me, okay?"

Jamie gulped down the surprise her reply caused and welcomed having her warmth next to him. Many things in life caught him off guard. Claire and her affections were healing some of the broken parts of his soul.

No matter how much he relaxed in her company, thoughts of Iliana and her death played at the back of his mind. It never ceased to rest, slowly biding its time.

CHAPTER FIFTEEN

Pain exploded inside his head. Coming 'round, his eyes ached and flickered from side to side. He caught sight of the fist coming down onto his face again.

"You think you're a big lad, do you?" Jack spat.

The relentless pounding of his father's fists broke the skin on Jamie's cheek.

Sonya cried. She put her hands on Jack's shoulders, trying to pull him back.

Jamie brought his hands up to cover his head. Disoriented, he took a few seconds to gather his thoughts before he realized he was the target for the night.

"Jack … please," Sonya said, her voice strained.

"Da …" Jamie raised his voice. "What did I do?"

"You're a filthy piece of shit." Jack grabbed him by the neck and didn't let go, not until he had pinned him on the floor. "I'll teach you to be gallivanting around town with the trollop."

Jamie wiped the blood from his swollen mouth and sucked in a deep breath. His reprieve was temporary.

Jack repeatedly ploughed his fists into Jamie's stomach.

"Da!" Jamie roared, wrapping his arms around his torso.

Jack knelt over his son. His eyes bulged. With heavy breaths, he stood and unclenched his fists.

"If I hear head or tail of you anywhere near the wee trollop, I'll gut you like a fish. Do you understand?"

Jamie sat on the floor, his face bloodied. His head pounded.

His mother stood by the bedroom door, covering her face with her hands.

"You told him about Claire?" he asked, shaking his head and squirming in pain.

"I had to before someone else did."

Sonya looked away, pulling the cuffs of her cardigan over her hands. She left the room, not once inspecting his wounds.

Jamie's eyes narrowed. He touched the side of his mouth. He had always suspected his father would find out about him and Claire. He never expected his mother to be the one to leak the information.

Jamie tried to remember a time when his mother hadn't been the weak, broken thing she'd become. Even with the memories, all the happy times, the woman she was now overshadowed the woman from his past.

Angry, he stood, slammed his door shut, switched on his lamp, and walked to the mirror to inspect his war wounds.

"Fecking prick." He cursed under his breath.

It would always be this way. There would be no escape. The knowledge coursed through his veins with every breath he took.

He'd cowered behind Emer's death, unwilling to meet the devastation of his grief head on. With Claire becoming a part of his life, he would never get away with being with her or parading her around town. Not without his father sticking his oar in.

Glaring at his reflection, Jamie pursed his lips, fighting the urge to cry. He stared hard, hating what he saw staring back.

Shimmering ripples appeared across the mirror's glass surface.

"Not now, Iliana," he muttered, shaking his head.

A new kind of pain ground in his ears. Jamie tilted his head, intent on shaking the discomfort away. He hit the side of his head repeatedly.

From within the mirror, flesh swam toward him, crawling out of the glass.

Jamie stepped back, wanting to avoid her touch.

Her clammy fingers reached for him. Black veins traced over her skin. Her mouth opened in a silent scream. Dark matter dripped from her swollen lips. Her unblinking eyes stared hard into his. She moved closer to him, her dislocated jaw and broken teeth in full view. Without warning, a piercing screech erupted from her mouth and she charged towards him.

Jamie's stomach churned, bile rising to the back of his throat. A stream of warm liquid ran down his leg. Tears burned his eyes.

"Iliana, please ... not now. Don't do this." His voice ached.

This level of fear was new to Jamie. Up until the episode in the extension, he had come to accept Iliana's visions. She now pulled him into something he wasn't prepared for.

Jamie listened to the drips of water and the temperature dropped. Evil had been awoken. Everything had changed. The ball no longer in his court, his life was now ruled by the undead. He wasn't sure how to appease the anger and sadness radiating from Iliana.

Iliana couldn't control it.

She didn't want to be a monster. Yet she found it impossible to ignore the surrounding darkness. Iliana reached out to Jamie. She saw the pain, the sadness, the anger, and sensed his frustration.

The sight of his swollen, bloodied face made it even more real. He was a living, breathing reminder of the torment she suffered during her last moments alive. The night she'd stepped onto the causeway came back to haunt her. The hands broke her nose, the bones crunching with every blow. She tasted blood, and her ears rang.

The violence of her death left an everlasting stain on her soul. Regardless of how and when she would be released from her jail, she would forever be tainted with the blood of her murderer.

Iliana inspected the wounds on Jamie's face. The broken skin under his eye looked painful. The metallic scent of his blood wafted into her nostrils. She turned her face away briefly, unsure if she was strong enough to finish what she'd started. Reaching her hand out to him, she saw the fear in his eyes.

"Don't be scared," she whispered. "I just want to help. I won't hurt you."

Jamie shook his head and scrambled away. "Don't … don't touch me."

Iliana kept her simmering temper under control. In her current state, she was unpredictable. She had no power over her wayward emotions. One minute, she was sad and angry. The next, she unleashed the unthinkable. She didn't want to be this way, but the darkness of her afterlife made it impossible.

"I thought when I died there'd be light, but there was nothing," she mumbled. "There is no heaven, not for me anyway.

There's just so much darkness."

She glanced at Jamie, her dark eyes locked on his. She coughed and black matter spilled from her mouth.

"Help me."

She waited for Jamie to react.

He covered his face with his hands. His fingers trembled.

She had pushed a little too hard.

"Go away, Iliana. I don't know what you want from me," he said.

Iliana's anger bellowed through her chest. The pressure in her throat felt like a volcano, moments away from eruption. Her mouth opened, the tar-like matter oozed down the side of her chin.

"Please, please, help me," she begged. "Only you can do this. Do you not understand? I want to be free from this. You have to help me ... please."

Iliana held out her arms. Water dripped from her, pooling at her feet. Her swollen fingers, bent at odd angles, reached for Jamie.

"Don't leave me," she cried. "I hate the dark. I'm so cold. I just want to go home. Please, Jamie, let me go home."

Jamie froze where he stood.

Water and black matter dripped from Iliana. Her torn skirt revealed deep welts on the side of her grey legs. As she moved, her body trembled. Her eyes darted from left to right, and then focused back on him.

His mind refused to fathom what he saw. The room was cold. The lamp by his bed flickered a few times and went out. Jamie stood in the darkness, unmoving.

A cold, rancid scent burned the back of his nostrils. Jamie held a hand over his mouth and nose, trying not to breathe in the odor. Repulsed by the scent of decay, he stepped backward, attempting to make his way to the door.

A hand dropped onto his shoulder. Dampness seeped into the material of his T-shirt.

"You need to see," she whispered in his ear. "You need to witness everything."

Jamie squeezed his eyes shut. Shaking his head, he ignored her presence. Ripples soared through him before he had the chance to cry out. A deathly silence hummed in his ears. No longer in his room, all control had been taken from him. In its place, he became little more than a puppet in his own horror show.

Iliana took center stage within him. She pulled him back to the causeway, to the very moment her fate had been sealed.

CHAPTER SIXTEEN

"Y̶ou think you're some big woman, sneaking out, acting like some trollop from town," Jack spat. "I'll teach you a lesson or two, lassie. I've warned you before not to cross me and you just keep pushing."

Emer swung at her father, slapping his face hard. "I hate you. I wish you were dead."

Jack grabbed Emer's arm and stomped across the causeway.

She fought and kicked.

Jack refused to allow her the upper hand. "Your mother is in the house breaking her heart over you, and this is what you do? What kind of wee bitch are you? Because your mother and I didn't raise you to go around drinking, smoking, and doing God knows what else."

"I hate you both. You ruin everything I do," Emer shouted.

"You've ruined yourself." Jack grabbed her cheeks and glared into her face. "The carry-on of you … You should be ashamed of yourself." Jack pulled Emer's hair and pushed her out in front of him.

"I'll tell the peelers you tried to touch me. Let's face it, Da, you're nothing but a miserable old man who's jealous because I can do whatever I want," Emer threatened. "You're an old creep. A desperate, dirty old man. No wonder Ma won't let you near her anymore."

Jack glared at the back of Emer's head. He gritted his teeth and clenched his right hand into a tight fist.

"I'll bloody kill you."

"Go on, then. Give it your best shot." Emer spun around and moved closer to her father's chest. "Go on, I dare you, Daddy. Kill me. Go on. It's all you keep saying, so do it."

"Don't test me, Emer," Jack warned. "You're already on thin ice."

Emer laughed. She cackled like a demented witch and stuck her middle finger up at her father.

"You're a joke. You haven't even got the balls to teach me a lesson."

Rage contorted Jack's face. His brow furrowed. He took several deep breaths. His eyes had a deadness within them. They were darker than night. He stared at Emer and drove his fist against her jaw.

Her strawberry-blonde hair swung over her face. Blood trickled down the side of her mouth.

"Is that it?" she cried. "Is that all you have in you? You're a bloody joke, Da."

Jack's posture grew rigid and exuded hostility. His face reddened with rage. He resembled a snake ready to bite and release its deadly venom.

"You haven't a clue, do you, lass?" he mumbled. "You haven't the slightest idea of the bad things that can happen, do you? You think you're smarter than me? Well, let me tell you something— you're not in control of this situation. I am. And no daughter of mine will walk the streets of this town thinking she's above the laws of her father."

"I don't give a shite," Emer roared. "I hate you, do you hear me? *I. Hate. You!*"

Jack's jaw set. His nostrils flared. He narrowed his eyes.

Emer took a step back. The atmosphere changed dramatically.

Without uttering another word, Jack hit Emer hard with the back of his hand.

Her head shot to the side. Blood leaked from her nose.

Another slap followed. Jack's fist smashed against bone. Emer's nose bled rapidly, and her face became a mess.

"I hate you," she mumbled, and spat blood at him.

Emer stumbled and fell onto the stones. She looked up at her father and smirked.

Jack didn't waste time. He moved closer to the kneeling Emer and kicked her in the stomach.

Emer fell back and rolled over onto her side. She clutched her abdomen.

Jack pulled Emer up by her hair.

She screamed, trying to prise his fingers open.

Jack dragged her down to the shoreline and threw Emer onto her knees. He held her hair in a tight grip and pushed her face towards the water.

Emer screamed. "No, Daddy, no!"

Jack's face darkened. His eyes bulged, his mouth tight.

Past the point of rational thought, everything he ever stood for or believed in had been pushed to the back of his mind. His wrath now controlled him. Jack held Emer's head under the water, the waves crashing over his arms.

Emer kicked her legs. Her arms thrashed beside her.

Jack's grip tightened.

Emer's body grew limp. Her struggles ceased. Her hair drifted around her head, the water lapping against her body.

Jack released his grip and straightened his body. Walking away, he turned his head to take one last look at the motionless body of his only daughter floating in the water. He wiped his mouth and glanced up to find *her* standing there.

Jamie came around and fell to the floor in his room. Retching, he wrapped his arms around his abdomen, unease turning his stomach. Not able to withstand the taste in his mouth, he vomited. He had clearly seen his father beating his sister to death, but something felt off about the vision. Maybe it had just been a bad dream. Perhaps the sick and twisted nightmare had little meaning.

It's not real. It can't be real.

Iliana came into view and stared down at him.

His face drenched in tears, he looked up at her. "Why would you show me such a thing? What cruel game are you playing?"

Iliana tilted her head. Her brows furrowed. She closed her eyes briefly and opened them again. Her body dissipated. Before she finally vanished, she met Jamie's gaze.

"He will kill you all."

Jamie sat on the ground, gazing at the spot Iliana had been standing in mere seconds ago.

Why would his father do this?

Jamie's hurt and anger deflated rapidly. What he'd seen, he would never be able to forget—not in his lifetime. The vision of his father holding Emer's head under water floated around in his head. He focused on something other than the monster his father had become. Yet there was no running from the truth. Dumbfounded by the revelation, he tried to stomach everything, but his heart broke all over again.

The thought of his father hurting his sister repulsed him. He would never be able to look his father in the eye again. It was bad enough knowing what he had done to Iliana, but now Emer—his father had crossed the line.

Jamie walked to the window and drew back the curtains. The sun glowed—picturesque; beautiful and majestic.

Despite the beautiful morning, a storm lurked on the horizon.

Claire waited for Jamie inside the bus shelter. Her face lit up when she saw him. The closer he got to her, the more her smile disappeared.

"Oh, my god, what happened?" she asked, touching his jaw.

Jamie stepped into the shelter, resting his back against the wall. "What do you think?"

Claire clutched the vial of her necklace and stared at the ground before looking back at Jamie. "Is this because of me?"

She wasn't stupid.

"I'd like to say it wasn't, but you know how it is," Jamie replied. His shame was hard to hide.

Claire's expression dimmed. He never understood the stupid feud.

"How did he find out?"

"Me mother."

She rolled her eyes and stared at the ground. "I guess this means ending things before you end up with another beating or worse."

"Are you mad?" Jamie said, his voice rising slightly. "I'm not listening to the fool a moment longer." Jamie pulled Claire towards him and wrapped his arms around her neck. "If my oul man has a problem, it's his to deal with. I like you, Claire. You're the first real thing that's made me happy in a while. Why should I let him ruin it?" He refused to allow his father near her or anyone else again.

Jamie leaned in, rubbing his nose against Claire's. He inhaled the sweet scent of her perfume.

When their lips met, the kiss was intoxicating, full of the urgency of newfound desire. Immersed in their mutual affection, they never heard the bus pull up.

"Me old mucker is here," Lenny shouted, stepping off the bus and laughing.

Claire smiled and snuggled into Jamie's chest, hiding her face.

"Shut up, you dose," Jamie replied, grinning.

Lenny's amusement soon changed. He glared at Jamie's wounds and shook his head.

"I am getting sick of seeing what that prick does to you."

"Ah, this," Jamie replied. "This is nothing. War wounds, that's all."

"What did you do this time?" Lenny asked, rolling a cigarette.

"Oh, this one is all on me," Claire piped in.

"Ah, so the great feud continues." Lenny chuckled. He lit his cigarette and took a long drag. "Wouldn't it be old news by now?"

"You'd think," Jamie said and shrugged. "I guess some things will never change."

Jamie washed the embarrassment of his wounds away with light banter. Claire and Lenny were both aware of the shit storm Jamie lived with at home. Unable to let down his guard, he wasn't sure how to deal with the atrocities committed by his father.

Iliana had chosen him. Why? He didn't know. One way or another, his father had to be brought to justice—by the hands of the law, or by other means.

"So, are the two of you exclusive, then?" Lenny asked, raising an eyebrow.

Claire looked up at Jamie and blushed.

He smirked, enjoying how bashful she became.

"I guess we are," Jamie replied, running his hand up and down Claire's back. He enjoyed the feeling of belonging to her.

"Get in there, my son." Lenny cheered and winked at Claire. "What's the plan with you today, then?"

"We," Claire spoke up, "are going to spend the day doing as little as possible, but doing it together."

"Fair enough," Lenny stated. "I'll be putting in a few extra hours in the shop before I chase destiny tonight."

"What's happening tonight?" Jamie gave Lenny a curious look.

"Now wouldn't that be tellin' ?"

Jamie laughed and winked at Lenny. "You can't leave me hanging, you dose."

"I've a date with a certain good girl dying to be bad."

Lenny shot Jamie a look. A huge smile spread across his face.

"I guess the owl charm is working a treat, then?"

"Plus, you've been chasing her skirt for the past six months." Claire giggled.

"Ah, now, Claire, that's not fair." Lenny smoked the rest of his cigarette and stomped the stub into the ground. "I'm selective when it comes to my lady friends."

Claire burst into laughter. She glanced at Jamie before looking at Lenny.

"Did you know? Maria has just broken up with Ryan."

"Indeed, I do, so therefore, I have to strike whilst the iron's hot," Lenny said with pride. "And let's face it, can she really say no to this?" Lenny stepped back and held out his hands before him. "She'd be mad to let a good thing down."

Jamie laughed. "You're such an idiot."

"Aye, but what's a lad to do?" Lenny took out his phone and frowned. "Best be on me way. I'm late for my shift. I'll give you a buzz tomorrow. Maybe plan to meet up, have a few beers?"

"Dead on, lad." Jamie nodded. "Don't be doing anything I wouldn't do."

"Ha, are you mad? I've every intention of letting Junior out to play." Lenny laughed and walked away.

Claire took Jamie's hand in hers and nodded for him to follow her.

"Where are we off to?"

"I know someone who might have some kind of advice to offer you with your whole ghost thing," she replied.

"Yeah." Jamie cleared his throat. "There's something I need to tell you."

CHAPTER SEVENTEEN

The old house sat at the end of a weed-infested driveway. Jamie's grandmother used to clean and prepare meals for the priest. He remembered how pretty the property had once been. The trellised roses, which had once given it an air of coziness, had grown wild. Patches of paint peeled along the old wooden window frames. The entire house drooped to the right, the foundation subsided.

It seemed like the house had simply given up any hope of ever being a home again. Jamie hated it. He avoided walking along the path and came to a stop in front of the house. Part of him wanted nothing more than to turn his back and run.

"Seriously, I'm not going in there," Jamie insisted, looking at the windows of the old dark house. He glared at Claire, pursed his lips, and shuddered.

"Why not? Don't tell me you're scared."

"Not fair." Jamie zipped the front of his hoodie and pushed his hands into the pockets of his jeans. "They say he's mad."

"So? People say my mother's mad, but it doesn't mean I believe every rumor going around. He's a harmless old man."

"He's a priest, one who was basically sacked by the diocese. He had a breakdown in front of the whole parish, Claire."

"And?"

"And this isn't a good idea."

Jamie didn't want to be the coward hiding behind his girlfriend. Yet there he stood, letting her take the lead.

"Suit yourself, but I'm going in." Claire pushed the gate to the driveway open, walking on ahead of him. The stones crunched under her feet.

Jamie swallowed a hard lump before running up behind her. "I still say this is a bad idea."

"Whatever," Claire replied. "Just relax, okay?"

Jamie nodded and raised his eyebrows.

Claire rang the bell. After a few minutes, the door opened.

"Ah, Claire, I've been expecting you," the old grey-haired man mumbled. "Come on in."

"Did you tell him we were coming?" Jamie whispered.

"Nope." Claire glanced back at Jamie and smiled.

"Great, just what I need. Another bloody spook."

The old man led them into a large living room, where he signaled for them to take a seat on a brown settee. Barely any sunlight came into the room. The curtains were partially drawn across the large bay window. Dust fragments visibly floated in the air. The walls were cream colored with a few pictures hanging at odd angles.

It took all of Jamie's willpower to not walk over and straighten them.

"Would you like a drop of tea?" he asked.

"No thank you," Jamie answered.

Claire shook her head. "We're grand, Father Murray."

The old priest sat down in his armchair. He gawped at Jamie, frowning and sucking on his dentures.

"I've been expecting you, lad."

Jamie sat up straight and held his breath.

"Don't be alarmed," Father Murray said. "Sometimes, we never can truly explain the mysteries that surround us."

"So, you can tell there's something going on with Jamie?" Claire took Jamie's hand in hers, holding it tight.

"Aye, indeed, I have. I've been waiting for him to call on me," Father Murray replied, staring at Jamie. "I can sense her energy on you. Her most recent appearance, did it involve her taking possession?"

Dumbfounded, he found it hard to focus. He nodded and glanced at Claire before turning his attention back to the priest.

"Can you tell me anything about what happens?" Father Murray sat back and folded his arms.

Jamie cleared his throat, feeling foolish for even thinking about telling the old man about Iliana, never mind having Claire listening in on the conversation.

"Well, I guess everything goes cold, like freezing cold. I always end up shivering and feeling unwell. I become aware of her presence. The darkness around her scares me. It's so different compared to the first time I saw her."

"When did she first present herself to you, Jamie?

"Several weeks ago down by the old lighthouse on the causeway. I sat beside the tower, getting ready to head to school. She stood nearby, her face covered, just staring at me." Jamie's cheeks flushed. "I thought I imagined her standing there—I thought I was going mad. But she's as real as you and me."

"Hmm, and before that day?"

"Nothing." Jamie shrugged. "I never believed in ghosts. But everything that's happened since … let's just say I've had a huge wake up call."

Jamie closed his eyes and grimaced. He hated having to face the truth.

"You're drawn to the lighthouse," Father Murray said. "I can feel the connection you have with it. I, of course, am aware of your poor sister perishing there. God rest her soul." The priest blessed himself and cleared his throat. "Whatever is drawn to you shares a connection with you. The causeway being the catalyst of her first manifestation."

Jamie tried to smile at the priest's kind words, but found it difficult to do, considering the whole nature of his visit.

"Why has everything begun to turn nasty?" Jamie asked. "In the beginning, she showed me how she died, where she died. But now, when she comes, it scares the crap out of me. It's like she's angrier."

"Jamie, there are things you need to understand about the afterlife." Father Murray sat forward. "This girl, she's an earthbound spirit. She may or may not be aware that she's dead. She is trapped here and hasn't passed into the light, not yet anyway. She has latched onto you because there is a bond present. Not a bond in the sense that you are connected by blood, of course. There is something deeper than blood here, and you might already be aware of the link. The problem is, if she continues to take possession of your body, regardless of her intentions, you leave yourself open to all the malevolence of the afterlife."

"What do you mean?" Jamie's eyes widened.

"The walking dead will be knocking at your door for many

moons to come." Father Murray bestowed him with an understanding smile.

Father Murray's words sent a cold shiver down Jamie's spine. Bile rose to the back of his throat.

"What do I do to stop this?"

"Has the girl asked you for anything? Has she communicated with you other than taking possession?"

"She's asked me to help her," Jamie confessed. "But mostly she keeps showing me how she died, and she showed me where to find this." Jamie reached into his pocket and pulled out the pendant.

Father Murray's eyes glazed over. He fumbled with the buttons on his cardigan, and remained quiet for a few seconds. The strain etched on his face, his lips tightened and turned down at the sides. His demeanor changed in a matter of moments.

"Where did you find this?" Claire asked, staring at the pendant.

"Down on the causeway, a few feet from the lighthouse," Jamie replied, running his thumb over the inscription.

"When she showed you where to find this, had she taken possession prior?" Father Murray asked.

Jamie nodded. "I lay on the ground inside the tower and saw the killer through her eyes, feeling the pain she suffered … until she was gone." He paused, clearing his throat. "It's the most brutal thing I've ever witnessed. Almost as bad as seeing how my sister died."

Both Claire and Father Murray gawped at Jamie. Their mouths opened.

Claire broke the surrounding silence. "What do you mean?"

Unable to control it, the cold crept through him, stinging him from the inside out. Every nerve in his body stood on edge. He felt like a child again, shackled by his own fear. Jamie's insides swarmed with anxiety. He admitted to the horrors Iliana had shown him. Sweat pooled in his palms. He tried hard to control the knot twisting in the pit of his stomach.

"She showed me the night Emer died," he whispered, sniffing and wiping his hand across the sleeve of his hoodie. "I saw it all. What happened, and who did it."

The words left his mouth. Jamie's mouth went dry. His pulse pounded in his temples. Panic set in. He didn't want to be there a moment longer.

Can't breathe. Need air. Get out of here.

Before Claire or the priest could ask anything more, Jamie jumped to his feet and ran to the door. He refused to remain there a minute more. He needed air. The tightness in his chest constricted his lungs.

The front door creaked. Jamie left it open, falling to his knees and gasping for breath. He closed his eyes. The dizziness warped his sense of balance. A hurricane descended upon him, wreaking havoc inside his body. The surrounding darkness engulfed him and he struggled for air.

Warm hands slid across his shoulders. The noise of screeching seagulls brought him 'round. Claire bent down beside him.

"Are you all right?"

Pay no attention to it, and it will go away.

Jamie clutched his middle. Sweat dotted his brow. The jitters refused to stop.

"Jamie, what can I do to help?"

Jamie turned his head. The worry on Claire's face filled him with guilt about introducing her to his problem.

"Nothing. There's nothing anyone can do."

"He's right." Father Murray muttered from behind them. "He is the only one who can put a stop to all of this. The power is in his hands. He just needs to find the courage."

Claire narrowed her eyes. "But how can I just sit back and allow this thing to take over my boyfriend and be okay with it?" Claire peered down at the vial on her necklace and rubbed her thumb across it.

"Because, Claire, pet, the girl is lost. Jamie is the key to her release to eternal life."

"And the killer?" Jamie asked. "What do I do about him?" Tears streamed down his cheeks.

"You need to make a decision soon. I have a feeling you already know what to do." Father Murray nodded, his gaze never leaving Jamie's face. "As troublesome as it seems, you are stronger than you give yourself credit for. Stop searching for ways to avoid this. Instead, reach deep inside. Unleash the courageous young man you are destined to be. You are the very key to your own salvation."

Jamie stood and brushed the dust from his knees. He wiped his face and felt stupid for breaking down in front of them. He held his hand out to the old man.

The two of them exchanged a firm handshake.

"Thanks for your time, Father," Jamie said.

"Remember, Jamie, there's a whole other world out there, one many of us are blind to. For the most part, they walk among us, day in, day out, and we never know. When the mind is opened to their existence, it's then we truly become aware of the great beyond. Don't lose your mind, and always keep your faith. Without prayer and faith, you doom yourself." Father Murray slid his hands into the pockets of his cardigan and sucked on his dentures again. "So, if there's nothing else, I'll be getting on with my day."

"Thanks, Father," Claire said.

"Not a bother, pet. Just look out for him. He may need you more than he lets on." The priest stepped back inside the house and closed the door behind him.

Jamie walked away from the house.

Claire followed close behind. "Jamie."

"What?"

He avoided looking at her. Shame coursed through him.

"Are you going to be all right?"

He shrugged. "I'm not sure anymore."

"You're going to have to give me more than that. You've shared so much, don't cut me out now."

"Claire, I don't know what I am meant to say here."

"You say nothing if you don't want to, but after what you said in there, it's going to be impossible for me to ignore it." She tucked her arm in under his and walked beside him. "I'm on your side here. I'm not the enemy."

Jamie's cheeks burned. "Do you think I'm mad?"

"Absolutely not."

"Then I guess we need to figure out how I'm going to do this." He sighed. "And fast, because I've a feeling she's getting impatient with me."

Aware of how crazy he sounded, knowing Claire and Father Murray believed him eased some of the burden. He needed to find a way of freeing Iliana, however. From what, he had yet to discover. Iliana would guide him, regardless.

CHAPTER EIGHTEEN

What began as high winds and a few isolated showers built into a raging storm. The wind screamed. The rain pounded, hard and merciless against the window. Thunder rolled across the darkened sky. Every few minutes, the *bang* shook the roof of the house. Branches hit the window.

Jamie sat on the edge of his bed, listening to the storm, too far gone to sleep. The sense of being watched didn't make for a restful environment. Iliana made her presence known whenever she chose to do so. He couldn't shake the jitters from his bones.

He hated being in the house. The thought of having to look at his father sent chills down his spine. Every time he closed his eyes, he saw his father's hands pushing Emer down into the water. Those images would be with him for the rest of his life. Knowing what happened to Emer didn't make things better … it made them worse.

So many things needed to be addressed. Afraid of having to take responsibility of all he knew, the burden lay heavy upon his heart. More alone than ever before, he didn't know who to turn to.

Jamie wasn't a fool. No one in their right mind would believe him. Claire and Father Murray were an exception to the rule. It baffled him, but he was glad he had been able to offload some of the secrets.

Holding the pendant between his fingers, Jamie looked at it and sighed. "Where are you, Iliana?" he whispered, and peered around his room.

Silence.

Desperation filled his head. He dreaded seeing her, equally driven to help her and bring the haunting to an end. He didn't have the energy to fight the battle he'd soon face with his father. The moral dilemma would end in blood, a prospect he feared but accepted.

Not able to stand another moment under the same roof as his father, Jamie decided to take a late-night walk, regardless of the storm. It would help him to clear his head. Everything always seemed right at the time.

He silently slipped out of his room and crept along the landing. The soft breathing of the twins sound asleep and safe in their slumber echoed nearby. Thoughts about them and little Sarah weighed heavily on his mind. He needed them to be safe. Letting them down wasn't an option.

Quiet and steady, he stepped down the stairs and tiptoed along the hall and into the kitchen. Beer cans and half a bottle of whiskey sat on the counter. The odor of stale booze turned his stomach. Once he stepped onto the back porch, he closed the kitchen door and made as little noise as possible.

He slipped his feet inside his trainers and bent down near the back door to tie the laces. Standing up, he took one last look through the glass of the door of the dark kitchen, making sure he hadn't disturbed anyone, and reached for the latch.

Thump.

Jamie turned his head to the side and held his breath.

Thump.

Thump.

Thump.

He tensed.

It happened again, only now the thumps were coming in quick succession.

Thump. Thump. Thump. Thump. Thump. Thump.

No, no, no. Not in there. Go away. Go away!

Turning on his heels, he faced the plastic sheeting and stepped a little closer. Coolness swept around him. It crept up his legs and didn't stop until he shivered. He exhaled. His breath froze before him and fell to the floor where it shattered into pieces.

Iliana stood in the darkness, waiting for him.

Jamie thought about running out the back door and not stopping, but she would always find him. They had connected in a way he'd never understand. There was no running from something that could take over your soul in a split second.

Jamie's legs grew heavy with each step he took. His mind screamed, "Don't go in there," but Jamie ignored it and kept pushing forward. He refused to allow his fear to control his actions.

Jamie stepped inside.

The room across the threshold of the extension had a distinct odor. Something rotten lay nearby. Jamie found it hard not to vomit, but pushed past the barrier of disgust and walked over to the wall.

Thump.

The thud from behind the wall made him jump. He clenched his hands. His nails dug into his palms. Swallowing the bile rising to the back of his throat made his stomach turn further.

"Iliana." His voice shook. "Is that you?"

A long pause followed. The room got colder and the dripping sound of water replaced the thuds.

Looking down, Jamie noticed the puddle beneath his feet.

"This can't be happening," he whispered. Confused, he lifted a foot and shook it, his shoe sopping wet.

"What the …?"

The words left his mouth, and the wall swelled before him. It stretched outward, like a balloon filling with air and reached for him. A face hidden beneath the plasterboard took shape. A mouth opened. Eyes like an endless pit of darkness peered out at him.

Jamie stumbled backward and freaked out. He fell onto his back, hitting his head hard.

The mass continued to grow, moving down over him. A distorted visage hovered over him, mouthing words he could not hear.

Every nerve in his body stood on edge. Paralyzed by his fear, he tried to scream and call for help. To his dismay, his voice escaped him. Closing his eyes, he silently prayed for the monster to go away. The harder he ignored it, the more persistent it became.

Something cold and damp stroked his face.

Jamie's eyes opened. They flickered from left to right, searching for whatever had touched him. Nothing but a huge swell floated over him.

"It's not real. It's not real," he muttered repeatedly.

A noise pierced his skull. The swollen mass retreated, and the wall returned to its previous state. Like nothing had happened.

Her presence surrounded him. As he sat up, she materialized before him, and stared at him with a desperate expression on her face. Her eyes, sunken in their sockets—a pitiful sight. Her face, more emaciated than Jamie remembered.

He didn't like the way she moved towards him. She was more menacing than before.

"Stop," Jamie mumbled.

Iliana ignored him. Jamie's pleas were drowned out by a rattling noise coming from her mouth.

Her jaws opened wide. Her face tore at either side. Dark matter seeped out of her cracked flesh, revealing the skeleton beneath.

Jamie turned his face away in horror. He would never be able to unsee the sight.

Jamie's breathing grew labored. The tightness in his chest squeezed hard. He struggled. The room spun around him. His mind grew blank.

Slipping towards unconsciousness, dark eyes appeared in front of him.

Iliana, please stop.

"Help me before he destroys you," she whispered.

Her eyes were wild. Her body reeked of decay. The dark liquid oozed from every crevice of her body.

"What ... do I have to do?" Jamie struggled to remain conscious.

Her voice echoed inside his head. "Release me."

As quick as she appeared, she disappeared.

The temperature of the room warmed. The chill no longer made his bones ache. His body thawed.

Jamie sat on the ground and coughed, intent on making sense of Iliana's request. He didn't have the first clue about how he'd free her or what it would achieve. His thoughts were interrupted.

A light came on. Jack stood by the doorway and glared at Jamie.

"What are you doing in here?" Jack asked, his voice flat.

"I ... I thought I heard something." Jamie scrambled to his feet, eyeing the hammer on the workbench.

"What have I told you about being in here?"

"I know, Da. I just came down to check ... to make sure no one was in the house."

"With your shoes and jacket on?"

Jamie's insides twisted. His heart raced. He ground his teeth together and tried to control the threat of the stutter on the tip of his tongue.

"I hate coming in here without something on me feet," Jamie replied.

Jack moved in further, eyeing the wall, and then gawping back at Jamie. "If you thought someone was in the house, why didn't you come and get me?"

"I didn't want to disturb you or Mammy."

"Hmmm." He made a noise and eyeballed Jamie. "You wouldn't happen to be sneaking out, would you? Maybe the wee trollop has got you up to badness, hmm? The wee bitch has you wrapped around her finger, doesn't she?"

Jamie shot a look of contempt his father's way. "No, Da."

"You ought to remember a few things." Jack sneered. "Look at what happened to your sister after she snuck out. You remember, don't you, son? Do you remember how broken your mother was? Is it your intention to cause this family more strife?"

Jamie's mouth went dry. His father's remark filled him with

disbelief.

"What do you mean?"

Jack let out a dry snigger and shoved his hands into the pockets of his jeans. He strolled over to the boarded window and glanced back at Jamie.

"The night your sister disappeared, she snuck out, didn't she?"

"Well, yeah."

Jack glared at Jamie once more. He narrowed his eyes.

"And look what became of her. The sneaking about didn't end well, did it?"

Jamie shook his head. His father was a devil standing there, brazenly talking about the life he'd stolen from his own flesh and blood.

Jamie's hands grew clammy. He had to get out of there before he said something he'd regret.

"I don't want to talk about Emer."

"Funny old thing, that," Jack replied, stepping an inch closer to Jamie. "Neither do I."

Jamie turned his back on his father and rushed from the room. It took every bit of courage not to break down. He didn't want his father witnessing his delicate state of mind.

While the house slept and the floorboards creaked, Jamie sought refuge in the twins' bedroom. He sat behind the door, watching and listening, making sure his father came nowhere near them. He nodded off a few times, but he refused to allow exhaustion to consume him.

His worst fears had been confirmed. His father was capable of hurting them all. Now, it was only a matter of time.

CHAPTER NINETEEN

The clocked chimed midday.

The smell of lavender from the scented candle filled the room. Sonya stood by the window, holding Sarah in her arms. She bit down on her bottom lip, her eye swollen. No amount of make-up or a different hairstyle would hide the fact that she'd been Jack's punching bag.

His father's continued tirade of abuse against his mother irked him. The frustration brewed beneath his skin like a storm waiting to burst forth. He clenched his fists tight, his knuckles turning white. Bitter resentment rose to the surface.

His brothers sat beside him. Silence surrounded them.

Jack stood in the kitchen, distant from his family.

Jamie preferred his father not engaging with him or his brothers. It meant he didn't have to put on a show, something he dreaded more than their impending visitor.

"What time did he say he'd be here?" Jamie asked, clearing his throat.

"Half eleven," his mother replied, and kissed the top of Sarah's head, rocking the baby from side to side on her hip.

"He's late." Jamie shifted from foot to foot, unwilling to wait for someone who hadn't bothered about them since Emer died.

"I've things to do."

Sonya turned her head and glared at him. "You'll wait and do as you're told."

"Jesus, Ma, he hasn't exactly made an effort since … well, you know what I'm talking about." Jamie rolled his eyes and stared at his feet before turning his attention to his brothers. "Want to go to the park for a wee while?"

The boys jumped up and clapped their hands.

Jamie smiled, catching sight of the glee spreading across their little faces.

"No, they're staying here," Sonya said. "And so are you, Jamie McGuiness. Don't dare and push me today. It's bad enough with him in there, pretending everything is fine. You should know better than anyone else that I've enough on my plate without this."

Jamie couldn't keep the surprise off his face. Ma rarely put her foot down. *Silly woman.* She'd lay down the law with him, yet she was happy to bend backwards and take a beating whenever Jack decided to prove himself a man.

Double standards.

Jamie had wanted to step up and talk some sense into his mother so many times. She angered him in a way no other had before. All the while, he wanted to protect her, to take her away from all of this. There was no talking sense into someone who was so badly broken and unable to think for themselves.

The doorbell rang. Sonya walked into the hallway.

A few moments later, his grandfather walked in with Sonya following behind.

He hadn't changed a bit. Standing at just over six feet tall, Pat McGuiness had the build of a rugby player. With huge callused hands, he reached for Jamie.

He took a step back and avoided making contact with him.

"Well, look at all of you," he said. "I can't believe the size of the twins." He turned his head and looked at Sonya, who put on a brave face. "And, Jamie, you're a man now." He glared at Jamie before turning and looking at Sarah. "And this must be the wee darlin' herself."

Jamie didn't say anything. He stared at his grandfather as if he were a stranger.

"Jamie, don't be so rude," Sonya scolded. "I'm sorry, Pat. I don't know what's gotten into him."

"Ach, sure, it's the youth of today, Sonya." His grandfather made light of the situation and frowned at Jamie. "A chip off the old block, aren't you?"

Jamie shrugged and looked at the boys. His creep of a grandfather sickened him more than his father did. Being in the same room with him repulsed Jamie. In his mind, Pat was a menace to society. His mind refused to fathom why his mother allowed him to enter their home.

"And where is the man of the house?" Pat asked.

"He's out in the kitchen. You know how he can get," Sonya said. "He's a bit worse for wear these past few years."

"Hmm. I see he's good with the hands." Pat raised an eyebrow and pointed at Sonya's face.

Sonya touched her face and blushed.

Jamie grimaced and shook his head.

"Ah, this?" Sonya replied. "It's nothing but a war wound from playing with the boys. They can be a little rough."

"I see." Pat grunted.

Her lie didn't sit with him either.

"I'll head on out and see Jack." Pat walked to the door, taking one last look at Jamie.

His bald, mottled scalp reminded Jamie of the last time he saw his grandfather. Jamie turned his face away in disgust, wanting to hide his shame of the memory.

June 9, 2012

"Those pikey bastards better not come knocking here for money, or so help me God," Jack warned, pacing the floors of the kitchen.

"Relax, son. Let me deal with the Brannigans," Pat said, pouring them both a tall glass of whiskey.

Jamie stood by the cooker and listened to his father's complaints about Denny Brannigan.

"The bastard screwed me over one too many times," Jack said. He lifted the glass and downed the drink in one gulp.

"Let sleeping dogs lie and then sort your troubles out, but only when the time's right," Pat suggested. "You've enough going on here without taking up arms against that lot. Be wise with how you handle this."

Even though it had only been a few months since they had buried Emer, Jack insisted on keeping his small business afloat with several jobs. It just so happened he'd hired the wrong people.

"What do you say, son?" Jack asked. "Should I go around there and bust Denny Brannigan's face?"

"No, Da, you can't be doing that," Jamie replied. His father's patience had been tested. "Just do as Grandda says and let it rest a while."

Jack sat forward, bristling with anger. A muscle twitched along his jaw. His fist clenched, and his eyes bulged. His breaths grew heavy. He stared at the tiles of the kitchen floor.

"Talk about taking the bit out of a child's mouth," Jack said. "And all whilst we buried our only daughter. What kind of person would do such a thing?"

"Now, son, you have to think clear before you go and do something stupid." Pat topped up Jack's glass and pushed it towards him. "Just do as I say, I'll make a few calls. Maybe have Denny roughed up a bit. Just enough to make them realize they can't get away with this malarkey. You have to keep your dignity intact, understand me?"

Jack sat upright and listened to his father.

Jamie stood still, resting his hands behind his back. He wondered what kind of things his grandfather meant.

"Jamie, leave us alone for a little while," Jack said, nodding at Jamie to leave the room.

He glared at his grandfather, and then at his father before finally conceding defeat. The grown-ups wanted their grown-up time. It meant one thing to Jamie—crime.

Jamie closed the kitchen door behind him.

Sonya sat at the bottom of the stairs.

Walking up the hallway in her direction, he asked, "Are you all right?"

"Aye, I'm just feeling a little tired." Sonya closed her eyes and pressed her fingers into her temple. She turned her head to the side and looked at Jamie. "Where are you going?"

"I'm going to pop over to Lenny's for a wee while. Do you mind?"

"Not at all. Off you go, just be home before ten," she said, forcing herself to smile through her obvious pain.

"Okay, thanks. Later, Ma," Jamie said. He bent down and kissed her cheek.

"Bye, pet."

Jamie left the house, wondering what his grandfather had meant by roughing up Denny Brannigan. His grandfather wasn't a saint. Pat had a reputation for being a notorious bully. A man who always got his way. Jamie wasn't stupid and noticed the growing change in his father. Having his grandfather around added to the growing unease in the house.

Fifteen minutes later, he stood outside Lenny's house. A couple of lads from school out on the green playing footie. He rang the doorbell.

The door opened.

"'Bout you, lad?" Lenny said, and nodded for Jamie to come in.

"Thought I'd stop by for a few. The oul man is going 'round the bend over something Denny Brannigan did," Jamie replied. "You know, the usual shite, lad."

Jamie followed Lenny up the stairs and shut the door behind them when they entered the small bedroom.

"Aye, something about copper piping being took from your old man's yard." Lenny raised his eyebrows and smirked. "As they say, there's money in the old piping."

"So my grandda keeps telling me da." Jamie sat on Lenny's bed and lifted the Xbox controller. "How many times have you respawned today?"

"Not too many times, you smart arse. I'll show you how it's done." Lenny chuckled and grabbed the spare controller.

Jamie bellowed and sniggered away, attacking Lenny's character and making faces every time he got a clean shot.

"Did you hear the rumor about Michelle?" Lenny asked in between shots at Jamie's character.

With his tongue hanging out, Jamie shrugged and shook his head.

"Rumor has it she let Chris finger her." Lenny stared at Jamie, waiting for his reaction.

"No way," Jamie said and sniggered. "Did Chris tell you this?"

Lenny rolled onto his back and stared at the ceiling. "Yup, and he said he'd do it again."

"The dirty fucker," Jamie replied, before bursting into a tear-filled laughter.

"Aye. He beat me to it." Lenny chuckled and rolled over onto his stomach. "I bet I kill you."

"In your dreams, you dose."

The two boys laughed and joked until it was time for Jamie to head on home. He didn't want to leave, but staying out past his curfew would have ended in big trouble.

"I best head on back before they send out an envoy. You know how me mother gets," Jamie said, throwing the controller onto the bed. "I can't stand when me grandda comes 'round. He's hardly bothered about us since Emer died, and now suddenly, he's ready to sort me da's problem's out for him. I don't know about you, but I don't trust his crap."

Relieved, he was glad he had gotten it off his chest, much to Lenny's amusement.

"You do know your Grandda McGuiness is a crook, right?"

"Yup, hence why I can't stand him messing with me da's business, not so soon after everything."

"Listen, Jamie," Lenny said. "All the stuff over the past few months can't have been easy on you all, but you have to remember, adults deal with grief in the weirdest ways. Your da's anger with Brannigan might be his way of relieving some of the frustration. I'm just guessing here, but maybe you should give him the benefit of the doubt."

Jamie winced at Lenny's words. He wasn't the kind of lad to take advice from people, especially his best friend. For the most part, he preferred to suffer in silence. Yet in a few short sentences, Lenny made perfect sense.

"Aye, I suppose you're right," Jamie admitted.

"Of course, I am. I'm the fecking man, after all." Lenny winked at him.

"You're a fecking dose." Jamie opened the door and nodded at Lenny. "Thanks for this evening. I'll give you a bell tomorrow."

"No worries, lad. You know where to find me."

Jamie closed the door, ran down the stairs, and shouted a "see ya" to Lenny's folks before disappearing out the front door.

Silence surrounded him when he got in. His father's van was gone from the drive, and the TV hummed in the background. He wandered to the kitchen, grabbed a packet of crisps from the cupboard, and filled a glass of juice. Peeking inside the living room, he took a mouthful of juice and went upstairs.

A grunting noise caught Jamie's attention as he drew close to his room. It sounded like a dog unable to breathe coming from his parents' bedroom.

A soft whimper followed the bizarre sound. The word, "No." could be clearly heard from where he stood.

The door to the room stood ajar, and the lights dimmed. Jamie drew closer, knowing it was perverse, but something felt off. The closer he got, the more aware he became of his mother's cries and the groans accompanying her pained voice.

Peering inside, his stomach spun in a knot. The vitriol rose to the back of his throat. He couldn't look away.

His mother's pained eyes caught sight of him. Tears lined her cheeks.

Go away, hide, she mouthed, not wanting to disturb Pat.

Jamie wanted to kill him. He wanted to get the scissors from the bathroom and ram them up Pat's bare arse.

What he witnessed wasn't right. His grandfather raped his mother right before his eyes, and he didn't know what to do. He hated him, repulsed by the sight.

Something welled inside Jamie. He refused to let his grandfather get away with this. He took a deep breath and charged into the room.

Pat looked up. His eyes rolled in his head.

"Get off my mother, you dirty pervert!" Jamie roared.

Pat smirked and climbed off the bed. He pulled his jeans back up before fastening the belt.

"Testing the goods, lad." He winked at Jamie. "Just testing the goods."

How could a man who claimed to love his family do this? Especially after everything they'd been through.

"Get out of my house now before I call the peelers," Jamie warned. His hand shook. He pointed his finger at Pat before he turned towards his mother. "Mammy, are you okay?"

Sonya pulled herself off the bed and stumbled against the wall. "I need water."

"How could you do this?" Jamie cried. "She's on all those sleeping tablets and you rape her?"

"It's called fair game, lad. She was asking for it. One day, you'll be man enough to understand," Pat replied, running his hand over his balding, speckled head.

"Get the feck out before I call me da," Jamie warned, and swung at the man.

Pat laughed and shook his head. "You silly little shite. Who in God's name do you think you are?" He slapped Jamie hard across the face. "Be thankful she's still able to walk."

Jamie's ears rang. It didn't stop him from screaming at the top of his lungs.

"Get out, get out, get out!"

The twins stepped out of their room, rubbing their tired eyes. Their little faces were full of confusion.

"What's wrong?"

"Go back to bed, boys," Jamie said, pointing to their bedroom door. "Grandda is just leaving."

Pat smirked. He turned to look at the boys and winked at them.

"I'll be seeing youse," he said, stomping down the stairs and lifting his coat from the coat rail. He slammed the front door hard on his way out.

Jamie took his mother's hand and led her back to the bed. Tears stained his cheeks. His hands trembled as he tended to her, making sure she was okay.

"Don't be getting upset, pet," Sonya slurred.

"I should have been here. If I had, he wouldn't have done this to you," he cried.

"I'll be okay. I promise. I'm made of stronger stuff."

"But ... you ... you have to tell Da."

"No. We will never speak of this again. Not ever. Do you hear me, Jamie?" She grabbed his wrist. "Never."

"But—"

"No, Jamie, there are some things we never speak of. This is one of them," she said, her voice more controlled.

A glint flashed in his mother's tired eyes. She kept her eyes locked on his. Her grip tightened. She would never admit to what had just happened.

Jamie settled his mother back into bed. He checked on the boys and stayed up for the remainder of the night. He didn't want to risk his mother's safety. Not while his grandfather was in town.

That night was the last time any of them saw or heard from him. Jamie hated how his mother pretended there was nothing wrong.

Pat didn't bat an eyelid when Jamie made things worse. He was a man at peace with his actions.

BENEATH THE LIGHTHOUSE

This made Jamie more determined to bring his father down. What better way to hurt his grandfather than revealing the monster his only child had become? Or better still, taking his father out.

The thought brought a smile to Jamie's face.

CHAPTER TWENTY

J amie found it hard to chew the piece of meat. He avoided looking at his father or Pat—refusing to refer to the man as his grandfather. Every time he opened his mouth to speak, a knot twisted inside his stomach.

He turned his face and focused on his brothers and sister.

Sarah cooed away in the highchair, giggling at the faces Thomas made.

Paul blew raspberries in her direction.

They were blissfully unaware of the ugliness of the world. Jamie envied their innocence; their ability to carry on regardless of what stood in front of them. He stared at them, his heart sinking deeper into the well of anguish.

Jack stood by the kitchen sink, popping open a can of cider. The tension in the room was palpable, the air brittle. A look of animosity flickered across Jack's face whenever he looked in his direction. Jack's eyes narrowed. His lips curled downward, his breathing deep and slow.

Sonya kept her face down, not once looking up, shame etched across her face.

An overwhelming sense of panic consumed him. The ball in his chest propelled itself forward, ready to burst.

His father and Pat grumbled a few words to each other and kept their meeting formal.

"We're in for a warm one this year," Pat remarked, buttering another slice of bread.

"That's what they always say," Jack replied between sips of his cider.

Pat took a bite of his bread, making a slurping noise as he chewed. "Any plans?"

"Like what?" Jack asked.

"Like taking the wee ones away for a day or two." Pat smirked. "The things normal families do. Surely, you remember those days?"

Jack looked at his father and furrowed his brows. "Since when have you cared about what I do with my family?"

"Come on, boys," Jamie interrupted, and smiled at the little ones.

The tension brewed in the kitchen. Jamie didn't want the wee ones playing piggy in the middle. None of this was their fault.

"Sit your arse there, lad," Jack spat. "I'm done with you thinking you can take over and call the shots. I'm the adult. The man of the house, or have you forgotten? You're to do as you're told, got it?"

"Enough, Jack," Sonya said. Her voice quavered.

"Oh? Is it 'let's all gang up on Jack' day?" Jack glared at Sonya. "Shut your bloody trap before I shut it for you."

"Some things never change, eh, Sonya?" Pat remarked, and winked at her. "Forever the doormat."

At first, Jamie swallowed the retort about to escape. The more he stared at Pat, the intensity of his rage burned. Unable to control the storm within, his emotions were like an earthquake; an eruption of every feeling he'd kept locked away.

Jamie couldn't stand it a minute longer. Pat was more animal than human. The fire inside him hit boiling point. Tunnel vision took over. He focused his entire wrath on Pat.

"Shut the hell up." Jamie's voice dripped with hatred. If looks could have killed, Pat would have been dead on the floor in a pool of blood. Jamie lifted his fork and drove it down on Pat's hand, stabbing him repeatedly. "Don't ... ever ... talk ... to my mother like that *again!*"

Pat pushed forward and slapped his open left hand across Jamie's face.

The force of the blow disoriented Jamie. He took a step back and blinked a few times. He then stared at Pat, taking sharp, deep breaths.

From the corner of his eye, Jamie noticed Jack's posture changing.

Jack stood straight, inhaling deeply.

Ignoring his father, Jamie returned his attentions back on Pat.

"I will kill you for everything you've done to my mother."

"Jamie." Sonya stood and shouted, "Stop this!"

Sarah screamed.

Sonya gently rubbed her small cheeks.

The twins ran to the hallway to avoid the chaos.

Jack set his can down and ran a hand over the back of his neck. He glared at Jamie, and then at his father. He looked at Sonya and shook his head.

"Would someone tell me what the hell has been going on?"

"Jack, calm down," Sonya said, and reached for him. Her small hands trembled.

He shook his head again, this time, turning to look at Jamie. "It's always you, isn't it?" He marched over to where Jamie stood. "Taking a hand to your elder's results in a hiding you won't forget for a long while."

Jack unfastened the belt of his jeans and whipped it out. He wrapped it around his fist.

Pat stood, covered his small wound with a tea towel, and smirked.

Sonya looked at him, her eyes filled with tears. "This is all your fault," she roared. "Tell him. Go on. Tell your precious son what you did to me." Spit gathered on her chin as she cried.

Jack turned his head. He focused his eyes on Sonya and gritted his teeth.

"Tell me what?"

Jamie ran to Sarah and lifted her out of the highchair. He held her close and soothed her, pressing little kisses to the side of her head. He tried to block out the noise.

"She's mad," Pat said, and laughed. "She's been gone in the head since Emer died."

"What the feck did you do to her?" Jack turned his head, his eyes almost bulging out of their sockets.

Jamie took a step back towards the kitchen door.

The twins peered inside, their little faces ashen with fear.

Jamie absorbed the drama, digesting the anguish building up inside him. Once Jack heard the truth, the door to hell would be opened.

"Go on, Pat. Tell him why you've been gone all this time,"

Sonya goaded. "Or shall I? Shall I tell him how you crept into our bedroom after I took my sleeping pills? How you climbed on top of me and raped me? Shall I tell your precious boy how you hit our son when he saw what you were doing to me? Shall I?"

Her eyes wide, she wiped her nose on the sleeve of her cardigan. Tears streamed down her face. Her whole body shook.

Jamie's eyes opened wide. Startled by her outburst, his mouth hung open.

Pat sighed and shook his head. "You're talking nonsense."

"What in God's name are you saying, woman?" Jack snapped, and held a hand to his head.

"What do you think, Jack?" she asked. "Your father raped me in our bed when our baby was only months in her grave, barely cold. He abused our trust and he took, just like he takes all the damned time. You were too blind to notice what went on in your own home. Drinking, fighting, and God-knows-what. I'm done with this life. I am done. I deserve better than this."

Sonya turned her back on the two men. Her eyes were red and raw. She pulled Sarah into her arms and walked down the hallway to open the front door.

"Come on, boys. We're going away," she said to the twins.

The twins ran up to their mother and looked back at Jamie. No questions were asked. The front door closed behind them.

Jamie stood in the hall, waiting for hell to break loose.

Jack's nostrils flared. His breathing grew deeper, more enraged.

"Did you?" he asked. "Did you touch my wife?"

Pat, a few inches taller than Jack, shrugged. "What more do you want me to say?"

"Did you rape my wife?" Jack's voice sounded like thunder. "Did you force yourself on the mother of my children?"

Jamie stood near the doorway, cautious about being caught in the crossfire. He wanted the two men to hurt as much as possible.

"I wouldn't call it rape," Pat replied in a calm voice.

"I'll kill you."

Jack lunged at his father. He drew his fist into Pat's jaw, sending the man falling backwards.

Pat smirked and spat a mouthful of blood onto the tiled floor. He wiped his chin and cracked his neck from side to side.

"I've taught you better than that, son," he mocked. "You should make sure your opponent never gets back up."

Jack charged like a bull and roared, coming face to face with his father.

Pat ducked the blow with a smile. He avoided one flying fist only to collide with another. This time, he went down like a ton of bricks.

Jamie held onto the handle of the door. His knuckles turned white.

Kill him. Kill the bastard.

A smile stretched across Jamie's face.

Jack's fist curled in a tight ball, continuously driving into Pat's face. Blow after blow, Jack spent his fury on Pat.

Contentment filled him. His father and grandfather were now torturing one another. He had more pressing matters on his mind. His mother's safety took top priority.

Jamie walked through the back gate of his grandmother's house.

Sonya stood at the bottom of the garden, smoking.

Surprised, he didn't remark on it. Smoking was a coping mechanism. After the morning she'd had, he'd turn a blind eye to the cigarette.

He glanced back at the house.

His granny stared in their direction.

He waved at her and turned his attention back to his mother. "Are you okay?"

Sonya shrugged and took another drag. "I can't believe I said those things." She shook her head. "All this time I've kept that night buried deep and I cave now. What kind of woman am I? I've just destroyed everything."

Jamie reached out for his mother, but she winced, refusing his touch.

"What am I to do now, Jamie? The boys are asking questions. They don't understand any of this. I don't know what I am meant to do or how I can fix things. It's just a bloody mess."

"Anything is better than being hit by Da every time he has a drink," Jamie said. "Anything is better than being afraid of your own shadow. What Grandda did … It was bad, Ma, so bloody bad. You should never have kept it silent, not all these years."

Sonya spun 'round to face him. "And now it's all out in the open. How will it help me now? Imagine the talk in the town once everyone hears of it. I'll be the joke. How can I live like this?

How can I expect the wee ones to live like this? It's all so unfair. I just need to find a way of making things good again."

Jamie's stomach spun.

Despair spread across his mother's face.

"Granny won't let you go back. I'll make sure of it. I've had enough of it. Enough of walking on eggshells. Enough of worrying about food, the electric, or if Sarah has nappies. I won't have him hurting you or any of us anymore. I'd rather die than watch you suffer another day." Tears burned his eyes. "I mean it, Ma. I'd rather be dead than bear witness to any more abuse. This can't go on. Surely, you see that now?"

Taking Jamie's hand in hers, Sonya put a hand to her mouth and broke down. She bit her lip and tightened her fingers around Jamie's hand. She shivered and inhaled a thin breath, struggling for breath while she sobbed.

"I can't do this without you," she admitted. "You're my rock, Jamie. You always have been."

Jamie held his mother's hands. Running his thumbs over her knuckles, he sniffed, refusing to become a sniveling wreck. There was nothing he wouldn't do for her, even hiding his own secrets.

Sometimes, however, secrets were made to be uncovered.

CHAPTER TWENTY-ONE

J amie watched the rising sun peeking out from behind a cloud. The clouds moved slowly, creating shapes as they went about their way. His mind distant, it rested somewhere so far out of reach, he wasn't sure how he would claim it back.

A headache had presented itself, but never quite formed into the mammoth it had promised to be. Discontent, he half hoped the ache would grow into a migraine, wanting to succumb to sleep. But no, it remained like a dull pain in the ass, and this perplexed him.

Lying on the stones of the causeway, Jamie thought about Emer and how she had died on those very stones. Quite morbid, Jamie found solace in the macabre. It brought him closer to her. He now knew how she had perished. A different kind of love and sorrow for his sister consumed him. He had to make all the bad go away one way or another.

His whole world crumbled around him, yet a glimmer of hope existed. Perhaps life could be good again. He owed this optimism to Claire. She gave him courage when so much darkness surrounded him. There had to be a way through all the pain, grief, anger, and frustration.

Jamie sat up and took out his phone. He'd missed a few calls from Lenny. Claire had also sent him a text.

```
Your Da has just been arrested. Your
grandda was taken away by ambulance.
What happened? R U alright? Let me know.
I am really worried.
xx
```

Jamie, lost in his own world, had forgotten about the chaos back at the house. Sighing, he got to his feet. He squinted and gawped up at the glass of the old lighthouse. No matter how many times he thought about Emer and Iliana, his mind refused to make sense of how they had died. How his own father had changed in a sheer moment would never register with him.

It made him question the whole *seeing a ghost* thing. He'd never get used to it or want to admit it publicly. His whole life seemed like one big facade. Hiding behind his false smile, he never allowed anyone in. A sign of weakness, Jamie didn't want to be weak.

The only two people who got a glimpse of his world were Lenny, who had been there all along, and now Claire, the girl his father had forbidden him to date.

Gulping down a lungful of air, Jamie turned and began his fifteen-minute walk back to town. The rumor mill would be churning out fat laden bullshit. The shame caused by his grandfather tried to take hold, but Jamie switched off, intent on carrying on regardless of what happened.

The house was quiet by the time he got in. A few nosy neighbors twitched their curtains.

Jamie closed the front door behind him. The smell from the previous day's lunchtime fry-up wafted through the air—fried bread, burnt toast, bacon, and eggs.

He walked down the hallway. The clock ticking in the living room echoed in the distance. He pushed the kitchen door open. Blood coated the tiles, and the chairs were overturned. Smears of blood streaked the walls. The sight should have repulsed him, but it didn't. Instead, Jamie frowned and ran a hand through his hair.

"They should both be dead," he muttered.

The air around him dropped to freezing. Jamie shivered and cautiously looked behind him.

This is all I need. He did his best not to lose his courage.

"Iliana, is it you?" he called, his voice calm.

The cold gripped him tight, like a block of ice being forced down his throat, freezing him from the inside out. His hands were numb. The fingertips turned blue. He imagined this was how the dead felt. Cold and trapped, forever miserable.

Drip.

Drip.

Drip.

He recognized the source of the dripping sound. Slow and steady, he walked through the kitchen and out onto the back porch. He pushed the plastic sheeting to the side. Broad daylight outside, the sun wouldn't set for several hours. Nevertheless, the room had been cast in darkness.

His stomach churned. He stepped across the threshold, aware of her presence.

"I know you're in here." His voice shook. "I can help you, but you need to help me, too."

A long pause of silence surrounded him before she appeared before him. Her eyes were wild and feral.

Jamie swallowed his apprehension and stepped forward. "What is it about this room?" he asked, looking around. "Why here?"

Iliana remained mute. She raised her arm. Black matter seeped from her grey sodden flesh. She pointed to the wall.

"I don't understand," Jamie muttered in confusion. "Is something behind the wall?"

Iliana nodded and disappeared.

Afraid of what lay behind the wall, the last thing he wanted to see was the skeleton of the ghostly girl. The thought of her corpse didn't fill him with reassurance.

He grabbed the hammer from the table and walked to wall. Pressing his ear up against the plasterboard, he listened.

Drip.

Drip.

Drip.

To hell with it.

His grip on the hammer tightened. Stepping back, he looked at every inch of the wall. He roared and drove the hammer against the surface.

Plaster broke with each strike of the hammer. Harder and harder he hit, until random holes appeared. When the hammer had broken enough of the wall away, Jamie used his hands. He pulled and broke the makeshift wall, cutting himself in the frenzy. His fury took over.

Jamie's face became distorted. His mouth twisted and narrowed his eyes.

"What did you do?" he cried, pulling at the drywall.

The dust filled his lungs, but not enough to deter him from tearing the wall apart. Irrational, and at the mercy of his own temper, he steadied his pace until he gave up and glared at the mess he'd made. He stood in front of the wall. Dust floated around him.

His nails were chipped and covered in drywall.

Tap. Tap. Tap.

His head shot up. A tapping sound came from inside the wall. Taking a step closer, he pulled at a piece of the rubble. It crumbled when it hit the floor.

Taking his phone out of his pocket, he switched on the flashlight, searching for the source of the noise. The plastic piping was intact. No logical reason existed when it came to the dripping water. He stretched his head over the hole he'd made and struggled to make sense of what he heard.

The temperature dipped again. This time, his breath froze in midair as he exhaled.

"Iliana," he whispered.

Pain throbbed behind his eyes. Blinking a few times, Jamie struggled to fight off the ache. It felt like the hammer had been smashed into his skull. His stomach turned. His mouth dried up, his focus lost.

Jamie shook his head and the phone slipped from his hand. He bent down to pick it up and something caught his eye from a small dent in the wall. A piece of fabric poked through the crack.

Jamie brushed his fingers against the material. A surge of energy pulsed through him, like a small electric shock. Jamie's eyes glazed over.

An odd sensation consumed him. The sickness subsided, replaced by something else—his awareness of his own mortality.

Iliana knelt on the ground beside him. Her powerful presence enveloped him.

He turned his head and looked at her.

Her face wasn't as contorted as it had previously been. Her

pale grey eyes pleaded with him.

"Is this what you wanted me to find?"

He pulled at the fabric. A line shot upwards, a fissure spreading across part of the wall. The plaster crumbled away, revealing the bloodstained silken scarf buried beneath the rubble.

Jamie pulled it out and ran his thumb across the fabric. "Is this yours?"

A pained, gurgling noise burst from Iliana's lips. She nodded and reached for the scarf, her fingers lightly grazing the edge of the material.

"My blood," she whispered. "My blood … my blood … my blood." She repeated the words until her wails became deafening.

Jamie gulped down a hard ball of air. He hated hearing those words.

"Stop, Iliana. Please stop."

The cool temperature rose slightly. Iliana grew silent and nodded.

"Why did he put it here?" Jamie asked, turning the fabric over.

Jamie glanced at Iliana and studied her aggrieved expression.

Her eyebrows were pinched. Overwhelming sadness flashed in the depths of her eyes. Her mouth thinned to a tight line, her grey, blotchy skin sunken and decaying.

Jamie stared at her, his eyes welling with tears. He hated knowing his father had done this, unable to wrap his mind around what had been done. In a way, he felt responsible for his father's crime.

Iliana rested her cold, wet hand on the back of Jamie's and said, "Let me show you."

Oh, God, no, not again, Jamie's inner voice roared.

Jamie's head smashed against the stones as Jack dragged him along. A breeze blew past, carrying the saltiness of the sea with it.

No, no, no, no. Not this. This can't be happening. The panic and shock weaved into a horrible ball of dread.

He stared at the twinkling stars above. Inside, he panicked, wanting to move, to get up and hit his father. Being dead meant he would no longer be able to call any kind of shots.

Iliana meant for him to experience everything she'd gone through. The significance confused him, but he'd understand soon enough.

Vulnerable, his mind raced, anticipating what would happen next.

His head bashed against rock after rock. Pain shot through his skull. It was torture, a cruel end to an innocent life.

Jack stopped moving. He released Jamie's legs.

For a second, relief filled every inch of Jamie's body. He stared at the stars and wondered, for the briefest moment, if heaven truly existed.

Jack reached down to fumble with something around Jamie's neck. He stood, holding the silken scarf to his nose. Jack closed his eyes and inhaled. He wiped the scarf across his face and stuck it into his back pocket.

The odd move made Jamie scream internally.

You sick prick.

The pressure came in one swift act. Jack hauled Jamie up over his shoulder.

Jamie's arms dangled in the air, his eyes focused on the stones and rocks of the causeway. Blood trickled from the side of his head. The *drip* noise echoed in his ear.

I've heard the sound before. I know that sound.

Jack didn't give Jamie enough time to register what happened.

Down he went, falling hard into the cold calm of the Irish Sea. His head cracked against a rock. More blood appeared, mixing with the water.

Jamie fought for breath. His lungs ached. Submerged in water, his arms floated out by his side. A hard object pressed against his back. The urge to thrash, to turn around in the water, and swim to the surface consumed him.

He remained immobile, staring at the blanket of briny darkness above him. The sea muted the sound of the outside world. Death wrapped itself around him, tightening its grip, forcing the last remnants of life from his lungs.

Jamie thought of something other than the murky depths of the sea. Nothing came, aside from the darkness invading his mind.

Please make the pain stop.

Finally, he gave in. Jamie accepted his fate—the fate bestowed upon Iliana.

Iliana floated beneath him, her arms stretched out, reaching for him. Her mouth opened. Bubbles crept to the surface. Her wounds were a mangled mess, and her dark eyes bore into his.

"I'm here." Her voice invaded his thoughts. *"This is where you'll find me."*

Fear consumed him. The heavy pressure pushing against his

back increased.

Iliana continued to reach for him. Her fingers came in contact with his.

The more pressure she exerted upon him, the more the weight descended. A sudden stillness shrouded him in an odd embryo of darkness. Then, a sense of release overcame him.

Jamie gasped and opened his eyes before he fell to the floor of the room. Iliana had disappeared. The same scarf his father had smelled now lay in his hand. The pungent smell of Jack's sweat mixed with Iliana's blood nauseated him. Through the wave of emotions soaring through him, however, a light beckoned.

Jamie scrambled to his feet. The adrenaline coursed beneath his skin.

"She's beneath the lighthouse."

CHAPTER TWENTY-TWO

J amie ran as fast as his legs would carry him. Giddy and scared, the jitters drove him on. By the time he reached Father Murray's, he was out of breath and somewhat intoxicated by his newfound knowledge.

After running up the graveled driveway and finally reaching the door, Jamie knocked frantically.

When the door opened, Father Murray smiled. "I've been expecting you," the old man said, and gestured for Jamie to come inside.

Jamie entered the house and followed Father Murray into the sitting room. He sat on the old brown couch, his knees jerking up and down. The movement didn't go unnoticed by Father Murray.

"You've come to a crossroad, haven't you?" he asked.

Jamie eyeballed the man and nodded. "I know where she's buried. I've seen it and felt it. I'm not strong enough for this. I don't know how I'm meant to help her. What do I have to do?"

Father Murray sat across from Jamie. He sucked on his dentures and scrunched his face. The lines under his eyes multiplied. He made little grunting noises before taking a deep breath.

"You have to go to the very place she's been lost. Only there can you make the decision to open the doorway to set her free. Remember, you must be careful. Saving a soul is always the right thing to do."

Jamie shook his head and took the scarf from his pocket. "This was hidden behind a wall in my house. This is her blood. My father did this." Jamie almost choked on the words.

Father Murray's face was unreadable. After a short pause, he stood and gestured for Jamie to follow him.

"I want to show you something."

Jamie got up and followed the priest down the hallway into a dark back room.

"What?"

Jamie's heart thumped hard. Sweat seeped in his palms. Nerves took over.

"Tell me what you feel in here?" Father Murray asked.

An unbearable coldness buried itself beneath Jamie's skin, penetrating his bones.

"What is this?" he whispered.

The chill wound itself around his body, holding him tight.

"Ah, you sense it, too," the priest replied. "This has been here for as long as I can remember." He sighed. "It made its presence known the day I had the breakdown in the chapel. Everyone had assumed I'd gone mad. Maybe they're right in some way, but in all honesty, the thing in this room, it has been following me since I was a boy. I never opened my mind to its energy until the day I walked away from the chapel. Ever since, it's been getting stronger, feeding from my soul, waiting. It's been waiting for a long time. Patient, but hungry for more than I can give it."

Jamie glared at the man. "Aren't you scared?"

"Fear is a state of mind. It allows our brains to conjure up the most horrific things. It is true what they say. Mind over matter, so to speak. The truth is, I take comfort in whatever this entity is or wants. It reminds me daily that humans aren't the be all and end all of all things. There's something greater and much more powerful out there. It's how you handle the truth, my boy. That's where the matter lies."

Father Murray stepped back and allowed Jamie to experience the darkness of the small room.

A headache burst behind Jamie's eyes like a sledgehammer, smashing its way through his skull. The pulsing pain turned his stomach, whilst the pressure built up inside his ears. He didn't want to be in the room, hating how it made him feel. Nonetheless, Father Murray was right, somehow.

Mind over matter. He focused on the darkness, pretending the pain wasn't there.

It hurt to breathe. The coolness burned the back of his nostrils and airway. The room had no window or furniture, only the darkness as decor.

"What is it?" he whispered.

"I'm not entirely sure, but it's a dark force and it feeds on energy."

Jamie glared at the priest. Bewildered, he asked, "How can you live like this?"

"Because I can," Father Murray replied. "And given the choice, where would I go? It would follow me, regardless of how far I go. It will move on when the time is right."

A low groan erupted in the room.

Jamie's ears felt like they were about to burst. Holding his hands over them, he raised a foot to take a step back, unable to move a muscle. A magnetic field of energy erupted all around him and Father Murray. The heaviness in the air increased, like a thunderstorm erupting around him. No boom or lightning engulfed him, aside from the sudden pressure.

"What's happening?"

"It's reading you, sensing the darkness hovering around you. Believe me, you can't hide those dark secrets. It sees what others can't."

Jamie frowned at Father Murray. He raised his eyebrows. Confusion consumed him.

"What?"

"It can taste fear," Father Murray replied. "Remember, this entity, it's unlike any other earthbound spirit out there. It can sense, taste, and see things. The stuff neither of us would ever understand."

"I … I … want to go," Jamie admitted. "I don't like it here. Please."

Father Murray laughed and placed a hand on Jamie's right shoulder. "Relax, son, it won't harm you. In a way, it will guide you. It will open the door to your inner strength. Have a little faith."

Jamie shook his head, unsure of what Father Murray referred to. Perhaps the old priest was, in fact, a demented psychopath leading him to his death.

"Just relax. Allow it to look inside your soul. Fighting it is not a good option, might I add. I wear the mark of my war wounds." He lifted the sleeve of his cardigan, revealing scarred tissue on his right forearm.

Jamie held his breath, anticipating being torn in half. The pressure inside his head grew uncomfortable, something he found odd, considering the severity of the situation. The grip on his legs relaxed, allowing him to move. He had no control over what took place. Small prickly vibrations pulsed through his skull.

Strange. A giddy sensation overcame him.

Every part of him reacted to the numbness creeping from his head, right down to his toes. Slowly, he became aware of the entity's intention. The entity had seen inside him, read his thoughts, and knew what he planned to do. After a few moments, the spirit released its hold on him. The pressure lifted, and he stood looking at Father Murray confused.

"How's about a drop of tea?" the old priest suggested, and held the door open for Jamie.

Jamie didn't have the nerve to decline and nodded. What happened left something buried deep inside him. The small ripples in the pit of his stomach settled. Something had changed, though he wasn't sure if he wanted to find out.

His cold fingers reached for the small teacup. His hands trembled. No matter how much he controlled the shakes, he still managed to spill a few drops of tea.

"Now, tell me about your father," Father Murray said, crossing one leg over the other.

Thinking about having to admit to another living soul about the murdering monster his father became caused Jamie's stomach to churn. His lips were dry and a hard lump formed at the back of his throat.

"I don't know where to begin," he muttered, trying to retain his composure. "It's not the kind of thing I'd ever imagined having to tell anyone."

"How's about the man you're afraid of. Why are you afraid of your father, Jamie?"

Jamie met Father Murray's eyes. "The weeks before Emer died, me da became a living nightmare. He grew frantic about Emer's behavior and caught her outside a few times in the middle of the night, hanging around with a few older lads. It drove him mad. Me ma couldn't control Emer. No matter how many times I tried to talk to her, she just laughed in me face and refused to acknowledge what she was doing."

Jamie closed his eyes. "She was a complete bitch, pardon my language, but it's the truth. She wouldn't stop pressing me da's buttons and got off on knowing she undermined his authority. She had no respect for him, or me ma. Then, the night she died, none of us knew where she was. Me poor ma was in pieces, and he was out on the drink without a care in the world. The peelers were called—they didn't give a shite—and the next day, they found her down by the causeway."

Jamie's silence mirrored his sadness. "I'll always remember how me da stood by her coffin. He never really looked at her or touched her, which I found odd, considering my ma just wouldn't stop brushing her hair with her hand. And even when they put her in the ground, me da refused to help lower the coffin.

At the time, I thought the grief consumed him. Maybe he hadn't accepted she was gone. I kept making up excuses in me head, trying to condone how cold he became. Then, the drinking got worse. First, he drank a few cans in the evening. Then, it became a morning ritual watching him pop the top of a can while pouring milk on my brother's cornflakes. It was just awful, watching his decline. The way he treated me mother made being in the house unbearable. He stopped working, let the business slide, and then … Then, I saw Iliana on the causeway."

Jamie swallowed, unable to ignore the urge to cry. Speaking so candidly made the nightmare real.

"I'd never been afraid of me da, not like I am now," Jamie confessed. "He has this cold, distant look in his eyes. When he caught me in the back extension a few nights ago, he made my skin crawl. Fathers aren't meant to be like that. Surely, there must be a reason why he's changed? Or maybe he's always been bad to the bone."

"I see," Father Murray replied. "Do you think he knows?"

Jamie shook his head. "I honestly don't know. But with me grandda showing up and hell breaking loose, I'd say he'll be on the rampage. It's what he does."

"I'm sorry, Jamie. You've had a lot to deal with. It can't have been easy." Father Murray sat forward. "But Iliana chose you for a specific reason, one neither of us will ever understand. She is relying on you to set her free."

"Aye, and I've accepted this. I'm just a little cut up about the man my father's become. How are the wee ones and I meant to live with this? We'll be shunned in town, never mind what will become of me mother. We're the innocent party in all this, but people won't see things how they should be. People cast stones for the smallest of reasons. There's no coming back from this once everyone knows."

"Listen to me, son, burdening yourself with this kind of talk will do you no favors," Father Murray said. "You have to rise above your own fear in order to complete what needs to be done."

"I've never believed in ghosts," Jamie admitted.

"And now?" Father Murray raised his brows and smiled.

Jamie picked at the skin around his thumbnail. "Now I'm afraid they're all I'll ever see."

"Mostly people lie when they talk about ghosts. The one's who say they see them and know who they are—they're the ones living a lie. It's us, people like you and I, who daren't talk about our experiences, because we'd be institutionalized for our troubles." Father Murray sat back and folded his arms. "My suggestion to you, lad, is to go down to the lighthouse and open yourself completely to the energy. Because believe it or not, Iliana won't rest until she's been freed. I daren't think about the darkness she'd emit if her wishes aren't fulfilled."

Everything the priest said made sense. In a short period of time, he'd become more attuned to the world and the bigger picture. Who would have thought it even remotely imaginable for a young man like him to see beyond the veil of possibility?

He had to help Iliana.

"And me da? Do I confront him?"

Father Murray shook his head. "Under no circumstances, Jamie. I've a bad feeling where your father is concerned. For once, heed my words when I say be careful. Act with caution."

Jamie swallowed and stood. "After it's done, do you mind if

I call by? It's just … you're the only one who truly understands what I'm going through."

"Absolutely, I'd like nothing better." Father Murray smiled and held out his hand. "My door is always open to you. Regardless of what the locals say, I've my wits about me."

Jamie shook his hand. He had found a kindred spirit. Irrespective of what everyone else in town thought, Jamie had made up his own mind about Father Murray. A gentle old soul who was treated like a fool, Father Murray was far from being anyone's jester.

Jamie walked from the house with a new sense of the world around him. If someone had told him weeks ago he'd believe in the unbelievable, he'd have laughed in their faces and mocked them. Now, the way he saw the world, the seen and the unseen, awakened something inside of him. Scary and enlightening, he never expected to play an important role in something so strange, so farfetched, yet as real as anything he'd gone through in his short sixteen years.

Jamie slipped his hand into his pocket and took out his phone. He texted Claire.

> Do you fancy being my sidekick this afternoon?

Her reply followed quickly.

> I thought you'd never ask xo

Jamie smiled and replied.

Julieanne Lynch

`I'm on my way to yours :)`

Determined to do Iliana justice, Jamie picked up his pace. He turned the corner, aware of the shadow following in his wake.

I guess things are about to get even more strange.

He sucked in a deep breath. "Typical," he muttered.

CHAPTER TWENTY-THREE

"Claire Brannigan, if you dare test my patience one more time, I swear ..."

Claire's mother scolded her as Jamie walked up to the open front door.

"Ah, Jamie, she's inside, being a bloody nuisance."

"I'll tell her to behave." He smiled.

"The YouTube channel she's got her sister addicted to, bloody awful stuff. And they call that music," she continued. "Anyway, I heard about your grandda. Any news?"

Jamie opened his mouth to reply, relieved when Claire appeared.

"See you later. I'll not be late."

Claire's mother stood with one hand on her hip and scowled. "I don't want no bother. I've enough coming from your father."

"I promise I won't let her get into any kind of trouble," Jamie said with reassurance.

"Boys your age say it all the time." She winked at them and turned around, heading inside the house.

They walked along the path.

Claire slipped her hand into Jamie's. Her skin sliding against his sent little goose pimples prickling across the surface.

"So, are we doing something very dangerous and otherworldly today?" she asked.

Jamie raised an eyebrow and glanced down at her. "Yup. It's now or never, I guess. Or at least give it my best shot."

"Would it be wrong of me to admit I am slightly excited by all this?" She giggled, holding onto the small vial on her necklace.

Jamie laughed. "Well, I guess you were always a weirdo."

"Hey, I'm not the one who sees ghosts." She pointed a finger into the side of his face, and then continued. "Which, to be fair, is kinda sexy, in a weird kind of way."

Jamie blushed. He wasn't used to this kind of attention, especially from a girl who made him feel alive.

"I guess being weird is the new black," he remarked, shielding his shyness.

"Absolutely." Claire rested her head against his arm. "Besides, we can be weird together."

Jamie smiled at those words. He never thought he'd ever connect with someone like her. In his mind, Claire had been out of his league, making him feel inferior, especially when he saw the group of girls she chose to hang around with. Ever since she became his, he realized her public image had all been based on rumor. She wasn't at all like he'd imagined her to be.

"I stopped by Father Murray's," he said, changing the subject.

Claire cocked her head and looked at him. "On your own?"

"Aye." He sighed. "It seemed like the right thing to do at the time."

"Wow. So, like ... what happened?"

"Do you really want to know?"

"You're such a dose. What do you think?"

She would press him for more information, but he wasn't sure if she was ready for the truth.

"I know where the dead girl is."

Jamie's mouth grew dry. His heart hammered inside his chest. He anticipated her laughing at him and mocking his confession.

"Oh, my god, seriously? Like where? Is this what you plan on us doing today? Digging up old bones?"

"Possession is the weirdest thing ever," Jamie remarked. "When she appears, I know she's going to take me with her to the very place she died. But nothing ever prepares me for what I see or experience. It's indescribable."

"What does it feel like?" Claire asked, the look on her face innocent.

"It makes me feel so unwell. I always end up cold and can never warm up, even after it's stopped. But each time it happens, and this is going to sound peculiar," he said, looking at her. "I'm always relieved she's shown me something I never thought possible. I am not glad me da's this stone-cold killer, but I understand everything that's happened now and why it's happened."

"Being relieved for seeing a dead girl is kind of insane."

"I knew you wouldn't get it."

Claire's making light of his honesty annoyed Jamie.

"I'm sorry. I didn't mean to be insensitive." Claire looked at him.

An awkward silence descended upon them. It lasted for a few minutes before Jamie responded.

"I guess I get it. I mean, it's not every day you hear about the crazy goings-on of a ghost, right?"

Claire squeezed his hand a little tighter. "But still, I shouldn't have acted like an arsehole. Am I forgiven?"

Jamie smirked before glancing down at her. "Only if you kiss me."

In the light of the late morning sun, Jamie stopped walking and closed the gap between them with one swift motion. Jamie's heart pounded hard as their lips moved together. He forgot the minor awkwardness they experienced. The kiss was a promise of things to come, but first, they had to overcome several hurdles in their way.

"I could get used to this," Claire whispered, holding onto him tight.

"Me, too." He looked away from her, focusing on the horizon. "But first, let's help a ghost in need."

The two headed off in the direction of the causeway, determined to put an end to the haunting.

No more than a chill in the air, a shimmer of mist glistened in the evening sun. Slowly a dark figure materialized and stood on the causeway. She stared at them as they drew closer.

Jamie didn't pass any remarks—he didn't want to scare Claire. Energy surrounded the area. He turned his head and caught sight of her, more in tune with her presence than ever before. Her tortured frustration rippled in the distance. Their connection grew stronger.

Iliana's hair covered her entire face. Her clothes were nothing more than rags hanging from her bones.

Jamie hadn't seen her look like this in any of their encounters. She looked dead.

When she moved, she flitted in and out of focus, moving at odd angles and appearing distressed. The stillness of the air sucked the sound of his breath as he stared at her. Iliana's body became warped and twisted. Bones protruded through her ragged clothing. Deep, dark welts appeared on her skeletal frame, liquid seeping from the wounds. Water pooled at her feet. Small beads of ice rolled toward Jamie.

Jamie looked up from where she stood and caught her gaze. Her hair blew back from her face, revealing the dark holes where her eyes once were. His voice caught in his throat, the scream caged like a bird, before her presence faded completely.

Jamie turned his focus back to Claire.

"Are you okay?" she asked.

"Yup," he muttered. The skin on the back of his neck tightened. "Just up over there."

He pointed to the small trail dipping downward in front of the lighthouse. "In high tide, this part of the causeway is completely submerged in water. We don't have a big window." Jamie gazed at the waves lapping against each other.

"So, like, she's over there?"

Jamie took a huge breath and nodded. "Yes, I believe so. I just don't know what to expect."

"I can't believe we're really going to do this." Claire sounded scared.

"Me, too, but hey, someone has to help this girl, right?"

Claire nodded and fumbled with the zip of her fleece.

Jamie stepped across the stones, holding his hand out for her. "I'm glad I've got you with me. I can't do it alone."

Claire smiled at him. A breeze blew strands of hair across her face.

Jamie drew in a sharp breath.

She's mine. How did I get so lucky?

He winked at her, doing his best to hide his growing affections. He didn't want to let his guard down completely.

"Well …" Claire beamed, jumping across the stones and sliding her fingers between Jamie's. "Aren't you lucky that I've an open mind? And besides, between the two of us, we can put this girl's soul to rest. It's the least we can do to help."

As if she'd read his mind, Jamie didn't reply. He didn't need to.

Hand in hand, they passed the entry to the lighthouse and climbed up over the rocks.

The calm sea spread across the horizon. A few lingering boats sailed across the rippling surface. The gulls swooped low and back up again, making their odd little cries.

Jamie loved the sea. At one point in his life, he had loved the causeway and the old lighthouse more than anything. Now, it was a constant reminder of everything dark in his world.

He turned to look at Claire.

Her pretty nose crinkled when she saw the seaweed.

The sight of her being all girlie amused him. She didn't resemble the girl he'd known at school. Jamie chuckled.

"What's so funny?"

"You," he replied.

"Yeah, yeah, yeah."

"I used to love sitting out here when I was younger," he remarked, staring into the distance. "It always brought me a sense of calm. The great vastness of it all. I guess it awed me as a child."

"And now?" Claire asked.

"I hate it. It's tainted with so much sadness and death." Jamie sighed and looked at his feet. "It depresses me. I don't need the constant reminder of all the pain my family has gone through."

"It's okay." Claire reached out to him. "I'm so sorry about everything you've been through. I can't imagine what's been going on. I'm here for you, regardless of what your da might think."

Claire's sincerity moved him. She gently stroked his fingertips with the pad of her thumb, a sign she'd always be there for him. A glimmer of hope in his dark world.

"Thank you," he whispered. "When it all started with Iliana, I thought I was going mad. When she showed me those things—things I never would have imagined—she gave me a boot up the backside." Jamie paused and sat down on the rocks. "I'd all but given up on life. Me da had begun to suck every last drop of my courage away. Each day I'd get up, face the same crap, and struggle on. I put on a show, slowly dying inside. I remember envying everyone around me. I resented Lenny. Sounds mad, right? Why? I honestly don't know. I've been so stuck in the past and being drowned by the present, I saw no way out of it."

His nerves on edge, Jamie had to get a few things off his chest.

"Maybe this dead girl has helped you more than you know," Claire said, and sighed. "Her death, gruesome and just wrong, has been her legacy. She's giving you a chance to redeem yourself, to help you get out of this rut. She wanted to help you all along, while having herself set free."

"It's just so sad."

Claire's warm eyes met Jamie's. "I know."

"She had a whole life ahead of her, and then he came and took it away. Like her life meant nothing. It's wrong, Claire. Who gave him the right to make those kinds of choices? It's unfair, it's cruel, and he has to pay."

Claire shook her head and shrugged. "Who knows what goes on in the mind of a killer? Somewhere, someday, your father will pay his dues, I am sure. It's just a matter of time, right?"

The words sent a shockwave down Jamie's spine. No matter what, his father had to be stopped.

"You see the small group of rocks down there?" Jamie pointed to a little pool a few feet away. "He put her there, using rocks to weigh her down. When the tide comes in, it brings debris in from the sea, bits of wood, seaweed, and the like. He waded through the water to remove any trace of her. Just thinking about it makes my skin crawl. No one would have ever noticed her because no one really comes down this far. The current can be bad, and I suppose everyone is wary about the old stories of the lighthouse. It's the perfect dumping ground."

He shuddered, the words registering in his head.

Dumping ground.

"Emer was found over there." He pointed to a location along the stony beach. "It looked just like a drunken accident. She'd had a good few drinks in her, or so the toxicology report said. No one ever questioned the cuts and bruising on her face. They all assumed the way she fell caused her injuries."

"Jamie, don't do this to yourself," Claire whispered, and clasped his arm.

"Why not? I need to say this out loud. I've bottled it all up for so long, it feels like the truth is ready to burst through my chest. I've no idea how much longer I can take this."

Jamie stared at Claire in silence. His eyes burned from the tears pricking behind them.

"Have you ever hated someone so much it feels like a physical pain?"

Claire shook her head. "No, not really."

"I do, every single day. It's like a disease, only there's no cure. No escape. Just a bed of lies and deceit, and it's no way to live your life."

He wiped his eyes, angry for letting his emotions get the better of him. His cheeks burned. Jamie pushed up from the rocks and stepped down slowly, making his way to the pool.

Bigger than he remembered from the vision, water lapped against the rocks. The salty scent of the sea air assaulted his nostrils. He stared absentmindedly at the water. The turmoil evaporated. In its place, a new sensation swarmed. The darkness crept deep inside, consuming him a piece at a time.

He glared at the water. His mouth went dry, and he sighed.

Jamie had his work cut out for him. Afraid, he had to get in there, and God only knew what lay beneath. He unzipped his hoodie and threw it at Claire.

"Wait, are you going in there?" she asked, sounding surprised.

"It's the only way." Jamie bent to remove his shoes, but kept his jeans and T-shirt on.

"But," Claire mumbled, "there's going to be bones and creepy crawlies … just … Yuck, don't go in there." She scrunched her face.

"Listen, I've come this far. I'm not about to be a scared little shite. This has to be done. Just trust me, okay?"

Claire knelt on the rocks. Looking at Jamie, she closed her eyes and shook her head.

"How deep is it? Do you even know? What if something happens to you?"

"It can't be that deep. If something happens, then you run and get help," he said.

Claire sucked in a deep breath and nodded. She said nothing more.

Jamie sat down on the edge of the rocks and took a deep breath before lowering himself into the water. The coldness of the sea felt like little jabs of glass digging into his chest. Jamie took several small gasps, still holding onto the rock above. Nausea overcame him. The sensation brought the memory back to him. The fear he'd felt when he had been face-down in the water, staring at the blanket of darkness beneath him.

Small drops of rain trickled down. Jamie looked up. The clouds clustered into one huge, grey mass. A few low rumbles of thunder growled in the distance.

Claire gave Jamie a worried glance and bit her lip.

"Stop worrying. It'll be grand," he said before dipping his shoulders into the water, taking a deep breath and sinking under.

Submerged in the murky water, Jamie opened his eyes and held his breath for as long as possible. Little fragments of white matter floated before him. Bubbles escaped through his nose and rose upward.

Jamie became acutely aware of Iliana's presence. Every follicle on Jamie's body pulsed.

Her energy surrounded him. She rippled through him. Pulling him deeper into the abyss. Iliana led him down a dark hole and into her briny grave.

CHAPTER TWENTY-FOUR

Iliana found it impossible to hold back. She had waited all this time, and now she was so close to being set free. Her impulsiveness became too much to contain.

Jamie stood nearby, searching for her final resting place.

Her body was just a bag of bones buried beneath the rocks and sand. She needed Jamie to push past the boundaries telling him he needed air.

"Find me, Jamie."

Her voice rippled through the water.

His eyes shot to the right. Through the misty flow of the sea, he saw her. Startled, he swam away from her, reaching for the surface.

"No … no … no," she cried. *"Come back."*

Jamie shot to the surface. He gasped for breath.

Claire looked down at him, holding her hand out. The storm raged on, soaking her to the bone.

BENEATH THE LIGHTHOUSE

Jamie's heart thumped hard, ready to burst through his chest. The realization crashed down around him. Iliana caused the storm—he was sure of it.

"I think I've found her," he cried.

Something tugged on Jamie's foot from beneath, pulling him down hard. He reached out, only to grasp at nothing. Panic raced through him. Down he went, sinking faster than he ever imagined. He held his breath. His throat burned, as though blades had been plunged into it. He opened his mouth and gasped in water.

I need air. His chest tightened. A hot burning sensation rippled inside of him. *I don't want to die. I don't want to die.*

He thrashed his legs, struggling against the force propelling him further down. He squeezed his eyes shut, trying to stop himself from swallowing more of the briny sea. A noose wrapped around his neck, its grip tightening and forcing his mouth open. Then, silence descended upon him. Calmness overtook all the pain. A warm welcoming heat raced through his head. He opened his eyes and stared ahead.

Through strands of seaweed and floating debris, Iliana's face floated towards him. Her features distorted. Her eye sockets empty. Her flesh torn, bits hung from her face and dangled in the water. She opened her mouth, as though she were sucking in mouthful after mouthful of water. Instead, she moved her hands to her face and pulled at her flesh, ripping herself apart, until there was nothing but bones left.

Iliana's skull lay on the seabed beneath him. Her remains were scattered around her. Rocks and stones lay beside her. The same rocks he remembered his father using to weigh her down.

Jamie found it hard to look away from the horrific sight. Lost in the mess before him, the burning in his lungs pulled him from his reverie and hurled him back to the present. Sheer panic drove through him hard.

I don't want to die down here.

He swam towards the surface and pushed past the current pulling him back down. His legs grew tired. Above him, Claire's face peered down into the water.

Help me, he shouted. *Claire, help me.*

He faced the black barrier of water. The torrent of wrath engulfed him.

Iliana refused to let go of him. Her energy became an all-consuming magnet.

Unable to understand why, he thrashed in the water, the rocks cutting into his skin. Blood mixed with the sea. His head grew heavy. Disoriented, he didn't know which way was up or down.

Relentless in her pursuit, Iliana exerted her power over him.

Jamie struggled to fight the impossible force of something he had no control over.

Iliana clawed at his clothes. She tugged at his jeans, her fingers tracing the line of his pockets.

Jamie reached out for her and pushed her away, his hands slipping through her ghostly form. Her silhouette burst before him, leaving tendrils of bubbles behind.

From the side, Iliana reappeared. Like fire, her anger enveloped him. She held him still, both of them unmoving in the water. Her lethal stare pierced him. She screamed, the vibrations rippling through the water. Unable to stop it, fear made him pee, and his bodily fluid entered the deep.

Jamie's heart pounded behind his eyes. Flashes of red dots

lined his vision. Dizziness slowly consumed him. His arms ached, as though they were laced with lead. Heavy and tired, he yearned to give in.

The small pendant loosened from the depths of his pocket. The more Jamie moved, the more he forced the necklace outward.

Iliana continued to pull and tug at him, until finally the pendant fell from his pocket and sank into the briny water, landing next to her skull.

Jamie neared the brink of death.

Is this what it's like to die?

Visions of his mother and siblings flitted through his mind. Emer's face flashed before him, its waxy pallor more real than he remembered. His body jerked a few times, as though he were having a seizure.

Please, Iliana, his inner voice cried. *Don't do this.*

Silence.

Warmth.

A hand.

A bubble surrounded every inch of Jamie's body. Warm and safe, he relaxed and turned onto his side, sighing with contentment. Sleepily, he opened his eyes.

A hand reached for him.

"Jamie," a voice muttered his name.

The voice echoed in his head. Like the person behind the voice lay deep within a well, too far out of reach.

"Jamie," it repeated over and over.

His eyes flickered, his vision blurred.

"You have to live," the voice continued. *"Jamie, you must live."*

The fight that had all but slipped away from him came rushing back with a vengeance. Jamie crashed through the water, his mouth open, begging the air to fill his lungs. He swallowed a mouthful of the salty water before he coughed and gagged.

Tears streamed down Claire's cheeks, mixing with the rainwater.

"Oh, my god," she screamed. "Jamie, please. Come here. Get out of the water." She held her arms out to him.

The wind howled like a wild beast. Waves crashed hard against the causeway. The world grew darker, gloomier, and there wasn't a thing Jamie could do about it.

He reached out and touched the side of the rocks. Exhausted, his head pounded. The rancid water caused the bile to rise to the back of his throat.

"Jamie, get out of there," Claire begged.

Shaking his head, Jamie held onto the rock, intent on pulling himself out. Every ounce of his energy had been spent fighting for survival.

"I can't," he mumbled. His lips quivered.

Claire tugged at his arms, trying to coax him to exert one last ounce of energy.

Jamie panted, holding onto the side of the rock pool. Deeper than he'd expected, the strangest feeling of release had overcome him. He'd half-expected Iliana to pull him back under, but she had gone silent. Her presence had faded.

"Jamie, can you please get out of the bloody water?" Claire shouted.

Jamie noticed the frightened look etched across her face. He nodded and pulled himself up against the rock. His right arm bled. Somehow, he'd cut the back of his neck.

"We need to get you to the hospital," Claire cried, touching his face. "You're freezing."

Jamie shuddered, unable to control the trembling. His body refused to remain still.

"What happened?" Claire asked. She wrapped Jamie's hoodie around his shoulders and rubbed his back, holding him tight.

"I saw her bones and felt her rage. She wanted to hurt me." Bile burned his throat choking off his words. He leaned over and wretched into the water. He wiped his mouth with the back of his hand, then took a couple deep gulps of air. "She wouldn't let me go, and then I felt like I was asleep. Warm and safe."

He shivered. "The next thing I know, I'm crashing out of the water, my lungs burning from all the water I swallowed." He paused and looked back at the pool. "It was like a bad dream, only it was very real."

The storm clouds darkened. Out on the horizon, large swells topped with white foam charged through the sea, intent on making their way to shore.

Jamie rested against a large rock, letting the rain wash the saltiness of the sea from his face. He closed his eyes. He needed to gather his thoughts.

"She's still down there, and I need to get her out," he mumbled. "How do I do this?"

"You need to get the peelers involved. It's the only way, Jamie," Claire said, holding his hands.

Their eyes met. She had a point. He didn't have the guts to make the call.

"What do I say?"

"Honestly?" Claire looked defeated. "I'm not sure. Maybe say nothing at all. Maybe my suggestion is stupid."

The wind picked up pace, and Jamie sat forward. There was more yet to come, he just didn't know what.

"If I go to the peelers, I'll open myself to a load of shit I can't be dealing with. I need to do this on the quiet." He gulped. "I need to bring her remains to the surface, and it means going back down there."

Sheer terror spread across Claire's face. Her eyes widened.

"It's not a good idea." She shook her head.

"It's better than leaving her down there and letting her continue attacking me. And besides, who will the peelers believe, me or me da?"

"You have a valid point." Claire bit her bottom lip. "With his temper, your da won't let things slide so easily."

Holding his fingers to his head, Jamie said, "Let's go back to my house. I need to grab a bag."

"Why?"

"To put her bones in." Jamie stood.

He held a hand out to Claire and helped her to her feet. Taking one last look at the rock pool, Jamie walked over to the edge and stared at the water.

"One way or another, you're coming to the surface."

Iliana glared up through the water. Jamie's words filtered down towards her. She frowned. For a moment, she was compelled to pull him back in. She looked at the pendant, unable to do so.

It had been three long years since she last read the inscription. She'd often anticipated how she'd feel once she was reunited with her mother's precious gift. Nevertheless, she was torn. Her mind fragmented and hurt.

Jamie was the key—the very source to her freedom. A soul for a soul, it would never come easy, not as long as he believed he had to retrieve her remains. New blood had to be spilled. Though it caused her inner torment, she had to finish it, once and for all.

Humming a lullaby from her youth, she danced around the pendant. A melody so bewitching, she found herself drifting off to her happy place. Memories of her mother's embrace filled her with both joy and woe.

For the first time in a long while, Iliana's misery dissipated. A moment she savored, however brief it seemed.

CHAPTER TWENTY-FIVE

The lights were off in the house by the time Jamie got home. He had already made his mind up to pack a few things and take them to his mother.

Jack stood in the living room, holding a can of beer in one hand and a hammer in the other.

Jamie never took the possibility of being confronted by his father into consideration. Not so soon anyway.

"It seems you've been busy while I've been down in the cop shop." Jack glared at Jamie.

Fear rose to the back of Jamie's throat. His father had seen the mess in the extension. "I thought I heard water dripping, just like I did the other night."

A shrewd look spread across Jack's face. The man wasn't a complete fool.

"Funny that, isn't it?"

"Come again?" Jamie cautiously stepped back.

"You have a thing for snooping about, don't you?" Jack took a step forward and set his can of beer on the mantelpiece. "I mean, you had to be the one to catch me old man mucking around me wife, didn't you?"

"Da, he raped her. She didn't ask for it. It wasn't her fault."

"Even so, it always comes down to you. Jamie this, Jamie sees that, Jamie knows too much for his own good," Jack mocked. "Just like the wee tramp you're running around with. A bloody Brannigan, for Christ sake. Is she easy like her mother?"

Jamie's fist curled into a tight ball. "Don't talk about Claire like that."

"Why, is she a good wee ride?" Jack teased, making a face as the words slipped off his tongue.

Jamie's hurt and anger twisted like a storm inside, "I hate you."

"Aye, it seems to be the daily mantra in this dive."

Jamie hated when his father did this. Jack twisted every aspect of their lives into something ugly. His father's continuous referrals to Claire tore at his heart. An unexpected rage consumed him.

"So, the hammer," Jack said, lifting it and glaring at its head. "You made a mess of me wall." His mouth curled into an ugly snarl. "So much so, I don't think I'll have the patience to fix it."

Jamie prepared himself for the oncoming attack. Everything changed—his composure, his glare, even the way he breathed. Jamie wished he had the courage and power to withstand his father's brutality. At five-foot-eight, Jamie was a mouse in comparison to his father's brutish six-foot-three physique.

"I'll fix it up myself," Jamie replied. His voice shook.

Jack made tutting noises and stepped closer to Jamie. "And how the hell do you think you'll do that?" He laughed. "You don't have enough skill to wipe your own arse, never mind building a wall."

Jamie found himself pressed against the front door. He reached for the handle behind his back. Doing so was futile. The deadbolt was on.

Jack raised the hammer in the air and whistled. "All it takes is one clean swoop to the side of the head, and *bam*. You're a goner." He laughed, baring his teeth. "That's all it takes to wipe another person off the face of this earth."

"Is that what you did to Emer?"

Jamie held his breath, anticipating the hammer making contact with his skull.

"What did you say?"

The ball at the back of his throat expanded. It didn't stop him from repeating what he said.

"Is that how you killed Emer?"

"What in God's name do you mean?"

Jack's eyes bulged. His nostrils flared. His breath reeked of booze.

"Exactly what the question implies."

"What do you think I've done?" Jack raised his brows and smirked.

"I know you killed Emer and the girl who saw what you did. I know all about it, Da. You are the worst kind of human I've ever known."

Jamie's head spun, as though he'd been deprived of oxygen. His heart pounded like drums in his ears. He closed his mouth, afraid of what he would say next. He clenched his fists, anticipating his father's next move. He shivered from the onset of the adrenaline rippling through him. He looked at his toes before raising his head and catching Jack's eye.

"Well, if it isn't Sherlock himself," Jack mocked. "And who do you believe will actually buy into your fairytale? The peelers?

Your mother? The fecking clergy? Go on, enlighten me. Give it your best shot. Because the way I see it, and the way the authorities will see it, is you're a lad on the road to self-destruction. Sure, look what you've done to me home. You've trashed it. No one is safe around you. Not even the twins or wee Sarah. You're a liability, son. A danger to us all and yourself."

Jamie shouldn't have been shocked. He remembered what Father Murray had said—mind over matter. Jamie threw caution to the wind and ploughed on.

"Why did you do it, Da?"

Jack snarled. "Do what, son?"

"You killed our Emer, and you killed Iliana. You did it, Da."

Jamie's heart grew heavy. Sweat bubbled across the palms of his hands. His stomach twisted itself into a tight ball of nerves. Darkness hovered in front of his eyes. Bile rose to the back of his throat.

Jack took a step back and glared at Jamie. "Are you trying to twist with me? Is that what this is? Some sort of twisted little mind game, eh?"

Jamie shook his head. Sweat formed across his top lip. The corners of his mouth quivered. He didn't want to come across as a coward, but he feared his father more than he feared anyone else in his life.

"You can stop the pretense with me, Da. I know all your secrets. How you beat the shit out of Emer and left her out there on the causeway, bleeding to death. You made it look like a drunken accident." Jamie paused, his throat hurt just from admitting the truth. "I know how you caught Iliana. You could have let her go, but you didn't. You ran after her, dragged her into the lighthouse, and you beat her to death." Tears leaked out of the corners of his eyes. "But it wasn't good enough, was it? You had to drag her across the rocks and down to the rock pool. You hid her there beneath the water, beneath the lighthouse, knowing no one would ever find her. Sure, why would they? She was a nobody. Her life didn't matter. In fact, nothing matters to you, does it? You're just selfish and think about yourself."

A clear line had been crossed.

Jack stood with his head bowed low. His breathing grew ragged. His posture slouched.

It was time to run.

Jamie sprang forward and pushed past his father. He ran down the hall, into the kitchen, and out onto the back porch. He reached for the lock, but his fingers fumbled. The keys weren't on the hook.

Jack came into view in the kitchen.

"Where are you running to, Jamie?" Jack sounded deranged. "What's this? Cat's got your tongue?" He laughed. "It's a first for you."

Jamie panicked. The keys were always on the hook—always.

Jack rattled them in front of Jamie and chuckled. "I'm always two steps ahead, son. Which brings me to ask a question."

"What?" Jamie asked, wide-eyed.

Jack looked Jamie up and down, and tilted his head, "Why are you soaking wet?"

"It's teeming out there, or haven't you noticed?"

Jack sniffed around Jamie and tutted again. "Ah, it might be pelting down out there, but there's a distinct odor, pretty much like the sea surrounding you. Have you been swimming? In your clothes?"

Jack glared at Jamie. A stillness lurked in his eyes, almost like death.

Jamie swallowed hard, afraid to utter another word.

Jack lifted the hammer and pushed the head against Jamie's chest, smirking and forcing him back against the wall.

"You're very much like her, you know?" He cocked his head to the side.

"Who?" Jamie asked, his voice trembled.

"Emer," Jack replied. "The same eyes, the same chin, the dimple, right down to the backchat."

"Da, what are you doing?"

Jamie searched the back porch for anything he could use to defend himself. An umbrella sat near the window. A horrible feeling overcame him.

Jack reached out and grabbed Jamie by the throat. He squeezed until Jamie found it hard to breathe.

"The thing about all this," Jack said. "It could have been avoided. Every single thing I've ever done was for the good of this family. The little bitch, she had to push me. Taunt me. And all the size of her. Do you know how hard it's been for me? How I've been affected? Or have you been too wrapped up in your own little woes to even give a shit?"

"Da ..." Jamie gasped. "Stop."

Jack let out a guttural laugh and squeezed harder. "That's the funny thing about the youth of today. They think they call the shots. No respect for their elders, never mind themselves. Your sister was out there, walking the streets at the dead of night, nothing more than a nipper, flaunting herself and drinking. Who the hell did she think she was? As if I'd allow her to behave like a tramp."

A wave of dizziness overcame him. No matter how much Jamie

focused on the shallow breaths he took, his vision swirled from the lack of oxygen.

Glee flashed in his father's eyes. Jack sighed and glanced at the plastic sheeting. He then glared at Jamie and smirked.

"Let's go take a look at your handiwork." His grip loosened on Jamie's neck, and he pushed him to walk ahead of him.

Jamie gasped and sucked in as much air as possible. The back of his throat burned. He hated not having the balls to turn around and whack his father in the face.

Kicked across the backs of his legs, he fell hard onto the cold concrete floor. He glanced back at his father, who laughed in response.

"Jesus, you're an ugly wee bastard," Jack remarked. "Now, take a look at me wall, and tell me what you see." He used the hammer to point at the wall. "Are you looking close enough?" Jack stomped over to Jamie and grabbed him by the back of his neck. He dragged him over to the wall and pushed his face against the crumbling plasterboard. "Do you see what you've done?"

"You ... stop ..." Jamie stammered. His spittle dribbled down his chin.

"Now tell me, what was the point in all of this?" Jack shouted. "What was the point in you being a nosy little prick?"

Jack pulled Jamie by the hair and yanked his head back. He glared down into his son's face.

Jamie thought he was about to die.

"I thought ... I heard ... water," Jamie stuttered.

"Water, me bloody arse." Jack pressed the hammer into the back of Jamie's neck, twisting the cold copper head until Jamie squirmed.

"Da, stop this."

"Why? Isn't this what you've wanted all along? A showdown with your oul man, putting wrongs to right. Come on, then. You're a big lad these days, eh?"

His words unsettled Jamie. A beating was coming and his father would not stop this time. Not until he had claimed his life, too.

Jack undid the belt of his jeans and whipped it off. He wrapped the buckle around his hand.

"I'll teach you to meddle in what doesn't concern you."

The first sting hit him hard across the back of the head. His hands shot up, and he shielded his face. He ached as the leather strap slapped against him continuously. He wanted to cry so badly, but he swallowed the pain. Numbness soon took over, something he'd grown accustomed to. Despite how much he struggled, his father refused to let up.

The skin broke on the backs of Jamie's hands. Warm blood trickled over his knuckles.

Jack roared. "You never stopped to think about what you were doing to me." He kicked Jamie hard in the face, forcing him onto his back. "Forever the nosey wee brat, thinking you're some kind of match to me. Let this be a lesson you'll never forget."

This is how I'm going to die, Jamie thought. *He's going to kill me.*

A slight chill seeped into the room. Jamie had experienced it repeatedly the past few weeks. The bitter cold swarmed around him.

Jack didn't notice a thing, too enraged to see past his own fury. Not once did he stop the kicks or the lashing of the belt.

Jamie curled into a ball, trying to protect himself. He caught sight of Iliana.

She peered out at him from beneath the workbench. Iliana held a finger to her mouth.

Jamie soon forgot the relentless blows and focused on Iliana.

Intent on spilling blood, Iliana hadn't thought about the abuse Jamie suffered at the hands of the very monster who'd claimed her life. Her fingernails scratched along the floor, leaving a trail of black goo. Her hand reached out towards Jamie. His pain rippled through her.

"No, not like this," she cried.

Iliana hadn't seen Jack since the night he beat her to death. She found it odd looking at him from this angle. He seemed so much smaller now. Nothing like the intimidating monster who had taken great pleasure in smashing her skull.

Heat burned in the pit of her cold, sunken stomach. She hadn't experienced the sensation once throughout the past three years. It gripped her tight, sending a shockwave of blistering fury through her mangled remains.

She cried out. *"What is this?"*

She stuck a nail inside her wet flesh and sliced her arm open. Yellow liquid oozed out of her like molten lava. The potent substance filled the air with a scent unlike anything she'd smelled before. The odor of death, her own rotten existence, sent a wave of blood thirst running through her.

Fear spread across Jamie's face. It mirrored every inch of the fear she felt the night she'd died.

Glaring at Jack, she knew what she had to do. She crawled out from under the bench. Her bones cracked and crunched as she made her way over to Jamie. She hovered above where he lay. Putting another finger to her lips, she met his gaze and nodded.

Jamie understood.

She waited for him to close his eyes.

A few moments passed. Jack reached down, pulled Jamie by the hair, and punched him hard across the face. A crunching noise sounded when Jamie's nose broke.

Pain exploded against the side of his head. A ringing sound bounced around inside his skull, enraging her to the point she couldn't control herself. She didn't hold back a second longer. Closing her eyes, she let herself go and fell into Jamie.

CHAPTER TWENTY-SIX

Iliana evaporated and took possession of him—again. Her life force coursed through him. The small electrifying jolts of energy seeped through his veins.

Jack raised the hammer in the air and plunged it downward. He aimed for Jamie's head.

Jamie's arm shot out, his hand wrapping around his father's wrist.

Jack's eyes widened with surprise. "You're a big man now?"

The air in the room turned stale, the temperature well below freezing.

Jack stood still and glared at Jamie. His nostrils flared at the same time he took a breath. His eyebrows rose.

Condensation formed in front of him. Tiny droplets of ice fell to the floor.

"What the …?" Jack said.

A low moan burst from Jamie's lips.

Jack cocked his head and stood over his son.

Jamie's grip tightened. He rose from the floor, moving at an odd angle. His venomous glare never left his father's.

Inside his head, he struggled to fight the intoxicating power surging through him. In desperation, Jamie tried to push her out.

Iliana's possession was beyond anything she'd done to him before. Her control over him was like a vise, crushing his will.

"Iliana, please stop."

Iliana fought with him internally, controlling his every move. She refused to allow him any sway over her actions and rendered him speechless.

Jamie found himself no more than a puppet. All his movements were now at her mercy. From the moment her anger rippled through him, he knew she was intent on causing Jack harm.

Jack smirked at Jamie, baring his tar-stained teeth. "Are you in the mood to fight? Because I'm only getting started."

Jamie didn't respond. Instead, he lashed out. This time, his movements were fast. He plunged forward and twisted Jack's wrist.

Crying out, Jack shot his head forward, smacking Jamie's face.

Crunch.

The bones of his broken nose shifted. Jamie didn't flinch. Blood dripped from his nose, streaking over his lips. His position firm, he glared at his father. A broad smile spread across Jamie's face.

"I've waited a long time for this," Jamie whispered. The words were out before he realized where they were coming from. "Jack ... Jack ... Jack ... bad man in the night. Jack ... Jack ... Jack ... feck ... tinker ... stupid bitch."

Jack's face smoothed. His eyes sobered up.

"What is this?" He looked at Jamie from head to toe, bewildered. "What kind of game are you playing?"

"Don't run, you little bitch," Jamie whispered, lunging at his father.

The grip on his father's wrist tightened further. Jack fell to his knees.

"Get your hands offa me, lad."

Jamie bent forward, pushing his face into Jack's. Jack's eyes were full of fear.

"Like father, like son, eh, Jackie Boy?"

"What's gotten into you?" Jack spat, not once taking his eyes off Jamie.

Jamie struggled to control her, but Iliana had him at her mercy. With his arm stretched out, he bent down and took the hammer from his father. He straightened and sighed.

"Daddy ... or is it Jack? Or big bad man?" Jamie spoke, the demented words slipping off his tongue.

Jamie stepped around his father, watching the subdued and confused drunk. He sniggered a few times, and then spat in Jack's face. His bloody spittle had Jack recoiling in disgust.

"Killing ... drinking ... killing ..."

Iliana forced the words from Jamie. He hated having no say or control over what came out of his mouth.

"Iliana," he pleaded, *"let me handle this."*

"Shut up ... shut up ... shut up!" Jamie roared, tapping the side of his head. He closed his eyes and twisted his mouth, trying to fight the words sitting on the tip of his tongue. "Jack ... Daddy ... bad man Jack."

"No, no, no, no. Stop, Iliana," he screamed inside his head.

The confusion became all too much for him. He found himself losing the battle. He was no match for Iliana's wrath. Her temper flared like an inferno, ready to destroy anything in her way. When she moved forward, the ripples of her energy pulsed through his body. His veins throbbed on the side of his neck. He struggled to force his hand up, but it was like trying to lift a dead weight. His body was no longer his.

Iliana forced Jamie's foot back and slammed it forward into Jack's stomach.

A low groan escaped Jack's lips.

Jamie repeated the action. This time, he smashed the hammer against the side of Jack's jaw.

Blood splattered. Jack's eyes rolled in his head.

Iliana smirked, her mind raced with euphoria.

For the briefest of moments, Jamie feared what Iliana would do next. Lost within him, she used him as her vessel.

Jamie screamed internally, his voice unheard.

Jamie's voice became a distant echo. Iliana was done playing nice. She crossed the point of no return. Watching Jack's blood splatter gave her the little kick she'd long been waiting for. It was odd seeing him so weak.

"How does it feel, Jackie Boy?" she asked, her words coming together in a more coherent manner. "Not nice being the victim, is it?"

Jack glared at her. He shook his head.

"What ... is this?"

"Retribution, bad man Jack."

"Jamie, what's wrong with you?"

Iliana noticed how convincing he sounded. If it wasn't for

what he'd done to her, she might have believed him. He seemed genuine. Even his body language was different compared to how she remembered him on the night he'd killed her. The damned rarely showed sincere remorse, however.

"Come, get up," she ordered, holding the hammer against the side of his head. "Let's go for a drive, Jack."

"Jamie, will you stop this nonsense?"

"Nope. No, nah … can't. Not yet."

Jack gasped and got to his feet. He stumbled and reached out for the wall, using it to steady himself.

"Easy there, Jack. Don't go knocking down walls." Iliana's voice slurred before she laughed.

Jamie fought back against her intrusion.

Stronger than he gave himself credit for, it both pleased and irked Iliana. She closed her eyes and cracked her neck to the side. As she opened them again, Jamie's voice faded in the background once more.

"Much better," she whispered. "Now, where was I?"

Iliana smiled, like the cat that got the cream. Or in her case, the ghost that got the killer. Using the hammer, she pressed it against Jack's chest.

"Lead the way, Daddy."

Jack turned his back on her and walked away from the extension. Following close behind, Iliana stretched out Jamie's arm and grabbed the Stanley knife from the bench.

Pretty.

She stared at Jack's head. What would it be like to ram the head of the hammer into the back of his skull? Would there be much damage? Would he bleed like she had bled?

Hmmm, she pondered. *Soon, maybe.*

Jack reached for the back door. His fingers fumbled. He searched his pockets for the keys.

Iliana grew restless and pushed the hammer hard into his lower back.

"Patience is not my virtue."

Jamie's voice was a lot more commanding than she'd thought it would be. She spoke again, enjoying the sound of his voice.

"Hurry up, Jackie Boy. I'm getting bored back here."

Jack turned his head and glared at his son. He muttered something unintelligible and sighed.

"Open the fecking door," she roared.

Iliana jumped with glee from using the curse word. She'd never used such language before. It made her feel naughty and alive. The idea of crossing boundaries appealed to her.

Jack pushed the door open and stepped out into the rain. It washed over him, rinsing the blood from the side of his face.

Iliana stepped out of the back porch. Tilting her head back, she opened Jamie's mouth, tasting the raindrops. Simple things like this were what she missed the most.

Feeling alive.

Feeling the rain on her flesh.

Beautiful and bittersweet, it reminded her of everything she'd been missing and would continue to miss. She hated Jack more than ever.

She followed Jack to the small blue van. "And now, you let me in, and then you get in, understand?"

"What makes you think you can control me like this?" Jack stared hard.

She laughed and shook her head. "The thing is, if you don't do as you're told, there might be a little problem for you, Daddy. And we really don't want to go there, not just yet. Okay?"

"Jamie, I don't know what's gotten into you, but pull yourself together," Jack said, holding his hand against the side of his head. "You're not yourself."

"That's rich coming from the man who found it so easy to take the life of not one, but two."

Jack froze.

"Yup, Daddy. I know all your secrets. Remember, you made them, and all secrets are made to be uncovered."

Iliana loved the power she felt. The energy coursed through her and made her realize how much she craved being alive.

Jack unlocked the passenger door.

Iliana slipped inside and strapped the seatbelt around Jamie's waist.

Jack got into the driver's side like an obedient little puppy. "So where to?" Jack asked. He trembled and gripped the steering wheel.

"Hmmm, I want to visit the lighthouse. Great weather for it." Iliana clapped her hands.

Sweat spread across Jack's brow.

Iliana enjoyed his discomfort. For every punch and kick she'd endured at his hands, the payback would be sweet.

Jack pulled the van out of the small drive and drove towards the harbor. He glanced at Jamie and frowned, his mouth thinning into a tight line. His brows furrowed. "I'll kill you for this."

Iliana burst into laughter and shook her head. "Don't be silly, Jack. You can't kill me twice."

CHAPTER TWENTY-SEVEN

The waves crashed over the rocks of the causeway and white froth creeped over the sand.

Iliana sucked in a deep breath and gasped. She'd seen this splendor many times over during the past three years, but had forgotten what it was like to experience the noise of Mother Nature. The goose pimples on her skin brought it all back. The life she missed, her future—all gone, never to be explored. In death, everything had become stagnant and muted, all because of the monster sitting beside her.

Glaring at Jack, she found the tears almost impossible to control. Jamie had a good supply stored in his well. Although he became a nuisance in the background, Iliana ignored his pleas.

"Do you remember how you destroyed everything here?"

Jack shot her a look of contempt. "You're out of your bloody mind."

She revealed the Stanley knife she held in her hand and flipped the safety catch, sliding the blade out of its enclosure. "Get out of the van."

Jack gawped at the blade, raising his eyebrows before focusing on his son.

Iliana loved the confused expression spreading across his face.

Jack sat in silence, furrowing his brows and fumbling with the seatbelt. He glanced at Jamie, sucking his top lip into his mouth.

Iliana smirked. "Having a little trouble there, Jackie Boy?"

"Stop calling me that," he growled.

"Or what?"

Iliana didn't bother threatening him again. The metal tip of the blade sliced across Jack's cheek. A nice clean cut, deep and bloody. She beamed at the sight of her killer's blood and his obvious pain.

He roared and touched the side of his face, staring at the red liquid smeared across his fingertips. "What have you done?" he shouted, his hands shaking.

"Oh, this?" She pointed to the cut. "It's just the appetizer."

Jack opened the van door and stumbled out of the vehicle.

Iliana followed and inhaled a deep breath, swallowing the delicious salty air. "Now, start walking," she ordered, holding the blade towards Jack.

Jack grumbled and stepped over the small rocky beach.

His weak and obliging manner surprised her, considering the last time they'd met face-to-face, he had been a giant, a murderous beast who frightened her. A tower compared to her, Iliana was no longer scared. She didn't bat an eyelash, thinking about all the different ways she could end his life.

Just not yet.

In the back of her mind, Jamie fought to be heard. *"Don't do this, Iliana,"* he pleaded. *"Let me handle things. I promise I won't let him get away with what he did to you."*

Shaking her head violently, she smacked her cheeks a few times and shouted, "Shut up. Shut up. Just *shut up!* This is my time."

Iliana ignored Jamie. She had to be the one to break Jack. Nothing else would do.

"What are you're going to get out of this, Jamie?" Jack looked back over his shoulder.

Iliana laughed. "Jamie? What's he got to do with any of this?"

Jack stopped. He turned around and looked at his son. He shook his head, his face a mess.

"What are you on? Did you take something? Was it some of your mother's tablets? Has the Brannigan whore got you onto the hard stuff? Is that what this is?"

A burst of laughter erupted from the back of Iliana's throat. "This is too good to be true."

"I told you once, lad, and I'll tell you again. I'll kill you and they won't find you anywhere." Jack stepped towards Iliana, not once taking his eyes off her.

"Now, is this really how a loving father talks to their child?" Iliana asked. "But then again, these are words spilling from the mouth of a killer. Right, Jackie Boy?"

"Don't push me, lad."

"Or what? You're going to kill me, bust my brains out of my head, and dump me in the water? Is this your plan?"

Jack didn't respond. He rubbed a hand across the back of his neck and peered at the causeway. He looked at her from the corner of his eye.

"Yup. You have a thing about blood and water, don't you, Daddy?" Iliana took a step forward. The blade sliced through his shirt and cut into his chest. His blood oozed out, soiling the material. "As I said, you can't kill me twice. Now turn around, walk towards the lighthouse, open the door, and shut the hell up."

Jack clutched his wound, wincing in pain with every step he took. His eyes were white with fear, his face drained of any color. Blood seeped over his fingers, dripping down like scarlet rain. He stumbled, his knees buckling. Sweat drenched his skin, swept away by the rain.

Uncaring of how many times he lost balance, Iliana kicked him hard. She giggled and watched him struggle. The sight of such a brute of a man succumbing to being nothing more than a feeble wreck amused her.

Jack glared at Jamie over his shoulder and bared his teeth. He narrowed his eyes and mumbled.

"What's that, Daddy?" Iliana laughed, shaking the blade in his face.

Jack shook his head, his eyes focused on the lighthouse.

"This is just the beginning. See, Jamie, this is how you pay back the sins of the father."

Once Jack stood inside the lighthouse, Iliana walked in, closed the door behind her, and gawped at him. "Remember this place?" she asked, and sniffed the stale salty air.

Jamie's voice echoed eerily around the stone tower.

"What are you doing to me, lad?"

"Has it really slipped your mind? Like, seriously? This little place should bring back a few memories for you."

Jack panted, holding his fingers over the wound on his chest. "I don't know what you mean."

"Hmmm, shall we refresh your memory?" Iliana asked. A sly smile spread across her lips.

Jack shook his head. Blood oozed through his fingers. His eyes widened and lower lip trembled.

The odd turn of events caught her by surprise. She'd half-expected him to put up a bigger struggle, but he was nothing more than a drunk and a coward.

"Do you not recall the night you beat the shite out of your own daughter?" she asked. "Remember, Jack? It was right outside. You beat the girl until she fell to the ground, and then you dragged her to the edge of the water and held her down until she stopped moving. What kind of father kills his own? I mean, did you ever love her? Was your intention all along to kill the bitch, eh?"

"You're talking nonsense," Jack said, shaking his head.

"Hmmm, really, Jack, or should I call you Daddy? I mean, it's been a while since I've been able to call anyone Daddy. You took my life, my future, my entire existence, and you seem to have forgotten that."

Jack glared at her, swallowing hard. Spittle dribbled down his chin, mixing with his blood.

"You're trying to wind me up, aren't you, lad?"

"Nope, he's not," Iliana answered, and pursed her lips. "Jamie's here, but I've locked him away inside his own mind. It was quite easy once I got him on my side. Some things can't be hidden forever. There are things about the afterlife you know nothing about, Jackie Boy. I can't rest in peace. How can I? I'm trapped because of you."

Jack said nothing. He gazed at his son. His eyes opened wide.

The confusion spreading across his face amused Iliana to no end.

"Do you understand what's happening, Jack?" she asked. "From the moment I took my last breath, I promised myself I would not rest until the day you paid your dues. You took my life from me, and for what? For playing witness to the sins you committed against your own flesh and blood. Did you honestly think you would get away with it? No one gets away with murder, not really."

She glared at him, holding the blade out, swinging her arm in the air. "I was an innocent. I had done nothing wrong. Why hurt me? Why crush my skull against the floor? Why drag me across the rocks? Why dump me in a pool of water? Why, Jack? I found my soul mate and had fallen in love. I had a whole life ahead of me. A future we planned together, and then you came and took it away. Why?"

Tears filled her eyes. The emotional rage surging through her was hard to control.

"Come on, you owe me this much. Why?"

"You're talking utter shite," Jack muttered in a breathless tone.

"Nope, you're the one in denial. You're the one who's been drinking himself to death because you can't face the truth. You're the one who beats on his defenseless wife and son because it makes you feel like a man. You're nothing but a coward, Jack. One who deserves everything that's coming to him."

Jack straightened his back. "You're off your head, you wee bollocks. What are you on? A few yokes? Weed? Maybe something stronger."

"Keep it coming, Jackie Boy. Go on, and show your true colors. You've never given a shite about anyone but yourself. You're like your daddy, aren't you, Jack? A fiend who preys on the weak." Iliana pressed Jamie's face against Jack's. "I bet if you look close enough, you'll see me."

BENEATH THE LIGHTHOUSE

Jack closed his eyes, and then opened them again. He glared at Iliana. Realization swarmed over his face. He turned white. His mouth dropped open with surprise.

"It … can't be," he muttered.

"Oh, but it can be," Iliana replied. "Welcome to my world." She curtsied.

Jack's mouth trembled. He shook his head and gasped in pain.

"You're dead … long gone."

"In body, yes. In spirit, no."

"How can this be?"

Iliana giggled and ran the side of the blade against Jamie's cheek. "I guess you can say I had trouble letting go."

"My boy, is he a part of this?"

"Of course not," Iliana said. "He's an innocent, just like I was. I would never do anything to hurt Jamie. He's been good to me. He's helped me in more ways than anyone else. He cares about the truth. Unlike you."

"Then why him? Why this?" Jack assessed Iliana from head to toe.

"Because he was the key to getting to you. He has your blood running through his veins. He's what connects me to you." Growing impatient, Iliana retreated. "Okay, enough with being chatty. Go on up." She pointed to the stairs. "Go on, chop, chop."

Jack took a long breath before pushing himself up from the wall. He gripped his chest hard, trying to stem the flow of the blood oozing from the wound.

Iliana expected him to question why, but like an obedient mutt, he did as he was told.

Good ole Jack.

Jack slowly climbed the spiral stairwell. He struggled every step of the way.

Iliana smirked the whole time.

Once they reached the lantern room, Jack paused and stared out the glass for a brief moment before glancing sideways at Iliana. He opened his mouth to say something, but nothing slid past his lips.

"Don't worry, Jack," she said. "It'll all be over soon."

Iliana stepped up to one of the storm panes and reached for the door handle. She nodded at Jack and winked.

"Come on, let's take in the scenery." She held the door open. "It's a good day for storm watching, don't you think?"

Jack walked past her and stood shivering on the balcony.

Iliana closed the door and stood beside Jack. The wind whistled around the tower. Its eerie sound, mixed with the raging waves crashing against the rocks below, filled her with complete satisfaction.

The swirling grey storm clouds moved across the ominous sky. They looked like they were moving inwards, trying to get a closer look at what was happening on the tower.

Iliana raised her head and smiled. Rain poured over her face.

"This is glorious," she muttered. "I miss this so much. Have you any idea of how much I miss the simplest things? I used to run inside when the rain came. Now I wished I danced in it. So many things I took for granted, and I'll never get it back. And all because of you."

Jack didn't reply. He forced himself upright. Holding onto the handrail, his tight grip whitened his knuckles.

"Oooops, steady on there, Jack. We don't want you falling

to your death too soon." Iliana snorted.

Jack closed his eyes and cried. He shook his head.

"This can't be happening," he mumbled.

"Oh, but it is." Iliana stretched out over the railing and stared at the rocks below.

"Please … I'm sorry," Jack begged. "Just stop. Leave my boy alone."

"Your boy? The one you hit with the hammer? The one you were going to kill? Jesus, Jackie Boy, don't be going all soft on me now. It's no good. You're a monster. One who needs to face his demons."

Jack cried like a baby. His snot dripped down over his lips. His bottom lip quivered.

"Now, Jack," Iliana said. "Here's the thing, I can't let you live, but I'm also no murdering scumbag like you. So, I want you to listen to me very carefully. I want you to climb over this here railing, okay? Can you do that?"

He cried out, shaking his head. "Please, don't do this. I will hand myself in to the peelers. I don't want to die. Not like this."

"Sorry, retribution comes only in payment with blood. Now, be a good man. For once in your life, do as you're told. Climb over the railing."

Iliana moved towards Jack. She held the blade out in front of her, intent on slicing his throat from ear-to-ear if he ignored her again.

Like a trained animal, he did as he was told. Taking his hand off his wound, Jack cried and balanced himself on the railing. He struggled to lift one leg over the bar, and then the other. Jack gripped the rail and closed his eyes, refusing to look at the rocks below.

Iliana wanted to clap, but she controlled the urge. Instead, she held her breath.

"That wasn't so bad," she said, winking. "Now tell me what's going through your mind."

His lips trembled. Jack sobbed.

"Please, I don't want to die." His body shook.

Anger rippled through every inch of her body. "That's not what I asked, is it?"

"I don't want to die."

"Neither did I, but you didn't seem to care when I pleaded for my life," she spat. "Now you have to feel the fear I felt. Now tell me, what's running through your mind right this second."

"I'm sorry for everything I've done," he shouted. "I'm a bad man. I admit it. I don't want to miss wee Sarah or the twins growing up. I don't want to die like this, please."

Jack shook his head, wailing and clutching onto the railing for his life.

"Now, turn around. Take in the beauty of the rugged coastline," she commanded. "It really is something else."

Jack turned his head and stared at the water crashing against the rocks below. Carefully, he turned himself around. The ferocious wind howled, the gusts hitting him hard in the face. He breathed hard through his sobs.

Iliana stepped up onto the first metal bar and peered over the edge, looking at the side of Jack's face.

"Are you scared?" she asked.

Jack nodded, his mumbling incoherent.

"Of course you're scared. I was scared, too. But you didn't

care, did you? The way I remember it, you got a kick out of watching me die." She chuckled. "Funny how the tide has changed. Now, I want you to let go of the railing and let gravity do its job."

Jack wouldn't release his grip. He closed his eyes and roared.

Frustrated, Iliana used the blade to coax his fingers open. She cut small slits into his knuckles.

Jack rocked backwards and forwards on his heels. The tiny ledge where he stood didn't have enough space for him to remain balanced. He let go of the railing. Every inch of his body shook.

In a few moments, it would all be over.

"Jump, Jack. Go on, do us all a favor," Iliana whispered in his ear. "Jump. Jump. Jump."

"I don't want to die."

Jack looked her in the eye. His voice quavered.

Tutting, Iliana sighed and shrugged. "No one wants to die, Jack. But this, right now, this is your choice. This is your doing. All this is because of the choices you made on the night you killed me. Let's not forget your beloved child."

Trembling, Jack cried out once more and gritted his teeth. Blood leaked from the wound on his face. He wobbled and forced himself to keep his balance. Between the strong gusts of wind and Iliana's taunts, he was losing the battle—fast.

"Jump. Jump. Jump, Jackie Boy, jump."

Iliana laughed. She couldn't resist. It was much better than she had anticipated.

"Please ..." he pleaded.

Jack lost his balance and fell like a stone. Head first, legs sprawled, and arms flailing.

His body crashed hard against the rocks below. Blood pooled beneath his head.

Iliana tilted her head and smirked. She'd expected it to be more dramatic, but it was over before it began.

"Bye, bye, Jack. See you in hell."

CHAPTER TWENTY-EIGHT

Deep inside, Jamie cried upon seeing his father's lifeless body sprawled across the rocks. The tide came in fast. The waves washed over Jack and receded, repeating the sequence again and again.

For what it was worth, Jamie mourned his father. In all of Jack's ugliness, there was no denying they shared blood. Sometimes, when the blood of those you loved—or at least used to—was spilled, it was hard to distinguish between the hate and grief.

Iliana had refused him any say in her plans. She had used him all along.

The strong gusts roared in from the sea. Its chill was nothing compared to the feeling of dread. His blood ran cold through his veins. This wasn't what he'd wanted.

So much blood. So much sorrow.

Jamie fought hard. He needed to claim back his body. Past caring about the woes of the dead, he needed to care for the living.

"Iliana," he said, fighting through her barrier. "You need to release me."

Jamie fought to close off his mind to her overpowering influence. He struggled until he felt a *pop* and the weight lifted from him.

Gripping the handrails, Jamie cried out with alarm. "Oh, God, please forgive me. What have I done?"

Tears streamed down his cheeks. He gazed at his father. Sorrow consumed him and left him nauseated. His chest tightened, full of a sadness he wasn't prepared for. Guilt ran through his veins.

"What have I done?" he whispered, shaking his head.

Jack lay motionless. His blood mixed with the foam of the waves. The bitter wind chilled Jamie to the bone and he shivered.

He fought hard to be a man as unlike his father as he could be, but was what he had done any better? There were so many voices in his mind calling for the scars to be healed. Unable to stand it a second longer, he had to get out of there.

Wiping his nose along the sleeve of his hoodie, he raced towards the door. He ran inside the lantern room, panting and trying to gather his thoughts. His mind was full of poison and shame—so much regret.

Jamie grappled with the severity of what had happened. He had to leave the lighthouse before the peelers showed up, not wanting to risk being connected to his father's death.

A lump formed at the back of his throat. It kept him from swallowing and sucking in enough air to fill his lungs. Overwhelmed, Jamie let go. Brick by brick, his walls crashed down around him. The sobs punched through him.

"Oh, my god," he cried, holding the sides of his head. He paced back and forth, trying to control his breathing.

Breathe, Jamie, breathe.

Iliana's presence surrounded him.

"*Stop!*" he roared, holding his hands out in front of him. "This

... this stops now."

Iliana appeared in front of him. Her eyes narrowed, black as night. She stared at him hard, not once moving.

"Why?" she slurred.

"Are you serious? This is MY life, Iliana. You just can't barge in and take over just because you feel like it."

"Why not? He took mine from me, why can't I take yours?" she screamed, the force of her voice shaking the glass in the windowpanes.

"What he did to you wasn't my fault."

"I don't care. I want a second chance. I deserve it. I've suffered enough."

"Iliana, you have to stop this, you have to let go."

An angry look spread across Iliana's face.

Turning his back on her, Jamie walked down the spiral staircase. The stench of stagnant water wafted through the air. The memories of how she died in the tower weighed heavily on his mind. Now it was the very place where his own father lost his life.

The burden became an overbearing weight on his heart. There were many ways for him to deal with his father's crimes, but Iliana's choice was just as bad as Jack's.

"Jamie ... Jamie ... Jamie ..." Iliana's voice echoed down the stairs behind him.

"You can stop it now, Iliana," he shouted. "You don't scare me anymore."

He reached for the door's latch.

Iliana stood beside him.

He glared at her.

Her eyes filled with black tears. "What do you mean?"

"It means I'm done. I tried to help you, Iliana. I nearly drowned trying to find your remains. How much more do you expect me to do?"

Iliana remained silent. Her bottom lip quivered. Her face sank into itself, swallowing her up and the rest of her body followed. She disappeared.

Jamie nearly fell over running out of the tower. He turned his head and looked back at the rocks. The swell of the tide washed over the front of the lighthouse. His heart sank to new depths. He ached, knowing he would have to break the news to his mother. There would be no coming back from this. Not ever.

Jamie walked fast, heading back to town, wanting to get rid of the headache. His stomach spun. A sour taste formed at the back of his mouth. Unsure of where to go, he needed to talk to someone, but *who* was another question.

Fifteen minutes later, he stood outside Lenny's front door. He rang the bell and waited for someone to answer.

The door opened. Lenny looked Jamie up and down, and shook his head.

"Jesus, lad, what the hell's happened?"

Jamie fell to pieces.

Lenny looked behind him.

His mother peered out from the kitchen.

Lenny opened the door. "Come on up to my room."

"Is everything all right, love?" Lenny's mother asked.

"Everything's grand, Ma. Just go back to your programme." Lenny walked up the steps behind Jamie.

Once inside the privacy of Lenny's bedroom, Jamie stood by the window and broke down. The despair and pain erupted from him like a volcano, and soon his cheeks were wet and salty. Uncontrollable sobs wracked his body, the pain unyielding.

Lenny rushed over to him. Resting a hand on his shoulder, he shook his head.

"What's happened?"

"Everything has gone so wrong." Jamie sobbed.

"What has?"

"He's gone," Jamie cried, staring into his best friend's face.

Lenny glared at Jamie. "Who's gone?"

"Me da!"

Jamie covered his face with his hands. Admitting it out loud caused the reality of what he—of what Iliana—had done to fill him with complete dread. He opened his mouth to speak, but no words came out. Instead, deep, gut-wrenching sobs tore through his chest.

He fell to his knees, unsure of how to express himself. Full of pain, tears coursed down his cheeks.

"Jamie, you're really scaring me now," Lenny said, dropping to the floor beside Jamie.

Through tear-filled eyes, Jamie met Lenny's concerned gaze and shook his head. "He's dead. Me da is dead, Lenny."

Lenny's mouth opened.

"It happened so fast," Jamie muttered through several sobs. "I tried so hard to make her stop, but she wouldn't listen. She blocked me out completely."

"Jamie, lad, you're not making sense."

"She goaded and pushed him until he became a complete mess and did as he was told. I couldn't stop her."

"You're really scaring me now," Lenny said, and grabbed

Jamie's arm. "You need to slow down and tell me exactly what's been happening."

Jamie wiped his face on the back of his sleeve and took a few deep breaths. "Things have been so weird for me. Ever since Emer died, I've been so lost. My family's changing overnight, it … it became a living nightmare. I kept going back there, losing myself to the grief. I guess I became obsessed with the causeway and where she died. I just never understood, not until a few weeks back when I started seeing things."

"Jamie," Lenny interrupted. "Do you need me to call me ma? Maybe get you a doctor or something?"

"No," Jamie shouted. "You wanted the truth, so I'm giving it to you."

"But you're not making sense, lad." Lenny scratched the back of his head.

"Just hear me out, Lenny, okay?"

Lenny nodded and sat down beside Jamie. "Go on, then."

"I thought I was going mad. Maybe I had been for a little while, but the more she appeared, the more real it became. I kind of blame myself, because I left the door open for her. She saw the weak little boy in me, and I was such an easy target."

He swallowed past the lump in his throat and ignored the pain in his head. "She showed me things. Stuff I didn't want to believe to be true, but it all began to make sense. Me da had been hiding secrets. Sinful things he had done. I experienced everything she went through when she died. The pain, my father's rage—it's the kind of stuff no one else would believe, not unless you've experienced it, just like I have. But I can tell you now, she was out for blood from the get-go. I was just a vessel for her to use."

Lenny's expression changed from confused to surprised. "How do you mean?"

"She took possession. She took over my body." Jamie looked up and met Lenny's eyes. "It sounds mad. Believe me, I've trouble accepting the truth in all of this, but she was relentless. She would not leave me alone."

"Which girl?"

"The one me da killed on the night he murdered Emer."

Lenny's mouthed dropped open, his face full of bewilderment. He shook his head and bit down on his lip before running a hand through his hair.

"Are you telling me your da killed your sister and another girl?"

"That's exactly what I'm telling you," Jamie said. "And now me da is dead."

Lenny shook his head. "How?"

"He jumped from the lighthouse."

"But what about the girl? Who is she?"

Lenny shook his head. Disbelief spread across his face.

"Iliana, a traveler. She was here with the fair. She witnessed me da beating Emer to death. When he saw she'd witnessed his crime, he went after her." Jamie wiped his eyes. His voice softened. "He just left Emer there. He didn't care, Lenny. He was a monster."

"Are you on something? What have you taken? Because this isn't you. You don't talk like this. You're going through some messed up shite, but Jesus, lad, this is nuts." Lenny ran his hands through his hair and sighed. "I'm having a hard time accepting this stuff. I mean, it's not every day your best friend tells you he's been haunted by a girl his father killed, and then you find out she used his body like some kind of tool. This is crazy stuff, lad. It makes you sound like you're insane. Who else have you told this to?"

"I knew you'd never understand." Jamie choked back the tears. "I shouldn't have come here."

"Stop talking like a bollocks. If you can't come to me, who else can you trust with this?"

"Claire knows," Jamie admitted.

"Claire?"

"She was with me today when I went down to the rock pool beneath the lighthouse."

"Has she known all along?" Lenny sounded wounded.

"Well, you've been busy working and chasing skirts, so I just kept my distance. I didn't want to be bothering you with my troubles."

"For Jesus Christ, lad. Who's been there for you through everything?"

Lenny stood, walked to his desk, and sat down. He clasped his hands together, not once taking his eyes off Jamie.

"Aye, you've been there for me. I couldn't have gotten through all my crap without you. But Claire just happened to be there, and I opened up to her. She made it so easy."

"I understand, lad. I'm just ..." Lenny sighed. "Where's this ghost girl now?"

Jamie shrugged. "I don't know. I left the lighthouse and came straight here."

Lenny stood and grabbed his phone, cigarettes, and jacket. "Come on then. Let's go see the damage."

"What? Do you believe me?"

"Lad, I don't know what to believe, but I know you. You aren't crazy enough to be making this shite up," Lenny replied. "Come on. There's no point sitting here, crying and beating yourself up over this. You need to face this head on, whatever it is."

"I don't know what to do," Jamie admitted. "It's all a mess."

"Then let me help you, okay?"

Jamie nodded and stood. "I don't know what I'd do without you, lad."

"Good job, I'm a sucker for head cases." Lenny winked at him.

Jamie relaxed. He'd made the right choice by coming to Lenny. There was no one he trusted more, next to Claire.

As they walked towards the causeway, the darkness of the storm lifted. A rainbow glimmered across the evening sky.

Jamie looked up. Perhaps it was a sign he'd cast the evil aside. He hoped for something more. There had to be a brighter future ahead, regardless of how much doom and gloom surrounded him.

CHAPTER TWENTY-NINE

Jamie's stomach twisted once he saw the tower of the lighthouse. A part of him wanted to turn and run away. He wouldn't be able to avoid the reality of it all for long.

Lenny nudged his arm. "What's Claire doing here?"

Jamie looked over at the rocks where Claire gazed at the horizon.

"Honestly, I'm not sure." He shook his head. "Maybe she's looking for me."

"We'll see."

A few minutes later, they walked over to where Claire stood.

"Claire," Jamie called out her. "What are you doing here?"

She didn't respond.

Reaching for her, Jamie noticed the tears staining her cheeks. "Claire, is everything all right?"

Claire spun around and hit him hard across the face. Her eyes flashed with anger and narrowed. Her forehead creased. She spat at him.

"You just had to go ruin everything," she screamed, spit dribbling over her chin.

"What the hell?" he shouted, clutching his cheek. "What did I do?"

Claire shook her head and walked towards the lighthouse. She ignored Jamie. She didn't even acknowledge Lenny's presence.

"Claire," Jamie said once more.

"I told her you would screw it all up." She glanced over her shoulder at Jamie. "You were too soft. Too wrapped up in your own torment to allow her to finish what we started. You should have died along with your oul man."

Jamie couldn't make heads or tails of what she said.

Lenny stepped up. "Claire, why don't you shut your trap and stop talking in riddles?"

Claire's eyes glazed over. She glared at Lenny. Turning her head, she pointed a finger at Jamie.

"Ah, this is so you, Jamie. You need your henchman by your side because you have no balls of your own. And who the hell do you think you are, Lenny, butting your ugly mug in our business?"

"I've no clue what she's on about," Jamie said, looking at Lenny.

"She's a dirty Brannigan. Doesn't that tell you something?" Lenny sneered.

Claire turned her head and stared at the calm sea spreading out before her. The waves had settled, and the sun glowed in the far-off distance, a beautiful sight in stark contrast to what took place on the causeway.

"Everything is ruined now," she mumbled, not taking her eyes off the horizon. "All you had to do was open your mind, but you just kept on pushing her away. She needed you, Jamie. She needed you to let go, and what do you do? You destroyed our plans."

"Claire, you're really starting to freak me out," Jamie said. He looked at Lenny and shrugged, before turning his attention back at

Claire.

She turned to face him. "Why didn't you just let her continue what we started? Why did you have to go and play the hero? You're nothing, Jamie. Never have been and never will be. She'll never forgive you now, and neither will I."

"Who? What are you on about?"

"Are you stupid?"

Jamie flinched. "Am I missing something here? Because you're not making one bit of sense."

"Iliana, you dumb prick."

She glared at him and her face twisted, becoming unrecognizable. Gone was the radiant beauty of what he'd assumed to be first love. In its place stood the ugly fact that he had never known her at all.

Lenny strode toward them. "You need to explain a bit better, Claire."

"Really?" She laughed. "Me, explain to ghost lover here, just how he messed up? He got his own father killed, and it was perfect, right until the end."

A light suddenly came on inside Jamie's head. So many little things made sense.

"You've known about Iliana all along, haven't you?"

Claire laughed and nodded. "What do you think, Einstein?"

"The night at your aunt's, you knew how I'd react, just like when we were at Father Murray's. Has all of this been some sick, twisted game to you?"

"What the hell is that?" Lenny pointed at the tower of the lighthouse.

Jamie looked up.

Iliana stood on the balcony, staring at the three of them.

"That's her," Jamie replied.

"Oh, my god," Lenny whispered, gawping in astonishment.

"Close your mouth, Lenny. You look like a rat." Claire chuckled.

Jamie's heart sank to new depths. He covered his eyes with one hand and shook his head. The sweet girl he'd fallen head over heels for stood before him, nothing more than a stranger.

"I never once thought you were capable of being a twisted bitch."

A breeze blew around them. A coldness Jamie had become accustomed to surrounded him.

"Iliana," he said. "No more."

Iliana appeared in front of him. Her eyes were cold and black. Tilting her head to the side, she opened her mouth, black liquid spilling from its depths.

"How long are you going to do this?" he asked.

"As long as it takes," she said, her face completely covered in the tar-like substance. Her eyes shone, glaring at him. "Don't you get it, Jamie? Your soul is mine. You belong to me."

Claire clapped her hands together and smiled. "I told you he was stupid."

Iliana snapped her head and glared at Claire.

The look the two exchanged left Jamie feeling very much out of his depths.

Jamie took a step back. Dread washed over him like a wave pulling him under.

"Didn't you learn something when we met Father Murray?" Claire asked. "Surely you felt it in the house?"

She referred to the darkness in the back room of Father Murray's. Nevertheless, he decided to play dumb.

"I don't know what you're on about."

"How interesting," she replied. "How's about you, Lenny? Can you feel the swell of the storm living inside your bestie?"

Lenny grabbed Claire's wrist. "You're one twisted bitch."

A raucous laugh burst from Claire's lips as she threw her head back. She resembled a demented witch.

"Enough," Jamie roared. "I'm completely lost. Whatever it is you've concocted with the dead, that's on you, Claire. I'm through with this. Come on, Lenny. I need to report my father's death to the peelers."

Lenny nodded. "Sounds like a plan."

"Really, Jamie?" Claire shouted. "You're going to tell them what, exactly?"

"The truth. It's always a good place to start."

Iliana walked back across the stones.

Jamie turned his back on them both.

"And your version of the truth, does it fare well with what I've on video? Because it was so easy to follow you, to slip inside the lighthouse, and have a front row seat of your Oscar-winning performance." Claire crossed her arms and smirked. A menacing light flashed in her eyes.

Jamie stopped walking and looked back at her. "What do you mean?"

"How will it look to the cops when I show them how you pushed your father over the edge? How you drove him to jump. Not to mention using the blade to cut into him. You manipulated your father to the point of death and it doesn't look good. But it makes for great viewing," Claire said, never taking her eyes off him. "Now, this can all be avoided if you stop behaving like a stupid little shite and allow us to finish what we started."

Before Jamie had a chance to reply, a sudden influx of goose pimples appeared on his skin. Jamie looked at Lenny. How long would it continue before his fragile mind finally caved?

"Jamie, you need to stop fighting it," Iliana whispered in his ear. "It's time to allow me complete control."

"Get away from him, you ugly bitch," Lenny shouted, and lunged forward to hit her. He fell right through her ghostly form and landed on the rocks hard.

Claire laughed and snorted, watching Lenny writhe. "Serves you right, you stupid prick."

"Why, Claire? I don't understand," Jamie said, shaking his head.

"Don't you get it?" she asked.

"No."

"Hmm, shall we educate him, Iliana?" Claire smirked.

"I thought you'd never ask," Iliana replied.

Iliana entered his core before he had the chance to fight back. The ripples of her possession traveled through him, causing every nerve of his body to stand on edge. She took her place within him and showed him things from the past he didn't want to believe to be true.

Iliana's face beamed when she saw Claire walking along the path. Her heart thumped hard. The familiar swarm of excitement lit her stomach.

Bouncing down onto the wooden seat, Claire planted a kiss on Iliana's lips, and the two girls hugged tight.

"I've missed you so much," Claire whispered in her ear.

"I've missed you, too," Iliana replied, gently running her hand down the back of Claire's hair.

Breaking their embrace, Claire reached into her pocket and took out her phone. "I don't have long. I have to be home before nine."

"I told my father I wouldn't be long. He worries when I miss curfew."

Iliana took Claire's hand in hers and ran her fingers over the pale skin of Claire's knuckles. She found it hard to hide her feelings. The sheer joy she felt every time she saw Claire consumed her. No one would ever understand or truly accept them as a couple. To her, Claire was like a shining star within the darkness taking over her world. When Claire smiled, warmth radiated from her, reaching places the sun never could. A beacon of light, Iliana cherished every moment they spent together.

Claire rested her head against Iliana's shoulder and sighed. "I hate that you will be leaving the day after tomorrow. It's not fair. Why can't you stay just a little while longer?"

"I hate having to say goodbye," Iliana replied. "But I can't stay. We've to move on and work the other towns."

"It's the worst part. I'm not sure I'll get down to Granny's again before the summer." Claire's face paled as she spoke.

"We can still text," Iliana said. "And I'll try and call you at least once a week."

Claire sighed and stood, looking out over the stony beach. She smiled.

"How about we go swimming?"

"Claire, it's not exactly scorching. We'd catch our death." Iliana grinned.

"Who cares?"

Iliana shook her head and burst into laughter. "Or we can go get some chips and sit out by the lighthouse."

"Well, I suppose we can always go swimming another day. Chips it is," Claire said, and held her hand out.

The two girls walked hand in hand for a few minutes before letting go. It didn't look right, especially since Claire was thirteen-years-old. No one would ever accept their love.

"I hate having to hide the fact that you mean everything to me," Claire muttered as they walked up the high street. "It's stupid. Who's to say I don't understand how I feel?"

"Because people are still stuck in the old ages, especially in small-town Ireland."

"It's complete bollocks," Claire agreed.

"But there's nothing we can do, not until I've saved enough money, and you're old enough to leave." Iliana looked at Claire and her heart sank. "I'll be an outcast, but it will be worth it."

"That's what worries me the most," Claire admitted. "I hate the thought of something happening to you because of what we want. Your father will be a broken man, not to mention how this will affect your grandmother."

Iliana shrugged. "It is what it is, I guess. My mother always told me life is worth living. To make each second count, to take risks and savor the moment. I intend to do so."

"Your mother sounds like she was an amazing woman."

Iliana touched the back of Claire's hand. "She was incredible. She would have accepted me for what I am, and love you, but she's not here to fight in my corner."

"I'll always be there for you," Claire said, her soft voice full of hope. "I won't ever let anything bad happen to you. You know that, right? I would never hurt you, Iliana."

Iliana smiled. Her insides fluttered upon hearing the words. In a small span of time, Claire had filled the void her mother's death had left behind.

She never imagined having someone like Claire in her life. Not only had she become the only person in the world she trusted, she found herself head over heels in love with someone who never judged her for who she was. It meant so much to Iliana.

After they bought their chips, they walked back to the causeway and settled down on the rocks, watching the waves wash back and forth.

"I love it here," Iliana remarked. "It's so beautiful and peaceful."

"Really?" Claire sounded surprised.

"Yes, I'd happily live here. I love the water and the smell of the sea. The idea of something so beautiful wiping you out in a split second is invigorating."

Claire laughed and nudged her arm. "That's so bloody morbid."

"Maybe, but it's the truth. You've no idea how sick I am of moving from one place to the next. I hate it. We never stay anywhere long enough for me to feel settled or make proper friends. In a way, I'm the loneliest girl in the world."

Claire took Iliana's hand in hers, lifted it to her lips, and placed a gentle kiss on the back of it. "When our time comes, it will be so worth it."

"I know," Iliana replied. "I love you."

"I love you more," Claire said, and moved her head next to Iliana's.

Their lips met. The kiss was soft and tender, full of the promise of their future. Iliana didn't want to let go and say goodbye. It was the one thing she hated the most. The sad goodbyes, the eagerness of their next meeting—so many little things gave her purpose.

"I don't want you to go," Claire cried.

Iliana wiped her eyes, trying to hide her broken heart. Months would pass before they saw each other again. The knowledge left an ache in her soul.

"I'll call you tomorrow before we leave," she said, running her thumb over Claire's lips.

"I ... I hate this so much."

Iliana pulled Claire in close.

The two girls embraced tight. They held on to each other for dear life.

"I've got to go," Claire said. A pained sigh escaped her.

"Just go ... please," Iliana cried.

With one last kiss, Claire turned her back on Iliana, leaving her standing on the rocks of the causeway.

CHAPTER THIRTY

Jamie came 'round and stared at Claire and Iliana with contempt. Hot and flushed, Jamie's muscles tensed on the back of his neck.

"You disgusting bitches," he shouted. "What the actual feck?" His jaw clenched.

"What ... what is it?" Lenny asked.

"Them, they're ... They were together."

Lenny scratched the back of his head and shrugged. "What? Like lesbos?"

Claire folded her arms across her chest and scowled at Lenny. "It's just a label, isn't it? Typical of all of you small-minded pricks."

"So, all this has been about the two of you being in love?"

Tears burned in his eyes. A whirlwind of emotions erupted inside him. The sadness was like poison, killing his spirit. How had he not seen it? He felt stupid for thinking he loved her. He'd been duped by his so-called girlfriend and her ghostly lover.

Iliana screamed. She held her mottled hands to her head and roared. Her head shook. Black goo oozed from her nose and ears.

Claire cried out with alarm. "Shush, Iliana, please, we can fix this."

"How?" Iliana howled.

"We can still finish the possession," Claire said, sounding desperate. "He's here. We can just take him. Let's finish it."

Jamie's anger whirled inside him. His vision became tunneled. His rage focused on Claire.

"This has all been your fault, hasn't it? You're the one who instigated all this. What did you do, Claire? How did you raise the dead?"

"I didn't raise anything, you dumb shit," she roared.

"Then how did you know she was even dead?"

"She came to me in a dream and begged me to help her," Claire said. "When I hadn't heard from her, I knew something bad had happened. Her father came looking for her, asked me if I'd seen her, and I denied her. Denied the love of my life, and for what?" she cried, looking Jamie up and down. "When you love something so much, you can feel it in your soul, but how would you know anything about pain? You've only ever been concerned about your own problems. You've never loved like I have."

"This is bullshit," Lenny said. "I'm away to get the peelers. This is some messed up, twisted shite."

"Lenny, wait," Jamie called. "Let me sort this."

"How?" Lenny held his arms out on either side. He shook his head. "She's gone in the head. And this ghost thing ... We need a priest, or an exorcist."

Iliana glared at Lenny. Her face grew hideously distorted.

"A priest?" Claire scoffed. "Who do you recommend, Lenny?"

"I should never have suggested Jamie give you the time of day." Lenny squared up to her. "You're a dirty scumbag. You're just like your oul man, a dirty rat who's only ever interested in himself."

"Really?" Claire planted her hand on her chest. "I'm so wounded." She sniggered and looked at Jamie. "Is this the best you can do? Lenny the dose? The world's dumbest fool. Jesus, the pair of you are nothing but jokes. No one actually gives a crap about either of you. Or do you believe all the hype? They say Lenny here is some kind of Romeo." She laughed. "I bet neither of you have ever listened to what the rest of class has said about you. The pair of you live in denial. If only you saw yourselves the way the rest of us do. As if I could ever love someone like you, Jamie McGuiness. An insecure little freak who hasn't a notion about girls. Did you actually think I was serious? Is it any wonder why your own da hated you? Even he couldn't stay around long enough to tell you he loved you. You're pathetic and you make my skin crawl."

"Jesus Christ, what did I ever do to you?" Jamie roared.

Claire narrowed her eyes. "Has it ever crossed your mind just how awful your father treated my family? My da never did anything to your oul man, but he still went after him, time after time. Do you think we deserved that?"

"I don't care, Claire. That had nothing to do with me. I was willing to love you for who you are, not what my father labelled you." Jamie shook his head. "This stops tonight. Whatever you've done, or whatever is going through your head, you've got to let her go. She needs to cross over."

"No," Claire cried. "Don't you even dare."

"What's wrong with you?"

Claire moved forward and dug her nails into the side of Jamie's face. "I'll tell you when I'm done. I'm nowhere near ready to let anything go, alright?"

Claire pressed her hand to her neck. She gripped her fingers around the chain and pulled it off. On the end of it hung the small vial Jamie had seen her touch many times before.

Jamie glared at it, and then looked at Claire, her face wet with tears.

"Remember when we did this, Iliana?" She held out the vial to Iliana. "We made a pact, and I am sticking to it."

Iliana wailed, shifting in and out of focus.

"I told you I'd never give up on us, not as long there was breath in my lungs. I still stand by my vow. I will never give up on you— *ever*."

"Holy fecking Christ," Lenny said. "You're a sicko, Claire." Lenny paced back and forth on the causeway, the sun setting fast.

Jamie didn't waste another moment. He lunged forward, grabbed the chain from Claire's hands, and ran down to the rocks.

Claire screamed and ran after him. "Give it back to me. Give it back now."

Jamie ignored her. Tired, he wanted it all to stop. He had enough of playing piggy in the middle and being used as a means to their end.

"This ends right now. I've no idea what you wanted to accomplish, but I'm not losing my life because the two of you think you're soul mates."

"Jamie, please, don't do this. It's all I have left of her." Claire wailed, holding out her hands in desperation. "She's my everything. I can't let go. You don't understand. You would never understand."

"Tough shit," Jamie snapped. "There's been enough taken from me."

"What? Is this payback for your father?" Claire screamed.

Jamie laughed and rolled his eyes. "Seriously? You honestly think I'm into playing with people's lives? I'm not like that, Claire. I'm not some sick fool. I don't go around carrying a vial of—what is this? Blood? I mean, how bloody sick is this?" He shook his head. "I've never played with anyone's life ever. My father should never have done the things he did, but he didn't deserve to die the way he did. You crossed a line and are no better than him. You are a devious, murdering bitch. You and her both belong in hell."

"I can't believe you're even defending him," Claire cried.

Behind Claire, Iliana took form and reached for her hand.

Not once had Jamie considered Iliana's feelings in all of this.

"Iliana, is this what you want? Do you really want to live the rest of your days inside the body of someone who never had a chance at life?" Jamie asked.

For a moment, Iliana ignored him, but his words seemed to affect her. She closed her eyes and withdrew her hand. Shaking her head, she moved back and cried.

"I don't know." She trembled. "I just want to live. It's all I've ever wanted. I want to feel the sun on my face again and the cool crisp winter air in my lungs. To hug my daddy and tell him I love him, but it's something I'll never have. I will never be the girl I used to be again. She's gone. It's over." Iliana sobbed. "I don't want to linger like this anymore. I'm tired of only existing in this limbo. I want it to end. I'm so sorry, Claire, but the fight has gone from me. It's dying."

She held her hands out. The grey complexion changed. Water dripped from her arms. Her entire body rippled, as though she'd become a puddle, taking shape in her former likeness.

Claire spun around and looked at Iliana. She then turned her attention back to Jamie.

"Don't you dare do this. Don't even try to mess with her mind. She deserves a chance at life. If it's within your body, then so be it."

The words tore his heart apart all over again. "You used me all along." The lethal blow left little in its wake.

"If you just let us complete the ritual, it can be real," Claire said. "To the outside world, it will be real. You will be Jamie to everyone else, only Iliana will live on within you. Can't you see it's the right thing to do?"

"What? Are you off your meds, woman?" Lenny asked.

Iliana turned her attention to him.

In one fine swoop, Lenny was thrown back. The front of his head smashed against the rocks. Blood leaked from a cut just above his left eye.

"Jesus Christ," Jamie roared, running to Lenny's aid. "He didn't do anything to you."

"He's poked his nose where it's not wanted," Claire snapped. Her eyes were full of tears. Her posture grew rigid, and her anger swirled around her. "He was always sticking his nose in where it wasn't wanted. A bit of peace and quiet wouldn't do us any harm." Her eyes became glossy, as though she was lost in her own thoughts.

Jamie stood. He wrapped the chain around his fingers, lifting it into the air. Before Claire or Iliana could stop him, he plunged it down onto the rocks, smashing the vial to pieces. The liquid inside spilled out.

Iliana screamed. Her voice shook the ground beneath his feet. Her face sunk within itself. Her body trembled where she stood.

JULIEANNE LYNCH

The foul odor of death made him recoil. He held his hands over his face.

Lenny groaned where he lay bleeding.

Claire knelt on the rocks screaming, holding her hands out by her head. "*No,*" she cried.

Iliana hovered in the air, flitting in and out of focus. Her pained expression was soon replaced by something else. Her face relaxed. A beacon of light shrouded her, as though it were wrapping her in a loving embrace.

"I don't want you to go," Claire cried, reaching for her. "Please don't leave me, Iliana. I can't live without you."

Iliana looked behind her. A warm light lingered in the background. She gazed back at Claire. Her mouth moved, though no sound slid past her lips. The light swarmed around her. Her features changed. The mess of the decaying dead girl disappeared. In its place stood the healthy and beautiful glow of a vivacious young woman.

Sadness gripped him hard deep inside. The influx of speed played with his feelings.

"Iliana, please. We can still fix this. We can be together … please don't do this."

"Claire, just let her go," Jamie said. "She needs to go into the light. Her time here is done."

Claire dug her nails into the rock beneath her knees. Her nails snapped and drew blood.

"Don't leave me, Iliana," she cried. "I'm nothing without you."

Iliana was lost to the world. Her presence dissipated. The negative and overwhelming energy was no longer there. The weight lifted from Jamie in an instant. For the first time in weeks, he could breathe again.

Jamie and Claire saw Iliana take on an ethereal glow.

Her hair floated in the air. Spectrums of light emanated from her body. Iliana looked down at her hands and smiled, gazing at Claire before finally turning around. She walked into the light and disappeared. The luminosity evaporated.

Silence followed for a few moments before Claire sighed. She got to her feet and ran to the very place Iliana had stood moments before she'd blinked out of existence. She cried and pulled at her hair. Turning her head, she glared at Jamie. Tears streamed down her cheeks.

"Why?" she shouted. "Why did you do this?"

"Because it was time. You can't keep holding onto something that's no longer a part of this world." Jamie stood and walked towards her, trying to reason with her. "Claire, you have to let go. I'll never understand the bond you had with Iliana, but she was dead. Her time here was over. What you began could never be natural. It's wrong."

Claire snapped her neck to the side and scowled before throwing herself at Jamie. She dug her nails into his face once more and drew blood.

"I hate you, Jamie McGuiness. You've ruined everything."

The two of them fell back onto the rocky causeway.

"Get off me."

Jamie fought back, pulling at her hair. He'd never hit a girl before—not like this. As much as he hated himself for lashing out, he wasn't about to let Claire gouge his eyes out.

Crazed, she kept attacking him in a frenzied, animalistic way.

She bit his ear.

Jamie screamed, slapping her hard across the face.

The two rolled on the rocks.

"I'm going to kill you," Claire said. A murderous glint shone in her eyes. "I'll gut you like a fish, you filthy piece of shit."

"Get ... off ... me."

Jamie pushed her back. His face stung, and his ear bled. Through all the discomfort, he never once anticipated Lenny being fit enough to step in.

"Get your hands off him." Lenny growled, pulling Claire up by the hair. "Who do you think you are? Catch yourself on, woman, and stop behaving like a bloody animal."

"Go to hell, Lenny. This has nothing to do with you." She spat in his face.

Lenny wiped the spittle from his cheek and taunted her. "I can't believe you're this psycho. And a lezzer. Who would've thought it? Claire Brannigan, the muff eater."

He offered Jamie a hand and helped him to his feet. "Are you all right?" he whispered, never taking his eyes off Claire.

Jamie rubbed his fingers over the marks on his face and grimaced in pain. Dropping his hands to his side, he glared at Claire.

She paced back and forth, muttering incoherently to herself.

"Claire, please," he said. "I know you're hurting, but you've got to try and relax."

Stepping over to her, Jamie held out his hand, offering her friendship, even though inside he was broken. Betrayed and used, he cast it aside, intent on showing her he wasn't a monster. He wasn't his father.

"Jamie, be careful," Lenny whispered.

Claire shook her head when Jamie came face to face with her.

For a moment, he thought he had somehow made a connection with her.

She stared at him. Her eyes filled with tears. She didn't move or say anything.

Claire squeezed her eyes shut and inhaled a deep breath. On opening her eyes, she smirked at Jamie. She reached under her jacket and pulled out a knife.

Jamie's heart bounced. She was even crazier than he imagined.

"Not so clever now, are you, Jamie?" she remarked. Her eyes were dark, full of hate and anger.

Jamie glared at Lenny.

His friend moved towards Claire.

"I wouldn't do that if I were you, Lenny," she said. "Or I'll slice through his soft skin right now. So, better stay away."

"Claire." Jamie's voice shook. "You don't want to do this."

"Don't I?"

A storm lurked in her eyes. She brimmed with revenge. Claire focused on him and nothing else.

Afraid of Claire, he realized she was unpredictable. She had the look of an angel, but her true intentions had been washed ashore. She was a monster underneath it all.

"When you die, Jamie, I'll make sure you won't come back, mark my words. And as for your dear old murdering father, I'll make sure the world knows about him. I might even add in a tale of woe or two. Just to give it a little edge," she said, pointing the tip of the blade against Jamie's stomach. "One wrong move, and you'll be a goner."

Whichever way he moved, the blade would impale him. He silently prayed she'd come to her senses and stop.

"If you do this, you'll go to prison," Jamie replied, trying to keep his breathing under control.

Waves crashed in, water lapping over the rocks where they stood. Small droplets of rain drizzled around them.

Claire tilted her head to the side and met Jamie's gaze. "How does it feel?"

"What?" he asked.

"Being the victim."

"You don't have to do this. We can all walk away from this and continue with our lives."

His words fell on deaf ears.

"Do what? This?" Claire moved forward, the tip of the blade cut through his clothes. "This," she whispered, "this is a reminder to never meddle in other people's business ever again. Lights out, Jamie."

The coldness of the metal pressed against his skin. It happened quicker than he expected.

Claire lost her footing on the wet rocks and fell backwards. She grabbed a hold of Jamie, and pulled him down along with her.

Lenny's roars were mere echoes in Jamie's head as he flitted in and out of consciousness. An intense tingle, like a severe electric shock consumed him.

What's happened? Where's Claire? His mouth went dry and bile rose in his throat.

A burning pain coursed through him like nothing he'd ever imagined. He had no idea where it came from.

Claire's painful screams pulsed through his head.

Lenny bent down and grabbed Jamie, pulling him off Claire.

Jamie struggled and swallowed a shallow breath. Weariness seeped into his bones.

"Jamie," Lenny said, patting his face. "Jesus, Jamie, stay with me, lad."

Jamie lifted his head. The pain became too much.

"Don't move," Lenny shouted, and then turned his attention to Claire. "Jesus Christ, what have you done, you bad bitch?"

Jamie opened his mouth to speak, but the words wouldn't come out. He turned his head.

Lenny got to his feet. The first blow of Lenny's foot against Claire's face sent a tooth shooting out of her mouth.

She didn't fight back.

Lenny's kicks came one after another, until he bent down and used his fists. He smashed them into Claire's face until it became a pulpy mess.

She mumbled something, coughing on her blood.

"Go to hell!" Lenny roared.

He lifted her head on either side and smashed her skull down onto the rocks. Blood pooled out fast, leaking over the wet boulder. Another wave crashed in, washing some of the blood away. Lenny stood. He stared at Jamie, his eyes wet from tears, breathing heavy.

Jamie swallowed hard. The heat from the wound penetrated through his core.

"Help ... me," he gasped. He stretched out his fingers, reaching for Lenny. He shivered, the shock of his wound overtaking his body.

Lenny knelt by his side and lifted Jamie's head onto his lap. He took out his phone from his back pocket and made a call.

Jamie found the pull of sleep too much to resist. His eyes flickered closed. The coldness consumed him.

Can't ... hold ... on.

Lenny cried and spoke into the phone.

The haze filling Jamie's head muted Lenny's words. Nothing but his own thoughts rambled inside his mind.

Am I going to die? Is this the end? Me da ... he's gone. Me poor mother ... the wee ones. It's all a mess.

Lenny's desperate eyes bore into Jamie's.

Jamie blinked one last time, and then the cold darkness claimed him.

CHAPTER THIRTY-ONE

A thick, heavy fog took refuge in his mind. The outside world seemed so far away. In an odd change of events, contentment filled him.

No pain.

No ghosts.

Nothing but rest.

Worn out, mentally battered, his confidence shot, and all because of his father and Claire's betrayal. In the midst of his silent reprieve, a shadow lurked. A constant reminder of the darkness he'd lived with for the past three years. This time, it was different. The darkness seemed to take comfort in his rest.

Unsure of where it came from, a beeping noise echoed somewhere at the back of his mind. He didn't want to hear it, preferring the silence of being lost within the haze.

The strong scent of antibacterial cleaner filled his nose. His mouth grew dry. He smacked his lips a few times before his eyes flickered open.

The bright light hurt. He focused his gaze and squinted his eyes. Jamie lay on a bed. White walls loomed above.

The faint whispers of voices came from the window nearby. Turning his head, his mother's blurred face flickered in the distance. She was talking to someone.

Jamie felt like he had been asleep for months, but he was still so terribly tired. He ached like he'd never hurt before. Afraid to move, he closed his eyes again.

Just a little while longer.

An inexplicable and comforting warmth wrapped itself around him. He wanted nothing more than to be lost in the fog forever. It comforted him and eased the dull ache.

A hand slid across his arm.

"Jamie." His mother's soft voice called his name.

Jamie didn't want to wake up. The more his mother rubbed his arm, the more he wanted to see her face.

He blinked a few times and fixed his gaze on her. "Ma," he mumbled, letting out a gentle cough.

"Oh, Jamie," Sonya exclaimed. "Thank God."

"I'm so sorry."

Images of Claire and Iliana flashed before his eyes. Jamie didn't want to remember. He didn't want to have to face the truth.

"For what?"

She gently squeezed his hand, her way of reassuring him. She'd done so ever since he was a small child.

"I don't know … everything." His voice sounded strained.

Sonya shook her head. "Jamie, you need to rest. Don't burden yourself with apologies."

Jamie choked back his tears. Despite what happened, his mother put on a brave face.

"Lenny … Is Lenny okay? Where is he?"

Sonya touched his cheek and bent to kiss his forehead. "If it weren't for Lenny, you would have died out there. He saved your life."

She was right. Jamie owed his life to Lenny. The dread soon seeped through his veins.

Claire. All that blood.

He mustered the courage to ask the question burning at the back of his mind.

"What happened to Claire?"

Sitting down on the side of the bed, Sonya took Jamie's hand in hers. She cleared her throat before she spoke.

"Claire died, Jamie."

His heart raced.

"What … what happened?"

Sonya cried and wiped her eyes with her handkerchief. "She attacked you. The knife was still inside you when they brought you in. It was Lenny who saved you and got help."

"But …" Jamie stuttered.

"The police believe she was doing some kind of ritual down at the causeway. They found books about raising the dead and witchcraft in her room. In their minds, you got caught in the line of fire. She could have killed you."

Jamie swallowed and closed his eyes, remembering the demented look in Claire's eyes as she'd stuck the knife in him.

"That's not all, pet," she said.

Jamie opened his eyes and stared at her, ready for what she was about to say.

"I don't know how to say this, but your father's dead, Jamie. He was found at the bottom of the lighthouse." Sonya cried. Her hands trembled. "They said he had defense wounds on him, and are looking for your grandfather. It's all such a mess, but given their history, they're not looking for any other suspects."

The lump in his throat became unbearable. He would never tell his mother the truth. Jamie would take the secret to the grave with him.

"Ma," he said. "It's all too much to take in. I'm sorry."

"What can you say, son? I left him. I finally had the courage to leave after all these years, and now he's dead. I just don't understand." Sonya crumpled the handkerchief in her hand and stared out the window before looking down at Jamie. "Jamie, what were you doing out there?"

Jamie thought hard, unsure of what to say or how to explain himself. The words became muddled in his head. The strain pulsed behind his eyes. A headache loomed.

Sonya shook her head. "Don't worry about it. You can tell me later. You just rest. You had a close call, son, and lost a lot of blood. When they removed the knife, your heart stopped beating twice. You're very lucky to be alive."

"Oh, my god, I died?"

"Almost, but the surgeon did a great job. I'm just so thankful you're okay."

Jamie closed his eyes. Tears rose to the surface. He didn't want to break down. Doing so was a sure-fire way to reveal everything.

"How long have I been asleep?"

"Since you came out of surgery last night," Sonya said, and patted the back of his hand.

Jamie finally caved. The tears fell like an avalanche. The crying offered him a slight respite from the pent-up hurt, anger, and sorrow buried deep inside him. The wave descended upon him, pulling him under, not allowing him a chance to catch his breath.

His mother held his hand. Her own tears streaked her cheeks.

"I'm so sorry, Ma. I really am. I should never have gone after her. I should have stayed at home. I thought I was helping her. I'm so stupid. I'm sorry for causing you more pain."

Sonya opened her mouth to reply.

The curtain around his bed was drawn back. Lenny appeared.

"'Bout ye, lad?" he said, tapping Jamie's foot under the blanket. "You gave us all a bit of a fright last night. Typical Jamie style, eh?" He winked.

"Aye."

Jamie looked at him. Lenny was putting on an act for his mother's benefit.

"Thank God you were there, pet," Sonya said.

Lenny nodded and looked at Sonya. "Anytime, Mrs. McGuiness. Jamie's like a brother to me. I'd do anything for him."

"With friends like Lenny, you'll go far in life," she said, looking from Lenny to Jamie. "Are you going to stay a while?"

"Aye, if you don't mind?"

"Not at all, pet. I need to get home and bring a few things in for Jamie. Is that all right with you, son?"

Jamie nodded and cleared his throat. "Aye, it's no bother, Ma."

"Okay," Sonya replied, grabbing her bag from the table near the window. "I'll be back in a few hours. Do you want something nice brought in?"

"Nah, I'm good, but thanks." Jamie struggled to control his breathing.

Sonya planted a kiss on his forehead and patted Lenny's shoulder before she left the ward.

Lenny sat on the bed and shook his head. "Jesus, lad, you scared the shite clean out of me. I thought you were a goner. You were so cold. It was awful. I'll never forget it as long as I live. I'm serious. It's the kind of stuff you see in one of them slasher films."

"What did they say about Claire? I don't understand 'cause I saw what you did. How can you hide the truth from the peelers?"

"Aye, about that." Lenny sucked in a deep breath. "I lost control. I saw what she did to you. I wasn't going to let some lezzer hurt my best friend. Besides, she'd already had a pretty bad injury to her head before I got my hands on her."

Jamie gawped at Lenny. "You've always been there for me, even when you thought I was going mad." He took a breath and whispered, "Claire's death was a necessity, right?"

Lenny nodded and folded his arms.

"So, like, what's going to happen? Aren't the peelers looking to question me? Or you?"

"Aye, it's all part of the process, but the fact is, her mother's kitchen knife was plunged into your stomach."

"But her phone …"

"Never say I don't do anything for you," Lenny said, and smirked. "I made sure it was taken care of."

"Damn."

"Listen, lad, I'm a very resourceful guy. I've your back covered. Okay?"

Jamie rested his head against his pillow and stared at the ceiling.

Is it really over?

After everything he'd gone through, he didn't want there to be a reprisal. He was tired and ready to move on with the rest of his life.

"What happens now? Do we just pretend none of it happened?"

Lenny pursed his lips and nodded. "Now you get to live your life, minus a ghost and a crazy lezzer girlfriend, not to mention your bully of a father."

"How do you do that?"

"What?"

"See the good in all the ugliness?"

Lenny laughed. "Because unlike you, ye bloody dose, I know there is a life waiting to be lived. You got your head stuck in the past and left yourself vulnerable to God-knows-what. Look at you. Ye nearly died, lad, and for what?"

"I thought I was helping her," Jamie admitted. He closed his eyes and winced in obvious pain. "I should have known better."

"It's just your nature," Lenny remarked. "You're a gentle soul, lad, and it leaves you open to the unthinkable. But I've plans to help harden you up, or at least have a bit of fun trying."

Lenny hit the nail on the head. A lightweight when it came to his feelings, Jamie had learned a valuable lesson—never to fall in love so easily. He didn't intend on repeating the mistake anytime soon.

"Do you think Claire is at peace?" Jamie asked.

Lenny scratched the back of his head and shrugged. "Honestly, I hope she's burning in hell, if it actually exists. She was a bad bitch for even trying to kill you. I shouldn't talk ill of the dead and shite, but seriously, she was just bad to the bone. She even had me duped."

"Ach, I know," Jamie said. "Maybe if I had tried harder with her, perhaps she would have seen the error of her ways."

Lenny laughed.

"What's so funny?" Jamie asked, raising his brows.

"You," Lenny replied. "You'll never change, will you?"

"Probably not."

"I knew it."

Jamie sniggered.

Lenny rubbed his hands together. "I do love a good old challenge."

The two lads chatted for hours, often stepping back and going over the events of the past month. An agreement was made, one Lenny would soon set in stone.

"Listen, we will never talk about any of this again, all right, lad? Your da and Claire will be buried. They'll probably be taking a joint trip down to hell together, and you get your second chance at life."

"You do know I tend to screw things up?"

"Aye, and that's when I'll shove my size nine's up your hole. Do you honestly think I'll let anything slip by me again?" Lenny raised an eyebrow, and Jamie shook his head. "Exactly, now all you need to do is rest, let the wound heal up, and everything else will fall into place."

"Just like that, hmm?" Jamie pulled a face.

"Well, what else can you do?"

"True."

"But one thing is for sure, I've an awful, nagging feeling I want to get away from here for a while."

Jamie stared at Lenny, waiting for him to elaborate on his remark.

"How's about the two of us head away?"

"Are you serious?" Lenny's suggestion caught him by surprise.

"Deadly, no pun intended." Lenny smirked.

"What about your A-Levels?"

Lenny shrugged. "I've been looking for an excuse to avoid going back there."

Jamie sighed and turned his head, closing his eyes before he spoke once more. "Where will we go?"

"London," Lenny announced. "I've made the calls. I've some money stashed away. My brother will set us up for a while. You just have to be on board with this. Ready to walk away."

"Just like that?" Jamie whispered.

"Yes. It's that simple."

"I guess ye've got it all worked out, then?"

"One hundred percent, lad. I'm done with small town Ireland. I want to get out there, figure out who I am. You are in the same boat. So, how's about it?" Lenny winked at Jamie.

"Feck it, what've I to lose?"

"Now there's the lad I know." Lenny grinned. "The world's our oyster. It would be rude not to sample the goods, eh?"

The thought of leaving scared the life out of Jamie, but the idea of a new beginning washed away all the pain. It was the very medicine he needed.

Nothing relieved Jamie more than being able to miss the funeral.

Being stabbed had its benefits. He refused to look at his father. Not after everything they'd done to one another.

One thing still bugged him more than anything—how Claire had ensnared him, using him as bait in her plans. He'd never forgive himself for allowing her that kind of power over him. No one would ever manipulate him like that again. Not as long as he had air in his lungs.

Standing by the tree at the top of the graveyard, Jamie considered not even paying his respects. It had been two weeks since everything had happened.

Mustering up enough courage, he walked down the slope and stopped at the grave. Emer was buried next to the man who had claimed her life.

What an irony. Jamie read the messages of condolences written on some of the wreaths.

"Hypocrites," he said.

"Not so much hypocrites, son," a voice said from behind.

He turned his head.

Father Murray strolled towards him. "What are you doing here?"

"Making sure the dead stay dead," Father Murray replied with a chuckle.

Jamie furrowed his eyebrows and glared at the old priest. "Did you know Claire was as demented as my father?"

"In all honesty, she hid her intentions well. She had us both fooled."

"And now, what do you think about it all?" Jamie asked, furrowing his brows.

"Sometimes, I wonder about life and the beauty of this

world. What if underneath all the bright colors, smiles, and joy, something darker lurks?"

Jamie cocked his head. "How do you mean?"

"I mean, Jamie, once ye've seen things from the other side, it's very hard to see life through rose-tinted glasses. Not when you are well aware of those walking among us—the good, the bad, and the monsters."

The priest's words caused a wave of bile to rise to the back of his throat. "But I thought you said I had to put an end to Iliana and then I'd be fine?"

Father Murray shook his head and sucked on his dentures. "Hmm, I did, but then, I never took into consideration your aura, or the fact that your energy attracts them. You're like a magnet. They feed off the energy seeping from you."

"Them?" The blood drained from Jamie's face.

"Sure, by now you understand quite well who and what I am referring to," Father Murray said. "Of course, it's still all new to you, but you're a quick learner. Besides, there's nowhere to run, son, for they will find you wherever you go."

Jamie swallowed a lump. "Is this what I think you mean?"

The old man chuckled and turned his back on Jamie. "I'll be seeing you, Jamie," he said, and walked away.

"Wait," Jamie called after him. "What do you mean them?"

"Keep your wits about you, say your prayers at night, and remember when they come calling, don't open the door."

Father Murray left Jamie standing by the grave.

Jamie's insides twisted. The sting from the wound made itself known, and his heart sank to a new level. It was never going to end.

"Why me?" he muttered.

Turning his back on the grave and the memory of his father, he walked back to town. Something bad lurked in his future and followed in his wake. He sensed it, though he couldn't understand it.

CHAPTER THIRTY-TWO

Jamie packed the last of his clothes into the large bag and sat on the edge of his bed. He looked around his room and his heart sank. It was hard to believe he was going to spend one last night in his childhood home. Memories of all he'd been through filled his head. As much as it hurt, his newfound courage gave him the strength to face his demons head on.

A knock at the door pulled him from his thoughts. He looked up.

Sonya stood in the doorway. "How're you getting on?" she asked.

"That's the last of it." He sighed and ran a hand over his knuckles.

Sonya walked into the room and stopped by the dresser. She picked up a small photo frame and beamed.

"The pair of you were thick as thieves when you were little."

Jamie stood and walked over to his mother. He gazed at the photograph, and as much as it pained him, he found himself smiling.

"It's my favorite picture," he said. "It was, by far, the best summer we had. I never wanted it to end."

"Aye. Do you remember the merry-go-round and how Emer

was frightened of the horse? She wouldn't go on it without you."

"Yeah," he said. "But we ended up spending half the afternoon going around in circles."

Sonya laughed and held a hand to her mouth. "God, I miss those days so much."

Sadness washed over his mother. He rested a hand against her back.

"I won't go if I think you're not going to be okay, Ma," he said.

Sonya turned her head and stared at him.

"I mean it, I won't go." He took the photo frame and stared at the picture of him and Emer sitting on the beach, ice cream on their faces, completely happy.

"I'll not have you giving up on life because of me, son."

"I feel so bad leaving you all," he admitted. "It's like I am giving up on you and just moving on. I don't want anyone to think I am abandoning you and the wee ones."

Sonya laughed and wrapped her arms around him. "I promise you, me and the wee ones will be grand. Sarah is finally sleeping again. The twins aren't afraid to play or ask for things. And you got decent exams results. It has to count for something, considering what we've all been through."

"It's just …" he said.

"No buts, Jamie McGuiness. You are going to go off and make a good life for yourself. See the world, and meet a nice wee lassie. Anything is better than being stuck here and falling into the same old rut as everyone else."

Jamie hugged his mother tight. "Well, you know I'll be home the moment you need me, right?"

"You deserve this more than anyone else."

Jamie smiled. His mother knew him better than most.

"Does Lenny know what he's letting himself in for?" he asked.

"Lenny's a wise lad," Sonya said. "He's not one for making rash decisions. He'll have your back, otherwise you wouldn't be setting foot on any ship. Now come on down, I've made you a nice dinner and the twins have something for you."

Sonya let go of Jamie and left the room.

He set the photo frame on his bag, glancing around the room and sighing. It really was his final night.

Jamie sat between the twins on the sofa.

Paul held a card, and Thomas had a small box wrapped in handmade wrapping.

"I drew a picture of Captain America," Paul announced.

"And I wrote my name," Thomas added with pride.

"Is that right?" Jamie asked, opening the card and grinning once he read the inscription.

> *To the best big brother and son in the world.*
> *All our love,*
> *Paul, Thomas, Sarah, and Mammy xxx*

Jamie set the card down and gathered the boys into his arms.

"You two are the best wee brothers ever," he said. "And look at the writing, you are brilliant. I love it."

The boys laughed and hugged Jamie.

"This one's from Mummy," Paul said, handing Jamie another envelope.

Jamie slid his finger under the seal and pulled out a ticket and some money.

"Jesus, Ma, this is too much." He drew his lower lip between his teeth and fought back tears.

"We all chipped in. Your granny and uncles all wanted to make sure you've enough to get by," she replied.

"But—"

"Now open this," Thomas shouted, stopping Jamie from finishing what he wanted to say. He gleefully pushed a small box into Jamie's hand.

"What's in here?" Jamie asked, teasing the boys and slowly unwrapping the paper.

"It's really special," Thomas said.

Jamie removed the final piece of paper and opened the lid of the small blue box. Inside lay an old watch.

"Ma, you don't have to," he said, staring up at his mother.

Sonya stood in front of the fireplace with Sarah in her arms. "I want you to have it."

"But it was Grandda's."

"And he'd want you to have it. I don't have an awful lot, son, but the watch went to many places in this world, and I want you to have it. It will make me happy."

Jamie cleared his throat. His cheeks burned.

"I don't know what to say," he said, staring at the watch.

"You don't say anything. You just smile and put it on."

"It's class," Thomas remarked.

"And old," an excited Paul added.

Jamie sucked in a breath and wrapped the brown leather strap around his wrist, fastening it shut. He looked down at the large face of the watch and remembered admiring it when he was a little boy. A sense of great pride filled him.

"This is the best thing ever. Thanks, Ma," he said, looking up at his mother.

"You're welcome," Sonya replied. "Now come on, I've made a nice pot of stew and Granny baked a potato bread loaf."

The twins raced from the room, making their usual ruckus as they ran down the hall.

Jamie reached out for Sarah and drew her into his arms. Kissing the little girl on the head, he inhaled deeply, never wanting to forget her being so small.

She babbled away, hitting him on the face, completely unaware of the fact that she wouldn't be seeing him for a while.

"I'll dish up," his mother said and left the room.

Jamie stood by the fireplace, gazing at Sarah and his heart sank to a new level.

"You better be good for Mammy, eh?" he said.

Sarah cooed away. Her big blue eyes and long lashes reminded him of Emer.

"God, I'm going to miss you," he whispered, swallowing the urge to cry. "I'll miss you all."

Sarah chewed on her fingers and gazed at Jamie.

He chuckled, walking out of the room and heading down the hall. The sight of his mother dishing up the food, the twins sitting side-by-side chatting away with excitement on their little faces, was burned deep into his mind. Part of him wanted to stay, but he had to go. He had to try to find a balance in his life.

After dinner, Jamie helped build a tower with Legos, and then read to the boys. He was about to kiss them goodnight when Thomas sat up in the bed.

"Jamie," he whispered.

"Yup?"

"Do you think the bad man will come and get us?" he asked.

Jamie stared at Thomas and shook his head. "What do you mean?"

"The dark man, the one scratching on the floor," Thomas replied, rubbing his tired eyes.

"There's no bad man," Jamie said, his voice full of reassurance. "You're just imaging things. Have you been watching something you shouldn't?"

"Nope," Thomas said, shaking his head. "He came after Daddy went to heaven."

Jamie's insides knotted. "What do you mean?"

Thomas lifted his blue bunny and rubbed his ears. He shrugged and yawned.

"He came after they put Daddy in the ground. He sits in the corner, scratching on the floor." Thomas pointed to a corner in the room.

A chill ran down his back. The hairs on the back of his neck stood on edge. He turned and gazed around the room.

"Have you told Mammy this?"

Thomas shook his head. "Nope."

"Why?"

"Because he looks like Daddy," Thomas said. His big blue eyes remained fixed on Jamie's face. "Is it Daddy?"

Jamie swallowed. "No, it's not. It's just your imagination, Thomas. Have you said your prayers?"

"Yup, I prayed to God to keep us safe and you safe," he said with a little smile on his face.

"Good boy, always say your prayers, okay?" Jamie kissed his forehead. "Now go to sleep. No more thinking about silly scary things."

"I'll miss you, Jamie."

"I'll miss you, too, you little rascal."

Jamie tucked the covers up around Thomas's neck and proceeded to leave the room. About to close the door, he took one last look in the corner and waited, half expecting something to jump out of the shadows.

Nothing.

It's just my overactive imagination.

He left the door ajar and made his way down the stairs. The niggling sensation told him something wasn't quite right. Then again, Thomas had hit a nerve. Sometimes, his own imagination got the better of him.

He took a seat in the living room. The TV was switched down low, and he didn't disturb his sleeping mother. It was odd knowing he was leaving. He'd spent much of the past three years dreaming about such an escape. Now that the moment had arrived, it was bittersweet.

Everything he knew and loved lay under this roof. All the memories—the good and bad—could never be replaced. Excited and nervous, he looked forward to the prospect of starting anew somewhere else.

"God, please look after them," he whispered, gazing at his mother.

He worried about her the most. She had been broken for so long, he wondered if she'd ever truly recover. She hid her scars well, wearing a smile no one would ever suspect of being fake. It was her way of dealing with what lay on her plate. She lived for him and the wee ones. If it hadn't have been for them, she'd have been gone a long time ago.

Jamie got up from the chair and turned off the television. He gently shook his mother.

"Ma, go on up to bed, I'll lock up."

Sonya stirred and sleepily nodded.

Jamie made his way to the front door, locking up before checking the rear of the house. He stopped outside the back room, staring at the blanket of darkness.

He would never forget and accepted it. Everything that had happened sickened him to the core. His whole perspective on life had changed. He'd never see things like he used to. His whole mind had been opened to the impossible. Knowing there were those who walked among the living lingered in his mind the most.

Jamie stepped across the threshold of the plastic sheeting. He inhaled deeply. The putrid stench of Iliana remained, a scent he'd never forget. Though she had scared him, knowing he had released her and she'd crossed over filled him with ease. To where, God only knew. Nevertheless, the fact that she was finally at peace filled him with satisfaction.

He stood in complete silence for a few minutes, staring, testing his own nerve. He hated the room. Of all the places in the house that kept him on edge, this one scared him the most.

Standing there, the chill crept in, pricking his skin. He shivered and took a deep breath. The familiar sensation enveloped him. His heart thumped hard. Its rhythmic beating pounded in his ears. He held his breath and turned his head.

Slowly, he scanned the darkness, sensing an unexpected presence. It was neither the living, nor the dead. It was something else. The words to ask what it wanted failed him. He wasn't that bold.

Jamie swallowed, preparing himself for the attack. The chill lifted, and the pressure in the room eased. The presence had disappeared.

That night, as Jamie lay in his bed, he stared at the ceiling, listening to the noises the house made—pipes scraping, floorboards creaking. His mind raced. He didn't want to be in the house a moment longer and made up his mind to get his mother and wee ones out of there. His timing just had to be right.

One thing was for certain, Father Murray was right.

Don't open the door and all would be well.

EPILOGUE

J amie sat on the boat and stared out at the harbor. The beginning for him, a new lease of life had been granted. No matter how hard things had been in the past, he was thankful for small blessings. Having the chance to earn a living and make enough to give his mother a new start inspired him the most.

Saying goodbye was never easy, but he'd known the day would come when he'd have to leave. Life was about living, making each moment count. He had learned the lesson the hard way.

He sighed and glanced around the upper deck of the car ferry. The many faces of strangers surrounded him, each lost within their own thoughts. What secrets did they leave behind?

Jamie gazed back at Northern Ireland. Larne was now a dot on the horizon.

For a split second, his heart skipped a beat. He'd miss his mother and the children. It was one of the hardest things he had to get through, but he had to do this for himself. He owed himself a chance at happiness. It was one of the things he'd promised his mother and Lenny.

He swallowed the hard ball in his throat and fought the urge to cry. He didn't want to think about Claire, but she'd always be there. Her pretty face, her soft lips, her last words—her final moments on this earth were all marred.

"'Bout you, lad?" a familiar voice said from behind.

Jamie shrugged and looked at Lenny. "Nothing, lad, just thinking."

"Here, drink this," Lenny said, handing Jamie a bottle of water. "And less of the thinking."

"Aye." Jamie stared at the dot in the distance. "Will your parents forgive you?"

"Who knows?" Lenny took a sip from his own bottle of water. "But sure, what was I to do?"

"I just hate you thinking this was your only choice."

Lenny shook his head and laughed. "You're such a dose, it actually hurts my intelligence."

"So you keep saying," Jamie said, and smiled. "But in all seriousness, what we're doing is right. I can feel it."

"Listen, after everything that's gone on these past three years, leaving and beginning again somewhere new, this has been owed to you, Jamie. I'm just tagging along to make sure you keep your pretty little head out of trouble."

There was no better person to accompany him on the next phase of his life. Between the two of them, they had a bit of cash, some digs set up, and work ready and waiting for them in London. The journey down from Scotland would be interesting. Lenny would provide the lead counsel if any of the ugliness reared its head.

Taking a sip of the water, Jamie turned his back on the country he loved. "Wanna head inside?" he asked.

Lenny beamed and winked at him. "I thought you'd never ask."

The two of them walked away from the upper deck and settled in a seat near a window. Everything Jamie had left behind was now another bad memory, locked away in the confines of the past, never to be spoken about again. It was a small price to pay for his sanity.

Jamie had listened to everything Father Murray had warned him about. He heeded the priest's words with care and precision, refusing to tempt fate. But he wasn't stupid. He wasn't truly alone. Not anymore.

The boys smiled and laughed, excited about the journey ahead. Neither of them spoke about Claire, Jamie's father, or the night on the causeway. There was no point in revisiting painful memories.

As the ferry glided over the calm Irish Sea, a presence hovered in the dark recesses of his mind. It waited, knowing his day would come.

Jamie sensed its patience. Its memories flitted in and out of his subconscious. At first, he thought it was a figment of his imagination. No one would ever deny the magnitude of the memories, the faces, the screams, or the torture he'd gone through. Jamie closed the door Father Murray had talked about and pretended *it* wasn't there.

Equipped with enough knowledge to know that when the darkness came knocking, it was a case of either letting it in or running for your life. One way or another, he would find out what it wanted. It all came down to when, and that's what irked him the most.

Until the time came, he intended on living his life—memories included. He just had to keep his eyes open at all times.

ABOUT THE AUTHOR

Julieanne Lynch is an author of Young Adult and Adult genre urban fantasy books. Julieanne was born in Northern Ireland, but spent much of her early life in London, United Kingdom, until her family relocated back to their roots.

Julieanne lives in Northern Ireland where she is a full-time author. She studied English Literature and Creative Writing at The Open University, and considered journalism as a career path. Julieanne has several projects optioned for film.

www.julieannelynch.com
www.BeneathTheLighthouse.com